Jeremy Potter is a Londoner who lives in
Kensington with his wife, novelist Anne
Betteridge, and their two children. He works
as a magazine publisher and is currently
Chairman of the Richard III Society.
His historical novel, *A Trail of Blood*, also
published by Sphere Books, was selected as
Alternate Choice of the Book of the
Month Club in America.

Also by Jeremy Potter and available from
Sphere Books

A TRAIL OF BLOOD

Going West

JEREMY POTTER

SPHERE BOOKS LIMITED
30/32 Gray's Inn Road, London WC1X 8JL

First published in Great Britain by
Constable & Co Ltd 1972
Copyright © Jeremy Potter 1972
Published by Sphere Books 1975

TRADE MARK

Set in Intertype Times

Printed in Great Britain by
C. Nicholls & Company Ltd
The Philips Park Press, Manchester

ISBN 0 7221 6975 2

CONTENTS

The wound in his thigh was throbbing. He was used to pain.
At the BOAC counter his suitcase was weighed and labelled
HNL for Honolulu. A conveyor belt carried it off at funeral
pace, like a coffin gliding out of sight from a crematorium
chapel. Gloomily he laid bets with himself whether it would
turn up in Honduras or Kong Kong. He took his ticket
and boarding card. The girl behind the counter smiled reassuringly and wished him a good flight.

Helen had driven him to the airport. Outside in the
January mizzle he waited for her to rejoin him from the car
park. A news bulletin reached him from a radio in the cab
rank. Shipyards in the north were strike-bound. So were car
factories in the midlands. Postal services everywhere were
suspended – the result of a one-day stoppage by GPO
workers. Student violence had closed the London School of
Economics. Frost was forecast in all areas. Also snow on
high ground. The rest of the good news was lost in the
whine of a landing jet.

Was he glad to be leaving? Would he be glad to be back?
He didn't know. Britain was home, after all, and the stop-
go-but-mostly-stop Sixties were nearly over. Would he be
back at all? That was more the question. He saw Helen's
motherly form approaching and wished she hadn't stayed.

'Cheer up,' she told him. 'It's all right for some. You're
lucky to be getting away. I wish I were coming too.' There
were faint streaks of smeared lipstick radiating from the
corners of her mouth, like the pink prints of tiny webbed
feet.

He made no reply and she dropped her voice.

'It'll be dangerous, won't it? Do look after yourself.
Douglas. You're getting too old for this sort of thing.'

She squeezed his arm and he patted hers without affection.

7

'If you're still fretting about your friend,' she persisted, 'he's dead and that's that. Anyway you hated him, didn't you?'

Douglas supposed he did. He regretted telling her about his obsession with the famous Ashley Wyndham West. The disclosure had been a needless confession: a breach of security regulations made in a weak moment of post-ciotal togetherness.

They inspected the concourse. The rival El Al and MEA counters stood jowl by jowl, both deserted. Smart boutiques exhibited high-priced souvenirs. What could a miniature tyre be concealing worth more than eight pounds? A transistor? An alarm clock? A brandy flask? She tried to raise his spirits with a guessing game.

The call for his flight was due at 11.20. He bought a *Paris-Match* and they parted five minutes early.

'You should get yourself another job,' she said. 'As soon as you're safely back we must talk about it. That and other things.'

If he got safely back, she meant. He pecked dutifully at an overpowdered cheek and turned abruptly away to hide his lack of feeling. 'Other things.' What could that mean but marriage? If she had to pick herself another husband, why did it have to be him? Even the red-faced major in the ground-floor flat was a better proposition. Along with his temper he at least had a pension and a cosy job with the National Trust.

Passport control didn't worry him. The passport he showed was genuine and his automatic no concern of theirs. He wore it in an ankle holster strapped to his calf.

In the departure lounge he became wary. At some point in the journey the woman he was following would certainly notice him. The later the better. It was important to choose his own moment for scaring the fight out of her. He would hate to allow her the chance of a second pot shot.

Despite the pain he disguised his limp and crossed briskly to the queue at the duty-free kiosk. There was no sign of her en route. After buying a bottle of cut-price whisky he retired to the gent's and sat on a lavatory seat

8

reading his *Paris-Match*. Between paragraphs he wondered whether she had given him the slip.

It was 11.30 when the intercom announced the departure of Flight BA 531. At 11.35 he rose, adjusted his dress and emerged, not looking about him. The glass door out of the lounge slid open as he approached. After half a mile or so of artificial marble corridor he reached Gate 9 on the tip of one of the terminal's new fingers.

'Please Wait Here.'

A cluster of junior staff stood under the illuminated sign. One wore a peaked cap with a red top, another had a badge identifying him as an Australian immigration officer. A third had a coloured face, and the fourth a well-shaped pair of nyloned legs. Among the passengers gathering round this second pair he suddenly spied her and for an instant his leg stopped throbbing. She was thickly coated and closely kerchiefed, but unmistakable.

Relieved and at once tense again, he hung back and averted his face. Outside on the tarmac assorted minnows were busily servicing their leviathan: petrol tankers and freight vans, trucks with hoists and flights of steps on wheels. Another monster had just taken off. It was rumbling overhead, decorating the overcast sky with trails of fairy slipstream.

A forward surge told him that 'Please Wait Here' had become 'Please Board Now'. Red Hat led the way, Australian Immigration stood frowning, Coloured Face tore the boarding cards, Legs smiled. He boarded last, returning both frown and smile.

19F was a window seat towards the back. A quietly weeping Australian matron occupied 19D, and 19E had fallen to a loud-mouthed Texan. There were squabbling children across the gangway and a hiccuping baby immediately in front. The prospect of a peaceful flight seemed remote. Squeezing into his seat and fumbling with the safety belt, he kept his head down while locating the thick coat and kerchief at the front of the cabin.

They would shortly be leaving for New York, San Francisco, Honolulu, Fiji and Sydney, a disembodied voice told them. They would fly at thirty-five thousand feet and arrive at New York in seven hours forty-five minutes. Captain Gardiner was their captain. Some of the crew spoke French.

Stewards and stewardesses demonstrated lifebelts and oxygen masks. The baby's parents wanted to know when they would get to Sydney, but the stewardess wasn't sure. She thought it would be Saturday morning, but the international date-line made things tricky. She would be getting off at New York herself.

Twelve noon was scheduled departure time and they reached the starting line punctually. Five minutes later the airport buildings were disappearing at speed. The wing outside his window developed a fit of the shudders and he counted the engines for comfort. There were two, which must mean four in all. Gravel pits appeared below, then the river and the motorway.

At least the take-off had been smoother than Helen's warming-up manoeuvres with her elderly Cortina in Norland Square. He wondered whether she was back there now. Ahead a grey mass shaped itself into Windsor Castle. He pointed out the Round Tower and the windows of St. George's Chapel to Loud-mouth, who greeted them with an uh-huh.

They soon rose to the clouds, which were light at first and wispy, then thicker. It became like driving in fog. Higher still they emerged on the other side and blue sky stretched to the horizon above a layer of cotton wool. It tantalised him to think of this unbroken sunshine over England all and every January. Blurred snatches of countryside came into view down crevasses, but vanished before he could identify them.

Averse to a second dose of news, he refused a daily paper. Instead, to celebrate being safely airborne with his quarry, he ordered *Moët et Chandon*. A quarter-bottle. Loud-mouth refused to join him on the grounds that champagne tasted too sweet. He advised lacing it with a double brandy to kill the acidity and save his stomach.

The broadcasting system spoke again. This time the captain himself, to announce the last of England. It was Wales below now, and any minute it would be Ireland. In less than half an hour they would have passed Shannon and be out over the ocean.

Above the Irish coast the clouds broke up, uncovering a green and brown land edged with deep blue. The remaining wisps in the sky glinted with the reflection of rainbow sunbeams. Cocooned in ethereal peace, he asked himself why he bothered so much about the little worries of his life. Sipping his champagne, he tried to taste tranquillity, but the baby was still hiccuping and he couldn't forget he was a failure. Also Loud-mouth had poisoned the champagne for him. It tasted too sweet.

Who said it was a long way to Tipperary? They were there already. He examined the mileage chart in the Welcome Aboard booklet. Auckland, for instance – that really was a long way. 13,165 miles from London as the Comets flew. Compared with New Zealand, even Honolulu's distance was middling. Incautiously he mentioned the fact to his neighbour.

Twenty minutes later Loud-mouth was still talking about the size of Texas. How could any man become so garrulous on Coca-Cola, Douglas wondered. First he closed his eyes, then he began heavy breathing, until at last the deluge was diverted to unhappy 19D.

Left at peace to wander, his thoughts settled at once on Ashley and the previous day's memorial service to the nation's latest hero. Wilberforce and Wellington, and now Wyndham West.

According to the Archbishop, they had come together in that House of Prayer to remember Ashley Wyndham West and give thanks to God, the Giver of all goodness, for him and his life among them. They were not to feel sorrow as men without hope, but in the faith of their Lord commend him to the wisdom and love of God.

The House of Prayer was St. Paul's and those who had come together included enough celebrities to cover several pages of *Who's Who*. Only the Primate of All England was thought good enough to conduct the service, and he did it from bidding to blessing. The other Archbishop contributed only the address, while the Bishop of London, out-ranked in his own cathedral, was confined to the lesson and a junior partnership in the prayers.

The Queen was represented by Snowdons and Kents. From his seat at the back near the centre aisle Douglas had watched them arrive and followed the movement of their detectives with a professional eye. The Prime Minister came in person, discreetly flanked by private secretary and bodyguard, leaving two more at the door. The Foreign Secretary came with the Minister for Overseas Development, chummily sharing a detective between them. The mounting size of the force on duty amused Douglas, but he had to confess afterwards that he could have done with their assistance.

The University of Oxford had enjoyed the privilege of completing Ashley's education, and the Chancellor and Vice-Chancellor processed up the aisle in full academicals to honour him. They were followed by the President of his college and the Chairman of the Governors and Head-master of the school which took the credit for moulding his character. It had moulded Douglas's too and behind them he was astonished to see a familiar shambling figure. Darlybags had been considered rather older than Methuselah thirty years before, when Ashley and Douglas were in his house. He seemed no older now.

Colour was contributed by the diplomatic corps, which was out in force, especially the Indians. To judge from the size of his posse, the entire staff of the Indian High Commissioner had waived its religious scruples to accompany him in a national gesture of farewell.

A contingent of communicators was led by the Chairman of the BBC and the Editor of *The Times*, and what with life peers, prominent do-gooders and two Beatles in a crowd which overflowed from the rotunda, right down the nave and out into the street, Ashley would have been pleased at drawing a better crowd than finals day at Wimbledon.

When the organ's mourning discords faded and the service began, they all sang that the God of Love their Shepherd was and how Ashley was walking in death's shady
dark abode, but not in fear. At this point Douglas was
conscious of being scrutinised from further along his row.
But when he looked sideways to return the scrutiny it
seemed that he had been mistaken.

The lesson was taken from Revelations. The anthem
came from Mozart. Nothing but the best for Ashley. The
hymn, inevitably, was the old chestnut featuring India's
coral strand.

In the address they were told how God had inspired his
servant Ashley Wyndham West to great deeds and how the
world was the poorer for his passing. He was a sower who
had gone forth sowing good seed. This present act of worship (so the Archbishop believed) was a tribute to shining
virtue, from the whole nation and indeed from the whole
sisterhood of nations.

As a grand finale the choir treated the congregation to
Immortal, Invisible, God Only Wise (In Light Inaccessible
Hid From Our Eyes). While the basses thundered and the
trebles filled the dome with descant, Douglas mouthed the
words and told himself that Only Wise was about right.
The solitary wreath propped against the high altar was no
evidence of Ashley walking in death's shady dark abode.

In the middle of the second verse he glimpsed among
the forest of backs a rear view of Ashley's mother. She
had worn well, like Darlybags: an elderly beanpole in-
domitably erect. There had been no other children, and
she stood alone – the sole family mourner. Mr. West could
scarcely have been expected. Officially dead for many years.
there was strong doubt whether he had ever been alive.
Douglas prayed that Ashley's apotheosis wouldn't lead to
belief in a new Virgin Birth.

As a boy he had tried without success to discover the
truth about Ashley's father. Ashley himself, when pressed,
used to hint at an affair between his mother and a Royal
Personage. In the safety of his potting shed, however, the
Wyndham West gardener had once confided to Douglas

that Mr. West was the man who used to call on the first Tuesday of each month to tune old Mr. Wyndham's piano. When he turned to tuning the daughter too, he was paid to go abroad and not come back. Since the Wyndham family claimed cousinship with Lord Leconfield a misalliance had been unthinkable.

They also claimed kinship with the Earls of Shaftesbury – hence the Ashley – and whatever the truth about Mr. West, mother and son adopted aristocratic airs. Douglas had to admire her pose now. She looked a good deal more regal than the royals across the aisle. How much did she know of Ashley's recent life, he wondered. Not that it mattered. He couldn't imagine himself successfully extracting any worth-while information from that flat but formidable breast.

Blessed by the senior Archbishop and deafened by an organ voluntary extolling the triumph of resurrection, the congregation shuffled to its feet and dispersed in order of precedence. The first inkling of danger reached Douglas when Mrs. Wyndham West paused for a second beside him on her progress down the aisle. Like himself, she came under scrutiny from further along his row, but she gave no sign of recognition and passed on and out of the building.

This time he had identified the starer. A kneeling female mourner, head in hands. Her figure wore a faintly familiar air which he couldn't place. At the sight of her he was puzzled and uneasy. For her part, she seemed to know and dislike him. The hostility, at any rate, was recognisable. The menace in the eyes alarmed him.

She rose and moved deliberately against the stream as though inviting him to reveal his intentions by following her. The openness of the challenge disconcerted him, but this was what he had come for. Any sort of a lead. He hesitated, then accepted the invitation.

Struggling through coveys of oncoming diplomats, he nearly lost her. She was standing at the top of a flight of steps and hurried suddenly down when he appeared.

Below, he became suspicious too late. Only when faced with silence and darkness and a right-angle turn at the foot

14

of the stairs did he realise that she had been waiting for him at the top, making sure he didn't lose her. The menace was real.

They had the crypt to themselves. It must have been closed during the service and just reopened. There were lights but they were few and dim. He turned the corner cautiously and walked towards a chapel in time to see her disappear in the direction of a huge sarcophagus. She was moving too purposefully for a tourist, leading him towards darkness.

When they were both out of the chapel she spun sharply round to face him at a distance. Taking no chances, he dropped on one knee and reached for his trouser leg as he dropped. His eyes stayed on hers. She was clutching a handbag and her grip on it tightened. It could have been a threat or a nervous reaction.

She broke the tension by laughing – a high-pitched schoolgirl giggle more suited to someone half her age. Sheepishly he resorted to undoing a shoelace and doing it up again, worrying how to phrase the question about her interest in Ashley. When he was ready and looked up for her she had gone.

The laugh had disarmed him and he followed her off his guard, reckoning that an unobserved tête-à-tête would suit him well. He didn't bother to transfer the gun into his pocket and keep a finger on the trigger, as he should have done. He forgot that shots could be fired in the remote corners of the stone undercroft without being heard above.

The sarcophagus bore the name of Horatio, Viscount Nelson, and the revolver crack came when he was abreast of the inscription. He felt the bullet graze his thigh and heard it pinging and ricocheting among the arches. He fell to the ground, as much from surprise as in self-preservation. Then he crawled towards Nelson for protection. There were dark alcoves of tombs on all sides. It was impossible to guess where the shot had come from.

Lying on the cold flags, he prayed for himself more fervently than he had prayed for Ashley. The humiliation of being outwitted and winged by a woman was more pain-

15

ful than the wound itself. Gun in hand too late, he peered into the gloom, alert for the slightest twitch of movement.

When it came the movement was behind him, accompanied by voices. He sprang up to find other visitors in the chapel coming in his direction. A grey-haired couple went by and he joined them in inspecting the next sarcophagus. Inside were the remains of Arthur, Duke of Wellington. He discovered no one concealed behind.

In the company of other visitors he cautiously explored among the various tombs and memorial tablets of the great. Beatty and Jellicoe, Constable and Van Dyck, Arthur Sullivan and Alexander Fleming – he drew a blank at all of them. This was the company Ashley Wyndham West was to keep, but the woman had slipped away.

Loud-mouth was jogging his elbow to announce lunch. While they ate, and for what seemed a century afterwards, Douglas was treated to a survey of the American political and economic scene. With particular reference to the numerous iniquities of the late Franklin D. Roosevelt.

When he at last disengaged himself and looked out of the window the whiteness below was cloud no longer. A bay came into view, almost sealed by a narrow spit of land. Inhospitable, but transatlantic. They had made the crossing.

His watch said 17.40, which meant two hours more to New York. He craned over the seat backs to make sure that his friend in the thick coat was behaving herself. She wasn't. Her seat was empty.

In the panic of the moment he almost believed that she had slipped away a second time – by parachute presumably. But a minute later she passed down the aisle on her way from the toilet and he had to shrink back to avoid being seen.

Boston below became the next excitement. Then Kennedy was promised, with cloud, rain and a temperature of thirty-six degrees. Loud-mouth sneered at the news and the moist sky outside the window. The climate, like everything else, was better in Dallas.

The engines slowed and the long descent began. It lasted more than half an hour. At 19.47 they touched down in a sodden desert landscape. Long Island lay enveloped in the same grey mizzle as London. Time and distance changed nothing, this side of Texas.

Not for Douglas either. Memorial services offered no proof of death. After all those hours and miles his problem remained. Was Ashley dead?

Transit passengers were encouraged to alight for the stop-over. They accepted readily enough. His quarry disembarked with the others. But Douglas noticed that she left the thick coat on board.

He produced his passport and transit card for immigration, then dawdled behind the rest of the party, making a show of aimless leg-stretching. When they were out of sight round a bend in the interminable corridors he changed gear and made a brisk diversion through a door marked Chief Immigration Officer. There he showed another pass: International Air Transport Association, Security and Fraud Prevention.

Co-operation was prompt. His business took ten minutes. When he rejoined his group a stewardess was already explaining that there had been a mistake. Although only in transit, passengers technically entered the country if they left the aircraft. They must therefore complete the usual formalities. Instead of being shepherded on to the transit lounge they would be shepherded back through customs and immigration to the terminal entrance. There they would be given forms.

'Where were you born?' 'Where do you live?' 'What gifts are you bringing?' While filling in the answers he kept the corner of his eye on the woman. She gave no sign of recognition but must have seen him. She gave no sign of discomposure either, although one purpose of his manoeuvre was to rattle her. Faced with the possibility of a customs examination, she must have been congratulating herself on leaving that coat behind.

The form-filling provided him with his first opportunity to study her. She was of uncertain age. The even features and smooth skin suggested early thirties. So did the ash-blonde hair. Yet the skin had a dead appearance and the

18

hair might be a wig. In that case, well-preserved forties would be nearer the mark.

When they moved on, she walked with a slight awkwardness. Not a limp like his, but more of a bandiness. He thought he knew the cause. She was carrying her revolver in a favourite female hiding place. The inside of the thigh. How was she going to explain that to the customs? It would be a relief to have the thing confiscated, but they mustn't be allowed to put her off the flight. Or to take the coat.

Back at immigration again, the party met another hitch. The immigration officers themselves had not been told.

'Transit? How long are you staying? Leaving by the same flight in ninety minutes? Who told you to fill out forms?'

After a bout of confusion, word filtered through. It was okay. They needed forms. Yesterday they wouldn't have. Tomorrow they wouldn't have. But today was one of those days. They sure needed them today.

The woman in the queue in front of Douglas had no visa. It was 19D.

'No visa? What happened?'

She didn't have a visa because she had no intention of entering the States. She was en route for Australia.

'Then you should have stopped on the plane.'

She would have, she said, if she'd known how they treated passengers at Kennedy.

Tempers became frayed, hard words exchanged. She was taken away to the customs section in tears to be searched.

When the whole group was through he paid a second visit to the private office.

'Negative,' he was told.

'But she was carrying a revolver.'

'We stripped her right down. Nothing. Nix.'

They argued. He demanded her form. It was the wrong one. 19D had been searched in error.

'We're not doing a repeat. We told you one, and that's the lot.'

'But you picked the wrong one. I described the woman for you and distinctly said —'

'It's not our fault if the description was inadequate. You should have pinpointed your suspect more accurately. You guys seem to think we've time on our hands here. Why, the number of passengers we process —'

'My description was perfectly clear. You searched the woman you did because she started arguing.'

'Nuts. You didn't even know your party's name. Here, is this the form? Take it and say thank you.'

He took the proffered form. If they knew it was the right one, that proved the mistake was theirs. But what was the point in arguing? He put it in his pocket and left. He had long grown reconciled to bearing the brunt of other people's boobs. Douglas the fall guy. Douglas the scapegoat. Douglas the sucker. That was his role in life.

It took him a long haul from arrival to departure, but the exercise restored his equanimity. Up escalators, along corridors, past flight-information boards, he worked off his depression. Aeroflot and Air Afrique were due in. Braniff International and Irish International due out. Airports appeared all alike whatever the country. Apart from the odd names like soda fountains and drugstores, and tax-free for duty-free shops, Kennedy could be Heathrow.

Outside the window of the main concourse the flags of all nations drooped in the drizzle and the view was car park as far as the eye could stretch. This reminded him of Schiphol. There were so many airports in his life. A taxi pulled away and it occurred to him that his quarry might panic and do a bunk. If that happened he would have mucked it properly. She was his only lead 'in the game which Ashley – or someone else – was playing.

In the transit lounge a stewardess was apologising to a group of sullen passengers. The US Civil Aeronautics Board did not like foreign airlines crossing the States and therefore adopted a policy of haphazard harassment. BOAC were sorry for what had occurred but it was not their responsibility. Transit passengers were advised to stay on the aircraft when they reached San Francisco.

His quarry sat there listening impassively. How silly of him to imagine her flitting without her coat.

They re-embarked with relief and trundled along the runway for a second sight of Long Island's uninspired sound. He had not adjusted his watch and it registered nearly 22.30 his time. Six more hours until the next stop.

Flight over land became rougher. They bored and shuddered a passage over the turbulence of North America. Dinner was served at midnight – teatime below. Loudmouth had left at New York, heading for Dallas, but Douglas enjoyed no noise abatement. One of the children across the gangway seemed intent on howling non-stop round the western hemisphere.

The clouds cleared with the meal. Over a mind-healing cognac he looked down on a flat snowy surface meagrely dotted with lights. A near-nothingness as blank from above as the great Iranian desert. He asked the stewardess where it could be, and she asked the steward, who had to ask the captain. A hundred miles west of Minnesota. Well, at least he didn't live there. That was one failure he had avoided.

He took out the form passed to him in the immigration office at Kennedy. Sylvia Smith was the name and she claimed to be British. Born in London, January 1924. Resident in Hawaii. The words were laboriously spelled out in shaky capitals as though written by a centenarian or an alcoholic.

January 1924 would make her forty-five. Nearly Ashley's age and his own. Instinctively he glanced up to test for accuracy, but her back could have been any age. What about Smith? The most plausible of names, but one which made checking next to impossible.

The brat had been doped with aspirin, and one by one the other noises in the cabin subsided. Stripped-in-error 19D had moved across the aisle to be sorrowful alone. Time was telling on the whole plane-load. Lights were extinguished and, with adjacent seats empty, he put up the arm-rests, gathered all three pillows, took off his jacket and shoes, found a blanket in the rack above and stretched himself out beneath it. He would doze through the prairies

21

of the Mid-West and rock-a-bye across the Rockies.

Try as he might, sleep wouldn't come. A girl friend was out of character for Ashley, so she must be a business partner. But what would prompt him to make her his heir? Blackmail? That shouldn't be beyond her.

Against his will Douglas returned to the encounter in St. Paul's.

Emerging from the semi-darkness of the crypt into the splendour of the cathedral, he was hailed before he had time for more than a quick surreptitious inspection of his thigh. A flesh wound, luckily. Skin deep – little more.

'Douglas! I thought I recognised you skulking at the back during the service. Long time no see! How are you?'

'Oh hullo.' He jumped at the voice. 'I'm all right. Getting by.'

'You're looking rather washed out. There's nothing wrong, is there?'

'Nothing at all. And you? You're looking quite the opposite – disgustingly healthy and prosperous, I must say.'

Was it a lucky chance meeting Jack Willingdon just then, or not the mere coincidence it seemed? The girl had made off and he could hardly break away in belated pursuit.

'An appearance of well-being is a professional disguise. It inspires confidence in the clients. Who would consult a threadbare solicitor?'

'No one, I suppose.' He looked around. 'This is a sad occasion.'

'Indeed yes. As a matter of fact I organised the service. It went off rather well, don't you think?'

Douglas agreed.

'Poor Ashley! What a terrible tragedy! But what a terrific turn-out for him. Even you, Douglas. I wouldn't have expected any last respects from you.'

'Why not? I knew him on and off for forty years.'

'No reason at all. Except that, after that unfortunate affair in India during the war, we all seem to have lost touch with you.'

They were outside on the steps by this time and Douglas

said nothing, staring carefully at Queen Anne. He was pondering how to tackle Jack without arousing suspicion, when Jack solved the problem for him.

'I'll tell you what. Before you disappear for another twenty-five years why don't we have a reminiscing noggin? Better still, if you're free for tiffin what about a bite at my club? Ashley's mama is off my hands, thank God, and I've made the last free-will offering to the umpteenth verger.'

Taxis proved scarce, so they walked down Ludgate Hill. Douglas stepped out as normally as his leg would allow and hoped that nothing was noticeable. Jack delivered his own funeral oration on Ashley as they went.

'His death is unbelievable. A senseless accident on the other side of the world. I can't tell you how vital and vibrant he was, how full of life and gusto. Even if you haven't met him since the war you must have seen him on the box. No one would have believed he was nearly fifty. Still flaxen-haired and fit as a fiddle. Still charming the birds off the trees. It's difficult to accept the fact that a person like that is dead.'

Jack's glance was bland. Douglas hastily put on his poker face. Was the remark innocent, or bait for him to rise to? Best to ignore it.

'Ashley wasn't much interested in bird-charming when I knew him,' he said. 'He never married, did he?'

'No,' Jack replied. 'And yourself?'

Douglas fought down a flush. 'No, I've never married either. And not likely to. I travel a lot in my job and it wouldn't work. Sometimes I'm abroad for the best part of a year and always on the move.'

'You're still in government service then? The Foreign Office, isn't it?'

'No, no. Nothing like that. Commerce, I'm afraid. Export – import. It's just a tiny company in a very small way of business.' The lie came easily.

Jack's club was plushy. First, Douglas retired to the lavatory to inspect the damage to his thigh. The bullet had torn off a neat strip of trouser and a corresponding strip of

23

skin underneath. It stung like mad when he dabbed it with a handkerchief, but otherwise felt stiff rather than painful. With a pukka dressing it would soon heal. Meantime he was losing no more blood than a donor. He reminded himself to keep a hand over the tear.

Ashley had been a member of the club and his fellow members had attended the memorial service in force. The bar was full of them, drowning their sorrow. 'Terrible blow,' they were saying, and 'the worst thing to happen since Suez.'

Everyone except Douglas seemed to know everyone else except Douglas. It was a roomful of men who had arrived and he clearly hadn't. His clothes weren't either smart or aggressively shabby. His voice wasn't either booming or soft in the top-executive manner. Like flushing, he should have outgrown his sense of inadequacy but he hadn't. Maybe his triumph was to come, and wouldn't they all be astonished and confounded when he pulled it off?

Jack declared that nothing made him thirstier than a memorial service. Since they had a reunion to celebrate as well as a death to mourn, he insisted on champagne. It was served chilled in silver tankards and quickly loosened his tongue.

He reminisced about India during the war. Those were the days, weren't they? The days of the British raj. Did Douglas remember that Christmas in Bombay? The bathing? The Towers of Silence where vultures picked at human corpses? The frolics at the Taj Mahal Hotel? The Parsee women at the races? The prostitutes on offer in cages? What about that leave in Naini Tal when a fakir had walked stark naked down the main street at high noon with all the memsahibs and their daughters doing their weekend shopping? And none of the police dared arrest him because a fakir was as holy as a cow.

Douglas wished he was in a pub by himself with a ham sandwich and half a pint of draught Guinness. 'No,' he replied when the pause came, 'I don't remember Naini Tal.'

Jack apologised. Naini Tal must have been after Douglas's spot of bother. No need to go into all that again, although this he had to say: Douglas had been shame-fully treated. They must have another noggin of champers and then they really ought to eat.

By the time they reached the dining-room they were both awash with champers. Douglas allowed himself to be talked into caviare and an *entrecôte* and a bottle of *Clos de Vougeot*. When the wine had been sniffed and pronounced palatable he began probing for information about Ashley.

'I believe you handled the legal side of Ashley's Fund?'

'Not me personally. My firm, you know. And not all of it. A great deal has to be done in India and elsewhere.'

Through the meal they talked of the India Fund, which was Ashley's life work and his legacy to mankind. After the British withdrawal Ashley, almost single-handed, had maintained and developed charitable relations between the two countries. Britain was affluent, India was starving. The reviled imperialists who had exploited and plundered a subcontinent would demonstrate their true character by re-turning the loot of the nabobs in the form of charitable donations. That was his vision, and he made it a reality.

In a Gladstonian campaign in the early 1950s Ashley, who had come to love India as a wartime officer in the Indian Army, persuaded the British public of a moral ob-ligation towards the former Empire's brightest jewel. He evoked sentiment. He pleaded for compassion. He threw out hints of self-interest through a continuing connection beneficial to trade.

His fund-raising ran into millions of pounds. Wealthy companies contributed, and hundreds of thousands of in-dividuals – from retired colonels and church-going spin-sters to idealistic students and obedient schoolchildren. In a few years Ashley Wyndham West became famous as the creator and organiser of what quickly grew to be the best-known charitable enterprise in history. IF. Unlike the other giant foundations – Rockefeller, Ford, Nuffield and Gul-benkian – IF enjoyed wide public support and continual publicity. Other charities grew in its shade. Oxfam, Shelter, War on Want.

'We all thought of Ashley as a prophet,' said Jack, wiping the last of the caviare from his chin with a napkin, 'but of course he wasn't an airy-fairy waffler at all. He was bloody practical. That's what made the whole enterprise tick.'

According to Jack, funds had been collected by a well-disciplined field force operating on military lines. Once collected, cash was never distributed. That had been one of Ashley's strictest principles. The money was used to buy necessities or the machinery to produce them. In time of famine IF gave rice; otherwise it would be ploughs and combine harvesters and electricity generators. IF never used government or commercial channels. To prevent corruption and profiteering from eating into its funds, it established its own purchasing agents.

'Ashley was determined to satisfy people that what they gave wouldn't go the way of so much American Aid. He supervised all the buying himself.' Jack nodded approval over the *entrecôte* as he catalogued Ashley's virtues.

Ashley had been a showman too. An actor *manqué*. Each piece of equipment was presented personally to a particular Indian village or group of villages, often by Ashley himself. It always came as a gift from a particular English locality or body. Towns, regions and institutions were paired: 'Calcutta with Manchester, Kashmir with the Scottish Highlands, the universities of Cambridge and Benares. Mayors, governors, lords-lieutenant, chairmen of students' unions all exchanged courtesy visits. With Ashley as impresario.

'Who will become Director-General now?' asked Douglas.

'Difficult to say at this stage. The executive committee meets next month. It will have to be decided then.'

'I was wondering whether it would be George Paget.'

Jack Willingdon frowned at his last mouthful of steak. 'He won't get my vote. I can promise you that.'

George had been one of the boys in India. They all passed out of the same Officers' Training School into the same regiment, and George was Ashley's special crony. Almost as smooth as Ashley himself, he packed a sting in his tail like a scorpion, as Douglas had discovered since. A sidekick and a natural successor, one would have thought.

Like Ashley, George was sharp about money. Towards the end of the war he began cultivating business contacts with local army contractors. Instead of returning home he chose to be demobbed in India and set up shop in Delhi as a commercial agent and PR consultant. When the India Fund was launched he became the Indian end of it. Paget & Co.'s offices expanded into the India Fund Buildings, occupying a whole segment of Connaught Circus and enjoying semi-governmental status. Douglas had met him only that once since the war, but once was more than enough. If George Paget became the new Director-General it would be a short-lived appointment because Douglas intended to kill him.

Over the port and Stilton he probed deeper as Jack appeared to grow more and more fuddled.

'Weren't you Ashley's personal solicitor too? There'll be a lot of public interest in the will.'

Ashley had worn the Fund's millions like a halo. His public image projected him as an other-worldly do-gooder, a kind of secular clergyman. Although he lived among the rich and wined and dined with them, it seemed that he always did it for the sake of starving India. He held press conferences at the Savoy, attended charity balls at the Dorchester and was for ever flying round the world on a first-class ticket. But his expression and his aides left no one in doubt that he would have preferred a monastic life of simplicity and austerity. The Savoy and the Dorchester were in the line of duty. The first-class seat was provided by tender-hearted airlines keen that he should arrive at his destination fresh for the good works ahead.

'You knew Ashley. How much do you think he left? Have a guess.' Jack was becoming indiscreet at last. Or probing too.

'A million or two,' said Douglas incautiously.

'That's a bad guess, old boy, and a bad joke.'

'How much then?'

'You don't expect me to tell you before probate is granted?'

'Why not? I promise to keep it to myself.'

'Well, since you seem to have got Ashley all wrong and it'll be public knowledge shortly anyhow, I'll tell you.' Jack paused for effect. 'He didn't leave a penny.'

Douglas hid his surprise by taking a slow swig of port.

'Croft's '35,' said Jack. 'Do you like it?'

'Excellent,' Douglas pronounced, hardly tasting it. 'Is there no beneficiary?'

'That's the most extraordinary thing.' Jack leaned across the table in excitement. 'Beneficiary's hardly the *mot juste* in the circumstances, but he left all his nothing to a woman. It seems he met her in Hawaii and kept her to himself. So you may have got Ashley's sex life all wrong too.'

'What sort of age is this woman? What's her name? Did he marry her?'

Douglas had a vision of Ashley in one of his frequent television appearances. The sports coat and turtle-neck sweater. The handsome, smiling Adonis face. Then the earnest Boy Scout manner. Clean in word and deed. No womaniser he.

'Frankly she's a mystery. I didn't draw up the will, so there wasn't an opportunity of asking him about her. As executor I've written, of course, and asked her to come and see me. So far she hasn't turned up. She's not described as a wife, so they didn't marry evidently. Really the only thing I know about her is her name which doesn't mean anything to me. And wouldn't to you.'

'It might. I knew Ashley rather better than anyone else at one time, if you remember.' Douglas looked expectant, but it didn't work.

'I'm sorry, but the name has to remain confidential until I've made contact.'

'It wasn't Susan something by any chance?'

'No it wasn't. I know about Susan.'

Douglas gave silent thanks for small mercies. Everything pointed to the woman in the crypt and he couldn't have borne its being Susan.

'Why on earth do you expect her to show up,' he asked, 'if she lives in Hawaii and there's nothing here to collect?'

'Apparently she has been in Paris since Ashley died. She came to Europe after the funeral in Honolulu. I got a postcard yesterday saying she hoped to attend the service today on her way home but wouldn't have time to call at the office. I kept an eye cocked for her, but it was hopeless with such a mob. Particularly if one doesn't know whether she's nineteen or ninety-two. Her handwriting suggests a great-grandmother.'

'If you were to change your mind about telling me her name I might be able to help.'

'Why so interested, old boy?'

They had left the table and Jack turned a glazed eye on Douglas's face. From there it travelled down and fixed itself on the blood-stained tear in his trousers.

Douglas shrugged the question aside and moved his arm down to cover the tear. Later in the afternoon he rang Jack on the pretext of thanking him for the lunch. The woman's name remained on the secret list, but Jack had news for him. She had actually telephoned. They had cleared up one or two matters which were holding up probate. No, he would not be seeing her. She didn't reveal her London address and was flying back to Honolulu the next morning.

He must have slept eventually. The circling of the plane woke him. His watch said 4.20 and ribbons of light welcomed them from below. The couple behind were arguing which were Oakland and which San Francisco. A lonely fairy chain had to be the causeway, strung across the invisible bay.

The aircraft flew round and round like a kite on an off-day for prey. Local time had slipped back another three hours, making nine in all. It was nearly eight o'clock in the evening and they had dined at midnight five hours before.

On landing they all left the plane again, despite the lesson and warning at New York. Even harassment was preferable to staying aboard. But this time Douglas had no
29

business with immigration and the party stayed un-harassed.

The airport seemed less haphazard than Kennedy and more spacious than Heathrow. The mock marble was familiar, though. They walked on it all through the building, round the four sides of a gigantic square. The airlines on the arrival and departure boards were Western, Philippine and Japan. Outside the departure lounge their aircraft stood where they had left it for the Great March.

The exercise restored Douglas's circulation and roused him into wakefulness. His ears troubled him, blocked with the pressure of two long descents. His eyes he kept on Sylvia Smith. She had worried him by lingering overlong beside a shoplet called Shaw's Candies, but now sat docilely awaiting re-embarkation. He had tailed many suspects in his time but never a gunwoman who was heiress to a nil estate.

The line to Paris had been crackling with atmospherics when he reported Jack's information about the flight, but his boss's instructions were clear. 'Fly and pursue.'

They were airborne again at 06.00 his time. The last leg of the flight would take five hours, making twenty-three in all. He entered the exact time in his notebook. Details like that added authenticity to his reports. A full one would have to go to Paris, something routine to Montreal. He yawned, closed the window shutter on the Pacific and went to the toilet to dab his temples and wrists with Elizabeth Arden's *eau-de-Cologne*.

While dabbing he decided to change his seat in the cabin. A moustachioed and sideboarded stage Irishman had boarded at San Francisco with his missus and taken the seats next to his. Even before seat-belts were fastened the man had been breathing ill odours and overlapping his quota of space. His missus had come from New York and for her benefit he gave a dramatic rendering of an encounter with a highway patrol on the freeway from Los Angeles. Also, there had been storms in southern California, leaving ninety-three dead and hundreds homeless. Bad-breath was more interesting than Loud-mouth but less wholesome. Douglas would like to have taken the *eau-de-Cologne* container and spilled the whole contents over him.

The cabin lights were dim when he stepped out of the toilet. Most of the passengers had dossed down to snatch at what sleep was going. Sylvia Smith sat with a blanket up to her chin. Her eyes were closed. She was breathing deeply. The garrulous Irishman had produced a bottle of John Jamieson for a nightcap. The stewardesses had stopped clattering in the kitchenette.

One of Douglas's overdeveloped senses was a nose for danger. He smelt it now.

He had an instinct for recognition too. A figure lay sprawled across the back row of seats within touching dis-

31

tance of his left hand as he stood in the aisle. The wall of
the cabin behind, the tall seat backs in front, and the near-
darkness – these all protected the newcomer from sight. Except from where Douglas stood. The head was half-
covered in blanket but Douglas recognised it in half a
glance and felt the juices in his stomach curdle. This was
the man he intended to kill, the man who would kill him
first if he could, and make a better job of it than Sylvia
Smith.

George Paget's eyes were closed but Douglas knew him
for the kind who might somehow see through eyelids. He
ducked cautiously and threw himself horizontal across
three vacant seats further up the cabin.

What had brought George aboard? Was it by arrangement with Ashley's girl friend or unknown to her? If by
arrangement, was it a scheduled rendezvous or an emergency because of what Douglas had set in motion in New
York? Were they not sitting together for his benefit or the
customs'? Was her life in danger? If it was, how much did
he mind?

The questions ran on until his mind tired and turned
back. To the previous spring. Moscow in May.

It was his first assignment in the new job. After a spell in
MI8 he had been transfered to MI5. Someone in MI5
had decided, a few years later, to second him to Interpol.
After trying him out in various departments Interpol had
shuffled him into a subsection assigned to work with
IATA. That was his intelligence career in a nutshell. He
was the dispensable counter-spy, the disposable agent. The
one permanently available for transfer and secondment.
The former backroom boy wandering the world with a gun
round his ankle and a catalogue of conscientious failures
in his dossier.

His new chief at Interpol accepted him with due reserve.
A Frenchman with de Gaulle's nose and aloofness, he was
known in the office as *Monsieur le Président*. The subsection boasted only two other operatives – Sammy
Samuelson and Pierre.

Pierre had served in the Resistance as a boy. He had been a loner since the day he had come home from school to find the house burned down and the bodies of the rest of the family in a row outside, bound and shot in the back of the head by the Gestapo. He resented taking Douglas with him to Moscow, but *Monsieur le Président* had insisted.

Sammy and Pierre had spent the previous two years coordinating police action against the growth of what had become the largest of international gold-smuggling organisations. Heavy consignments of gold were travelling illicitly by air all over the world. Carriers were caught from time to time, but never anyone who mattered. Investigation revealed nothing except the existence of the organisation. In countries like India and Japan, where demand for gold exceeded the legitimate supply, the excess demand was being systematically satisfied.

The local police could make no headway in the consumer countries because dealers, even honest ones, refrained from asking questions. If they did, they ran the risk of being put out of business. The producing countries accused each other. The South Africans were adamant that all their gold reached world markets legitimately. In Johannesburg Pierre was told brusquely that he would do better to pursue his inquiries in Russia. When he made approaches to the Russians he was snubbed for his pains. In the view of the Soviet government the affair was a plot by Rand plutocrats to raise the world price of gold.

When the invitation to visit Moscow arrived out of the blue, *Monsieur le Président* fingered it suspiciously. Soviet relations with Interpol were currently below freezing point on all fronts, and Rand plutocrats were not the only people with a vested interest in the price of gold. There were excellent reasons, commercial and political, for the Russians to encourage gold-smuggling in the rest of the world. After being so understandably obstructive why should they suddenly change their tune?

The form of the invitation was a curiosity in itself. It came from Aeroflot and had gone to IATA headquarters in Montreal. A foreign businessman suspected of gold-smuggling was said to be expected in Moscow. Would IATA care to send one of its investigators?

IATA passed the letter to Interpol in Paris and Interpol made polite inquiries from the Soviet Ministry of Foreign Affairs, which claimed to know nothing of the matter. The Ministry co-operated, however, to the extent of agreeing to issue a visa. Provided the applicant was acceptable.

The wrangle about visas was intense but conducted at surprising speed. The Russians would not issue more than one, and *Monsieur le Président*, deaf to Pierre's pleas. would not allow him to go unaccompanied. Then the Russians conceded two and *Monsieur le Président* nominated Sammy. The Russians then stated that they could not accept a Jew. So, in the end, Douglas went with Pierre.

A Mr. Smirnov met them at the airport and took them to an hotel, but was otherwise unhelpful. Their man had not yet arrived. When he did they would be informed. Meanwhile they must consider themselves the guests of Aeroflot. A car would be provided. On all other subjects he was uncommunicative. Their whys and wherefores went unanswered.

Pierre accepted the situation with a bad grace. He claimed that they had other assignments waiting and could not hang about indefinitely. He insisted on a return flight to Paris being booked for the following week.

In the hotel they were awarded a suite of Edwardian grandeur. Ante-room. Bedsitting room complete with dining table and two king-size beds. Private bathroom and lavatory. There could be only one reason for such VIP treatment and they spent a concentrated ten minutes tracking down the bugging device. It was concealed inside one of the bedside lamps. Pierre decided to muffle it with a sock but not to tamper further. The weather was warm and they put their heads out of the window to talk business.

'I don't like this at all.' Pierre spoke in a whisper. 'I thought it might be a trap before we came. Now I'm sure.'

'They can't be interested in us personally.'

'Have you ever worked against them?'

Douglas nodded. 'Of course. And you?'

'Who hasn't? But we're not important, as you say. They must be going to use us to discredit Interpol.'

'Or they may intend us to do something they don't want to take responsibility for themselves.'

Pierre shrugged. 'It would be better if Sammy were here.'

'I won't let you down, I promise.'

'It's not that. Sammy speaks Russian. That's why they wouldn't have him. For us it's see Moscow and die.'

What they saw as they talked was a view across Marx Prospekt and 50th Anniversary of the Revolution Square to the walls and towers of the Kremlin. Beyond Red Square stood St. Basil's Cathedral with coloured domes like enormous peppermint whirls. In sunshine it all looked far from sinister.

They strolled across the square and entered the Kremlin without challenge. The days of Stalin had passed. There were gardens inside the walls and sights on display. A cannon too large to be fired and a bell too large to be rung. Wry specimens of tsarist megalomania. They inspected imperial regalia and court dresses in a museum and, outside again, the Kremlin's cluster of private cathedrals where tsars had been proclaimed and crowned. Proud exhibits of the citadel of a communist and atheist regime. Douglas did not feel reassured.

Nor did reassurance come as the days went by and nothing happened. Every night the red walls were illuminated and the towers topped with great red stars shining out of the darkness, a red flag floodlit above the tallest. For Douglas it resembled an illustration to a fairy story. He went to sleep with his automatic under his pillow, determined not to be lulled into false ideas. Yet every morning, with nothing else to do, they saw more improbable sights. Treasured icons at the Tretyakov. Gauguins at the Pushkin. Country houses of the nobility. Classical ballet in the Hall of Congresses and reactionary operas at the Bolshoi. If they went by car a guide accompanied them. When they walked they were discreetly followed.

On the morning of the last day of their week, while

Pierre was brewing an ultimatum, Mr. Smirnov reappeared to warn them not to leave their room. The man they were waiting for had arrived during the night and was in the room next door.

'What's his name?' Pierre demanded.

Mr. Smirnov was his usual evasive self. 'You must tell us.'

'The name in his passport? His nationality?'

'I cannot say. What does it matter? The passport will be false.' He smiled apologetically.

'Can we arrest him and take him out of the country?'

'On Soviet territory! Certainly not.' Pierre had shocked him.

'Are your police going to arrest him?'

'That is not for me to say.' At the mention of the police Mr. Smirnov became nervous.

'So all you are offering us is a chance to identify him so that he can be arrested when he leaves Russia? Is that it?'

The telephone rang and instead of replying Mr. Smirnov answered it. He spoke in Russian and the line at once went dead. They could hear the burring.

'Yes, yes, you may identify him. You have a camera? Good. We will tell you when he leaves his room. You may find that he is English.'

Mr. Smirnov addressed the last remark to Douglas and left the room in a hurry.

'That telephone call scared him,' said Douglas, 'What do you think is going on?'

'It smells,' said Pierre gloomily. 'If this man is buying on the black market they would arrest him themselves. If he is dealing officially they wouldn't have sent for us unless they had run out of use for him and wanted us to take him away. They must know who he is.'

The Soviet government was not as monolithic as it seemed. In a communist country, where no opposition is permitted, the opposition was within the government. Smirnov's reaction to the mention of police and the phone call suggested to Douglas that he represented one government agency but not all.

36

'You may be right,' Pierre agreed. 'Suppose one department has to earn foreign currency from the sale of gold and can earn more by selling it illicitly. Then suppose another department prefers to keep all available gold inside the communist bloc. It's illegal under Soviet law for our friend in the next room to buy gold and take it out of the country, but he does it with official connivance. If other officials stop him they start an inter-departmental war which they may lose. So what do they do?'

'Call in foreign investigators who take action on their own account and can be said to have exceeded their brief. We're meant to kill him, aren't we?'

Pierre lit a cigarette and flicked the match down on to the pavement below. They were talking at the window as usual.

'I suppose so,' he said. 'You'd think if there's one thing the Russians could do for themselves it's killing people. But there may be suitable occasions for doing it by proxy. No doubt they would use this one, too, to prove that Interpol is a criminal organisation.'

'What happens if we do kill him?' Douglas didn't relish the role of fall guy.

'That depends on who wins the inter-departmental power game. At a guess I'd say twenty years' corrective labour in Siberia. With our past records of anti-Soviet activities we might even rate a show trial.'

'Thank you very much,' said Douglas. 'In that case I'm leaving my automatic behind.'

'That would be even riskier. Our friend and his contacts may be armed. We must take guns. But only shoot in self-defence. Bring your passport and escape wallet as well. If anything goes wrong, get a taxi straight to the airport. The flight is booked. If we make it we can always write our thank-you letters from Paris.'

The telephone rang and Pierre stubbed out his cigarette on the window-sill. Douglas picked up the receiver and a voice told him that the gentleman in the next room was leaving to keep an appointment. In the corridor a maid pointed to the back of a man already halfway down the stairs. They followed.

He paused at the newspaper kiosk in the lobby and bought a postcard. Outside in the street he stood for a moment to admire the scene before turning towards Gorky Street. At the corner he went down the steps to the metro. They closed up so as to board the same train, but instead he continued along the underground passage towards Red Square.

On surfacing he again did his admiring act, this time directed at the queue for Lenin's tomb. It stretched downhill from the square into the Alexander Gardens and snaked through the park between lilacs and red tulips for half a mile or more. Casually he walked up the slope towards the head of the queue. An official let him in a few yards from the front.

Pierre and Douglas followed with the same pretence of aimlessness. All three of them were carrying cameras tourist-style. Douglas thought they would have to wait in the square, but by showing their passports they were allowed to join the queue near the front. This made them bogus pilgrims, shuffling forward to worship at the black marble shrine of the people's anti-god.

Armed guards protected the entrance. Inside they stood in formation round the body itself. It lay embalmed, spectacularly lit, waxy but well preserved. A neatly trimmed beard and well pressed city suit. Outside, in the sunshine again, the procession straggled along the Kremlin wall past the graves and cremation plaques of minor anti-gods and heroes of the revolution.

At the exit their man was joined by a loitering girl. She was plump and tumblable, to the Slav taste, with a skirt too short for a party member. She looked like a good-time girl picking up a foreigner, and Pierre muttered that he wouldn't mind being compromised with her. She talked animatedly to the man, as though practising her English. When he turned his head to answer, Douglas suffered a shock. A spasm of recognition.

A building like a cross between Selfridge's and Paddington station occupied the whole of the far side of the square. Inside, it became a Victorian version of an oriental bazaar. Shops ran in rows on three storeys, connected above ground level with bridges across promenades. The entire area was roofed with great glass vaults over a series of arcades. In each arcade and at every level shoppers swarmed like bees in a glass hive.

The perfect place to lose a tail. Before Douglas could snap them the man and girl had disappeared inside. Pierre accelerated, signing to Douglas to follow.

They climbed to the top floor where the crowds were thinner. Then along a gallery where the shops gave way to storerooms and there were no shoppers at all. They were high in a distant corner of the building, the four of them alone. Douglas began to feel alarm at the unexpected isolation. He could see a mass of heads below and hear the rising babble of voices, but immediately to right and left the galleries were empty. He hurried on round corner after corner chasing Pierre's back, until he rounded one too many and found, not Pierre, but the girl facing him.

For an idiotic second he imagined she had stopped to ask him a question. Then he noticed the revolver. She held it low, aiming towards the pit of his stomach and points south.

He pretended surprise. 'What on earth is going on?' he demanded.

Her mouth and eyes were hard and she didn't bother to reply. It really seemed that she meant to plug him from a distance of five yards. He allowed the surprise to fade from his face and pretended to catch sight of someone over her shoulder.

'Pierre!' he called.

The trick worked. Her eyes followed his for an unguarded instant and he fell forwards, clutching at the gun. While they wrestled, it went off. It made a noise like a popgun and a bullet tinkled through the glass roof. The girl fled with a scream, leaving her weapon in his hand.

The scream was drowned in the sound of a commotion below. He ran through to a gallery overlooking the central arcade and looked down. A man had fallen from one of the upper galleries and lay sprawled on the stone floor beside a fountain. His skull had split open but the face was still recognisable. It was Pierre. Or had been.

He turned at once and ran back along the gallery, throwing the girl's gun into a waste-bin as he ran. He tripped and stumbled down flights of stairs, then steadied himself to a calm walking pace at the bottom before leaving by the furthest exit. A squad of plain-clothes police rushing from a parked car to seal the store nearly knocked him over on the pavement. It was a trap all right.

He walked round to Red Square and out of it in the opposite direction to his hotel. Most foreigners stayed at the Rossiya and he picked up a taxi there, where a stranger asking to be taken to the airport would attract least attention.

He never thought he'd make it, but at Sheremetyevo there was no hitch at all. He could hardly believe his luck when they let him take up the reservation on an SAS flight to Copenhagen. For a long half-hour in the departure lounge he kept an anxious watch on the door, expecting arrest at any moment by the usual posse of licensed roughnecks. In the end they never came.

His relief as the aircraft rose through the birch grove was quickly succeeded by guilt. 'I won't let you down,' he had told Pierre, and what had happened? A quarter-bottle of *Moët et Chandon* drunk to his memory was no consolation to either of them.

Back in Paris *Monsieur le Président* exploded and Sammy was reproachful. Why had he lagged behind and allowed himself to be held up by a girl? If Sammy had gone, they implied, Pierre might still be alive.

Even the one success of the assignment proved an embarrassment. He brought back no photograph of the man the Russians declared to be gold-smuggler-in-chief, but he could swear to his identity. The man was George Paget, friend and associate of that hero of the world, Ashley Wyndham West.

Half an hour out of Honolulu the arrival of yet another printed form roused him. He sat up and bent over it, taking pains to keep his face out of George Paget's line of vision.

Had he 'plants, live animals, cultures, or soil'? If so, which of the following: 'plants, cuttings, bulbs, seeds, flowers, corn on cob, radishes, turnips, other vegetables, soil, peat etc., live snakes, other reptiles, birds (live), dogs, cats, other animals, cultures, micro-organisms'? He was required to answer by the Hawaii Department of Agriculture, under Section 26 of the revised laws of Hawaii (1955) 'violaters of the law shall be fined not less than $25 nor more than $100 or imprisoned not more than six months or both'.

It was difficult to take the questionnaire seriously with George a few seats away. How could one tell whether one was carrying micro-organisms? What would the reaction be if he entered Sylvia Smith and George Paget under live snakes? Did the state of Hawaii worry more about undeclared peat than illicit gold?

Midnight local time and a temperature of seventy-four degrees. 'Aloha,' the airport tower announced in neon lights. 'Aloha,' echoed a notice on the customs building. Aloha meant welcome and the customs practised what it preached. If you had no gifts, samples, radishes or reptiles to declare, you were in, bud, and glad to have you with us.

With the connivance of a stewardess, Douglas had contrived to disembark first. He stood in the shadow of a wing and watched for Sylvia Smith. She left the aircraft without her coat and he asked the stewardess to check whether it was still aboard.

He had intended to make sure of Miss Smith here by handing her over to the authorities complete with coat. But there was only one customs officer on duty, the easy atmosphere made him hesitate, and how could he do it if she didn't have the coat?

The stewardess reported that a coat answering his description was on the aircraft but it belonged to a gentleman who was travelling on to Sydney. It came as no surprise

that the gentleman answered to the description of George
Paget.

By the time Douglas had established this, Sylvia Smith
was through customs and off into the sultry night.

Concrete shacks and urban sprawl. Tumbledown wharves along the Nimitz Highway.

Open water at last. Honolulu harbour with an illuminated Aloha smiling from the pierhead tower. Shop windows displaying shirts with Aloha across the chest. Even the taximeter welcoming him with an Aloha while it ticked up the dollars and cents. He had entered the land of the big hullo.

The taxi set him back five dollars at eight and fourpence to the dollar. Too much. His masters were mean about expenses. This would lead to a flurry of memos between Montreal and Paris. He had better bury it in the hotel bill. With the help of BOAC he had selected a modest place to stay. Thirteen dollars a night. Plus fifteen per cent service and four per cent local tax. No Hiltons and Sheratons for the likes of him.

More of an apartment house than hotel. He prowled warily round his room like a cat accustoming itself to a new home. They had put him on the twelfth floor, where a breeze augmented the air conditioning.

Two divan beds. A desk complete with telephone and directories. A blotter with Aloha on it.

A television set and a radio. A dressing table and an eating table. A cooking unit with shelves and a kitchen sink. A family-size deep-freeze.

Private bath and shower. Basin and lavatory.

No back ways in.

He should have flaked out and slept his flattened metabolism back into shape. Instead he switched on the television. Goodies were triumphantly shooting it out with the baddies. Being a detective was child's play on celluloid. He switched it off.

After a bath he felt spry and clear-headed. It might be

43

the small hours here, but where he'd come from it was early afternoon. No time for sleep. He reached for the directories and looked up police headquarters. His little black book of contacts told him who to ask for. Sergeant O'Leary.

Some busybody of a duty officer wanted to know all about him and his organisation. Douglas told him O'Leary would know and he'd show his credentials in the morning. Meantime he had an emergency on his hands. If O'Leary was not on duty, where could he reach him? Busybody replied crisply that they didn't give the home numbers of officers to strangers calling in the middle of the night, even if they were Lord God Almighty. Sergeant O'Leary would be on duty at nine o'clock. Whatever was eating the caller would have to keep till then.

Douglas thanked him sweetly for his Aloha and put down the phone in a huff. What was eating him would certainly not keep. George Paget would be off the plane before nine. Douglas took pleasure in imagining friend George's feelings when the inquiry by the stewardess forced him into claiming ownership of the coat. But it meant he wouldn't risk going on to Sydney. He and the coat would disappear at the only intermediate stop. Fiji.

Determined not to let Pierre's killer escape, Douglas began telephoning through the O'Learys listed in the directory. Four irate awoken slumberers. Fifth time lucky. If that was the word.

He explained who he was and what he wanted, to an accompaniment of heavy breathing at the other end.

'You a Limey?'

The question sounded hostile, as though Limeys and O'Learys didn't mix. Something to do with Oliver Cromwell, Douglas supposed. Aloha must be reserved for the natives.

'Yes. What's that got to do with anything?'

'What's your hotel?'

'The Pagoda.'

'Jap job, huh.' O'Leary's suspicions sounded confirmed. Come to think of it, Pearl Harbour was just down the road.

'And what's that got to do with anything?' Douglas demanded.

'Keep your hair on, bud. I'll be with you bright and early. I heard about you guys. Your problems are our problems. So relax.'

'I won't relax. I must have a general Interpol alert. There's a man who simply must be arrested at once. Paget's the name. Yes, Paget. P for Peanuts, A for Aloha, G for G-string, E for Elephant, T for Two. Here's the description. It's important. He's sure to have more than one passport.'

Douglas described him. Unlovingly. 'And please, he must be arrested with the stuff on him. Otherwise he is not to be held at all. Yes, interrogated and let go. He's aboard BA 531 for Nandi and Sydney. I reckon he'll make a dash for it at Nandi.'

'Okay. Message received.'

'And don't forget the warning that he's dangerous. A killer.' But the line had gone dead. He rang again. The number was engaged already.

He went to the window. In a chasm between the apartment blocks moonlight reflected from the ocean, silver as a Russian birch. On either side of the reflection, the water barely stirred. A sea dark, calm and secretive. In it Ashley had been reported drowned. His body was still missing. Douglas had been on his trail, along with George's, ever since Pierre's death in Moscow. They were too clever for him, but he would get them in the end. What else did he have to live for? Only the undesirable Helen.

He stripped off his pyjamas and lay down on one of the divans.

From Copenhagen he had gone straight to Paris to meet the reproaches and plead for pressure on the Russians to bring Pierre's murderer to justice. Unfortunately, as *Monsieur le Président* pointed out with Gallic precision, Douglas had made such haste to escape that he had returned without any evidence of a crime. From his report who could say with certainty that Pierre had not fallen accidentally while chasing his suspect? What had Douglas actually seen? Nothing, except Pierre dead.

The Russians remained implacably uninformative, refusing even to admit to Pierre's death. According to them he had fled the country on the SAS flight with Douglas, and *Monsieur le Président* was sent a stiff note demanding an explanation for the behaviour of his staff in disappearing like a pair of fascist bandits leaving their work undone. After this insult to the Socialist Peoples his department need expect no further co-operation.

Douglas felt guilty and offered to resign, but Sammy forestalled him by emigrating without notice to Israel. Pierre had been his particular friend. This left Douglas on his own, since for reasons of economy neither Pierre nor Sammy was replaced. Interpol headquarters never liked employing people. Liaison, yes. Conferences, yes. Staff, no. So Douglas became the entire establishment of the Air/Gold Smuggling Subsection.

He at once made himself more unpopular by insisting on the implications of his identification of George Paget. It meant that the sacred India Fund and the blessed Ashley Wyndham West were in the gold-smuggling racket up to their sanctimonious eyebrows. *Monsieur le Président* shrugged in disbelief and warned him that incontrovertible evidence would be required before any action could be taken. Arresting Mr. Wyndham West would be like laying hands on one of the Apostles. Interpol itself might not survive the repercussions.

Douglas pleaded for a team to help him prove his theory and clear up the whole affair. He knew these men personally and how to deal with them.

The request was refused. He could continue work on the case by himself. And then only on the understanding that there must be no scandal. No mistakes involving well-known names.

Monsieur le Président read him a severe lecture on the importance of circumspection in international police work. One must be a politician and a diplomat as well as a policeman. He had been making inquiries about Mr.

46

George Paget and discovered that the gentleman had the CBE (for charitable services), the high respect of the Indian government, and influential friends in official circles in America. Interpol colleagues in London, Delhi and Washington had recoiled in horror from any suggestion that Mr. Paget might not be all he seemed.

Douglas didn't bother to argue. George Paget also had the Danish Order of the Elephant and other peripheral perks for international services rendered, but the man was a criminal. They had known each other during the war, when Lieutenant Paget became an instructor in small arms and unarmed combat – something Douglas should have warned Pierre about in Red Square, but didn't.

A week later he learned that *Monsieur le Président*, smelling a personal grudge, had written to M15 to inquire whether they would like him back. Fortunately M15 declined with thanks.

The formal attachment to IATA came the next month. He remained on the job, but Interpol had shifted some of the responsibility for him on to IATA's Security and Fraud Prevention Section. When he protested, *Monsieur le Président* told him that after the incident in Moscow the smuggling would soon cease. Then IATA would want him transferred to forged tickets.

Towards the end of the summer he got a break. Scotland Yard reported their suspicions of an unaccountably globe-trotting girl who had once worked for the India Fund as a typist. Douglas traced her to Beirut, where she was living well above her apparent means. With the help of the Lebanese police he discovered an interesting fact. A local smuggling ring was training her to walk naturally while carrying heavy loads.

One day she flew to Zürich, stayed the night and caught a plane to Bombay. There were more direct routes from Lebanon to India, and he tipped off the Bombay police to search her. They found her wearing a girdle of gold nuggets weighing twenty-five kilograms. His efforts to connect her directly with George Paget failed, but in his report he underlined her connection with IF. Paget himself was back in Delhi living like a raja and keeping his nose clean. Douglas could only suppose that he and Pierre had guessed right about the set-up in Moscow and George had had friends in high places who saw him safely out of the country. He wondered whether Mr. Smirnov had survived the aftermath of the affair.

The second break came via a colleague concerned with smuggling by sea. The Canadian Mounted Police had become suspicious of a Vancouver company which exported cans of axle grease for agricultural machinery. In twelve months it had exported nothing but several hundred cans of grease. Also, it appeared to have no home trade to stave off bankruptcy. Its consignments always travelled to the same destination. The India Fund's offices in Madras.

At Douglas's insistence the next consignment was seized by the customs on arrival. A hundred cans of grease were emptied. When nothing was found the inspector in charge gave Douglas the benefit of his views on Interpol. Douglas had flown specially from Paris for the occasion and while they argued he let off his feelings by hammering in the bottom of a can. The inspector seized it from him to throw into the sea and then noticed the absence of any corresponding dent on the inside.

Re-examined, every can was found to have a double bottom. Nuggets of gold lay embedded in white styrene between the two sheets of tin. The total haul weighed more than a hundred kilograms. The inspector was promoted.

This happened at Christmas and within a couple of weeks Ashley Wyndham West had made his timely exit from life.

The telephone woke him at six. A woman's voice insisted that he had asked for a call. At half past seven his own alarm went. He had forgotten to switch it off. An hour later he dragged himself out of bed, mindful of his rendezvous.

He didn't feel so good. Seasoned or not, how could an air traveller expect to rush headlong through day and night without a modicum of sleep and feel none the worse for it? He punished his metabolism with a cold shower, which it resented.

Punctuality was a small man's virtue and he went down to breakfast on the dot. En route he called at reception to leave a message for Sergeant O'Leary. And to satisfy himself that the six o'clock call had been genuine. He hadn't yet heard Sylvia Smith speak. One couldn't recognise a voice from the memory of a giggle. When the switchboard girl confessed to making the call in error he felt disappointed. It was more than time to come to grips with Miss Smith.

O'Leary had been right in describing the hotel as a Japanese job. The restaurant took the form of a teahouse. It stood in a Japanese garden, surrounded by a moat which was more carp than water. Miniature flora bloomed all round. Azaleas and a waterfall and a little stone pagoda in thirteen tiny tiers. The carp were as brightly coloured as the azaleas – red, white, purple, gold and all permutations and combinations. The waitress said there were a thousand of them, worth a thousand dollars each, and Douglas worked out whether they could be profitably smuggled.

He ordered papaya and coffee and waited.

O'Leary showed up half an hour late without apology. He was chunky with slanted eyes and a touch of brown. Douglas groaned to himself. A Polynesian Irish-American. No wonder the chip on his shoulder had been audible on the phone.

'Your mate didn't show at Nandi.' O'Leary spoke accusingly. No good morning. Just instant aggression.

'Then he must be going on to Sydney.'

'Nope.'

'What do you mean, nope? I tell you he was on the flight.'

'Nope.'

'Then he must be here. He must have come off the aircraft after I left.'

'He didn't clear immigration.'

'Then where is he?' Douglas fought down a wave of panic.

49

O'Leary shrugged. 'That's your problem, fella. He could have changed flights.'

'Wouldn't he have gone through customs in that case?'

'They could have nodded him through.'

'Then we must wait for a report. We've got him wherever he goes.'

O'Leary didn't look so certain. He refused a cup of coffee and sat picking his teeth while Douglas finished his breakfast and digested the news with his food.

'You did send out that general alert, didn't you?'

'Fiji and Australia. Yep.'

'Only those two?'

'I reckoned that would cover it.'

Douglas lowered his head into his hands and let the wave of panic come. He had notched up yet another failure. The chance of a lifetime fluffed.

The murdering swine of a Paget had been making his fortune out of gold smuggled into India. It had probably been going on ever since the India Fund started. In all that time he would never have touched a kilogram of the stuff himself. Carriers like the typist in Beirut took the risks. Not the Mr. Bigs like George. But yesterday in an emergency he had had to take over a load.

That thick coat belonged to the same system as the Beirut girl's belt. With practice it could be worn or carried provided no one else felt the weight. Leather and sheepskin, it could pass as either a male or female garment.

This coat-load would be a loose end being tidied up. Ashley's exit surely meant that operations were thought too dangerous to continue. Douglas took the credit for that, but it meant that this would be the last opportunity of catching one of the ringleaders redhanded. Fluffed thanks to a Polynesian Irish-American cop who suffered from an inferiority complex about Limeys and wouldn't do what he was asked.

'Relax,' O'Leary told him. 'We'll pick the guy up. I've a general call out now. That's what made me late.'

To relieve his feelings Douglas changed the subject to Sylvia Smith. He explained how he had followed her for the purpose of inquiring into Ashley Wyndham West's death. Now he must interrogate Miss Smith before George Paget got in touch with her.

While O'Leary went to telephone he reviewed the state of play. Sylvia Smith and George Paget had a rendezvous here in Honolulu with a consignment of gold. Dividing the spoil? By drawing attention to himself in New York Douglas had alerted them and, to save la Smith from being arrested, George had taken over the gold. Why was he prepared to risk arrest for her sake? Blackmail? Love?

O'Leary returned. 'I have the address. You wanna go?'

They went. Automobiles, highways and reinforced concrete made up the island paradise. It could have been Miami or L.A. At Waikiki giant hotels crowded the shore, leaving a niggardly strip of sand. At Kapiolani O'Leary pulled up grudgingly to allow Douglas a sight of the scene.

In the sea surfriders were crouching on sandbanks waiting for the right wave. Or were launched and clambering to their feet on the crest of the surf. Other holiday makers in long canoes were paddling themselves like teams of galley slaves. On the beach it was warm enough to sunbathe through the January showers. In the streets tourist housewives from mainland America wore Polynesian shifts in patterns matching their husbands' Aloha shirts. A cavalcade of open cars passed, bearing a load of valued VIPs. The number plates proclaimed Hawaii the Aloha State and the visitors were garlanded with flowers.

'I call them things Welcome Wreaths,' said O'Leary with a graveyard sneer.

They drove round the extinct volcanoes of Diamond Head and across the causeway of Hawaii-Kai. Round Koko Head the coast grew wilder, and wind lashed the waves into white spray against the volcanic rock. No swimmers or surfriders here.

O'Leary seemed more in his element. He stopped of his own accord so that they could inspect a blow hole. The sea drove up under the rock and forced itself through the hole in periodic gushes. A single jet shot high in the air, collapsed and rose again. The orgasmic effect brought a grin instead

51

of the habitual scowl. Americanised, touristified Honolulu lay behind them. Here was primeval Oahu.

'Your Limey pal was drowned this side,' he said as the road climbed higher above the ragged coastline. 'Out there. The weather can get pretty rough between here and Molo-kai. One minute it's sunshine, the next you're in a squall.'

'Was he alone?'

'He and the dame hired a boat, it seems. A small job with an outboard motor. It capsized in a storm in the Kaiwi Channel. They were both in it. She got ashore. He didn't.'

'What about the body? Is there still any chance of its being washed up anywhere?'

'I guess not. The Pacific's big.'

'And the boat? Did that disappear as well?'

'The boat was washed ashore with the dame. He couldn't have done a bunk in it, if that's what you're thinking.'

'Could he have done a bunk without it? Slipped over the side and swum ashore?'

'Only a loony would risk it. The weather can be God-awful this side of the island. I wouldn't give a nickel for the chances of a guy in the sea out there in a storm.'

Within a few minutes the weather proved his point. Light rain grew heavier, and all at once the heavens opened. Visibility through the windscreen dropped towards zero. Oncoming traffic loomed from nowhere. O'Leary pulled over and, misjudging the clearance, knocked against a trash can. Water poured down the slope of the hill, making rivers of the side roads. Pools formed on the highway itself, and rocks and dirt were swept down with the torrents. Fields of pineapples and sugarcane turned into lakes. Houses became islands.

'We'll never make the house in this,' said O'Leary. 'They told me it's way up a hillside beyond Kaneohe.'

He kept going at a grim crawl until they reached a police station. A gum-chewing detective welcomed them without enthusiasm.

'So you made it, huh?'

They sat on upright chairs in an office which must once

have been a cell. The house which Ashley had bought as a hideaway lay a couple of miles further on, inaccessible until the storm subsided. The dame was there for sure, the detective said.

He had been making inquiries. She had arrived from the airport in the middle of the night. She was alone. Yes, he had seen her once – at the Wyndham West inquest. She had given evidence about the drowning and arranged for the funeral. She kept herself to herself. Her visit to the island at the time of the drowning was her first. She had no friends, and folks respected her grief. No one knew her except the home help, who called her a real genuine person.

'This West guy,' said O'Leary. 'I heard he was a bigshot. Boss of the charity for Injuns. The Governor came to the funeral, didn't he, and they damn near brought the President from Washington DC.'

'A funeral without a body,' said Douglas.

'It happens.' O'Leary leaned forward and tapped the other detective on the knee. 'What were their relations?'

'Their sexual relations? According to her at the inquest, they were thinking of getting married, and he bequeathed her the lot. I wasn't under the bed, but I guess he must have been getting something for his money.'

'That will is a motive for murder,' O'Leary pointed out. 'The guy must have been well stacked.'

'It's a swell house, and real estate hereabouts is pricey. He wouldn't have got much change from a couple of hundred thousand bucks. If I had that kind of money and wasn't married, I'd fix myself up with a younger girl.'

'I must question her,' said Douglas. 'Can we go?'

'Not today we can't. If the rain lays off tonight I can take you there tomorrow.'

'Tomorrow may be too late. It's vital I hear her account of the drowning.'

The others looked at him in surprise.

'Why should tomorrow be too late?' demanded O'Leary.

'She knows about me. She'll slip away.' The storm was just his luck.

53

'No, she won't,' O'Leary reassured him. 'We'll see to that. She's a Limey like you, and Limeys stick out round here.'

'I can tell you what came out at the inquest,' said the local detective, shifting his gum into the pouch of his cheek. 'The pair of them hired a boat for the day. West ordered it by phone from a boatman at Kahaluu on the bay. When the boatman heard he was thinking of going to Molokai he told him, better put off the trip because the forecast was bad. West said he had a guest on a stopover and he had to take her out that day. If the weather became rough they would stick along the coast.'

'How did he appear when they set off?'

'He didn't collect the boat himself. She did. She told the boatman who she was and how Mr. West was bringing the picnic and fishing tackle down to the shore near the house. She said she was used to handling boats and would be picking him up. She promised to warn him again about the weather and against attempting the crossing.'

'And he took no notice?'

'Seems not. She said he laughed at the idea of danger. He was the adventurous type. Quite a guy, I'm told.'

'Quite a guy,' Douglas confirmed. 'But was he ever in that boat? That's what I need to find out.'

'No one but you ever doubted it.' The detective became defensive.

'Well, I'm certainly doubting it now. Do we only have her word for it or are there independent witnesses?'

'There may have been. They weren't asked to come forward. He ordered the boat himself, didn't he? The boat-clothes were washed ashore with the boat.'

'How could that happen if he drowned in them?'

'He stripped off to bathe. In his trunks, she said.'

'In a storm?'

'Before the storm blew up. He decided to make the trip to Molokai and they were nearly across when it hit them.'

'Let's suppose he was in the boat then. Why shouldn't he have swum ashore and hidden on another island?'

'What, in his trunks under a pineapple bush? You can

rule that out. The boat and the woman were seen a long way off. A boat put out from Molokai and took her aboard. There was no sign of him by then. They searched right away and had a flotilla on the job just as soon as the sea was calm.'

There were too many unanswered questions for Douglas. If Ashley had really been in the boat, why had he chosen to take it out on a dangerous strip of water when bad weather was forecast? And with a woman aboard. And why hadn't he collected it himself? And was it a coincidence that this had happened on Sylvia Smith's first visit?

'I won't believe he's dead till I see the body,' he said.

'Then you won't believe he's dead,' the detective told him.

O'Leary glared at Douglas. 'He was a God-damn hero, wasn't he? You got a grudge against the guy or something?'

Monsieur le Prèsident had made the same point rather more elegantly.

'You might say so,' Douglas admitted. 'Most people thought of him as a hero but I happen to know better.'

'Took your girl from you, did he?' sneered O'Leary.

He could say that again.

After hanging about in vain for the rain to clear, they drove back towards Honolulu through the eye of the storm. O'Leary decided to risk the short cut through the Wilson Tunnel, and while they climbed the Koolau range the going was barely possible. Only the main road was open at all.

Once through the tunnel, they met a different kind of weather. Over Honolulu and Waikiki the sun shone from a clear sky.

According to the car radio it had been like that all day, while people living a few miles away were being flooded out of their homes. There, rivers of water were still running through drawing-rooms and over the roofs of hillside bungalows. The Wilson Tunnel was closed to traffic five minutes after they had passed through.

The newsreader described the storm as a freak moving across the Pacific from Southern California, and Douglas remembered the Irishman's story in the plane from San Francisco. It seemed like disaster dogging his mission. Typically, ill luck had dogged his whole life. Thanks to Ashley.

More bad news awaited him at police headquarters. Messages from Fiji and Australia confirmed George Paget's non-arrival. Even while he read them a third was handed to him. The Japanese police reported Mr Paget entering their country on a flight from Honolulu earlier in the day. He had left the airport at Tokyo before the Interpol alert reached them.

O'Leary had the grace to look sheepish, but what good did that do? The Japanese, at least, had acted promptly and done what they could. George's hotel had been traced and his room discreetly searched. Alas, it contained no gold or other contraband.

'That coat could have concealed nothing after all,' suggested O'Leary, recovering and moving over to the offensive.

'It could have, but it didn't.'

'Where's your evidence? Did anybody see any gold?'

Douglas ignored him and put through a call to Paris to report failure. Renée was on duty and he spoke to her in French. It was one of his few accomplishments and it impressed O'Leary.

She took the message, clucked sympathetically and reminded him to send his account for expenses to Montreal.

After a late pizza lunch and a glass of beer he paid a visit with O'Leary to Ashley's bank. The manager received them nervously and expressed himself anxious to oblige the police.

Yes, Mr. Wyndham West had opened an account in the course of the previous year. It was at the time when he acquired his house on the island. Apparently he used to spend an occasional few days there, relaxing during his flights round the world on behalf of the India Fund. Apparently, too, he was using Honolulu as a financial base. The sums involved were substantial.

'How often did you see him?' Douglas asked.

'Not once. All transactions were arranged by correspondence.'

'Isn't that unusual?'

'Somewhat so. I would have expected him to visit here when he opened the account. But there was nothing irregular. He provided references and was always clear and precise in his instructions.'

'You say he kept a substantial balance here, but I learned in London that he died virtually without assets.'

'At the time of his death the credit balance of his account here stood at a few dollars only.'

'Do you find that peculiar?'

'No, it conformed to his normal practice. Substantial credits would be made from time to time, but they were always transferred to another account.'

'Always to the same account?'

57

'Yes.'

'Would it be an account opened in the name of Sylvia Smith?'

'Yes, that is the name. The account was opened at the same time as his own.'

'Would I be right in thinking that these accounts were opened last May?'

The manager looked up his records and confirmed that May was the correct date. Douglas inspected Ashley's first letter. It had been written ten days after the shooting incident in Moscow.

'Did he give any reason for making this arrangement about two accounts?' he asked.

'Yes, he explained the circumstances in a subsequent letter. Miss Smith was his personal assistant in his charitable work. Payments for goods purchased by him were her responsibility.'

'But these were private accounts. Did Mr. Wyndham West give any indication that the money belonged to the India Fund?'

'Re-reading the correspondence since his death, I find that he didn't. I knew who he was, of course, and had read of his organisation's practice of purchasing privately and through its own agents to avoid being overcharged. Naturally I concluded that these accounts were the method he used in handling the India Fund's transactions. In view of the way our own government Aid Programme in Asia has been used to line piliticians' pockets, I was sympathetic and thought it clever of him. The precise position was none of my concern.'

'Not if money provided from charitable donations was being siphoned off into another account?'

'That had been explained, as I mentioned earlier. As head of the organisation Mr. Wyndham West was presumably authorised to dispose of the funds in this manner. What did cause me concern, when the tragedy occurred, was the possibility of litigation, over the ownership of the funds, between Mr. Wyndham West's heirs and Miss Smith as Trustee for the India Fund. Fortunately, he had the foresight to make Miss Smith his heir.'

'What form do these funds take? Are they in cash or stocks? Or in precious metals? Gold, for instance.' Douglas asked the question without much hope. As the manager said, Ashley had foresight.

'Gold? Certainly not. Cash and securities. No precious metals or gems or anything of that kind.'

'Stock certificates or marketable securities?'

'The securities were always marketable. Bearer bonds. In case a large cash payment had to be made in a hurry.'

'Were the bonds in his name or Miss Smith's?'

'In Miss Smith's.'

'And the house? If he died penniless, presumably Mr. Wyndham West didn't own that.'

'The deeds too are in Miss Smith's name.'

'How much of the money paid into the first account and transferred to the second was paid out?'

'Up to the time of Mr. Wyndham West's death, none. I understand that these particular funds constituted a temporary reserve to meet some large liabilities due for payment in the near future. Meantime the cash was earning a good rate of interest.'

'How often have you met Miss Smith?'

'Since hers was a deposit account and there have been no withdrawals we have had almost no dealings with her. Until recently I believe she had never visited Hawaii. I have met her only once.'

Here Sergeant O'Leary intervened before Douglas could ask his next question. He had been following the exchange with his slant eyes narrowed and his mouth ajar.

'How's this for a phoney set-up? A guy spends nine months making over all his loot to a dame. He dies and she has the jackpot. No formalities. No waiting for the will to be proved. All nice and liquid. She can come in here tomorrow, scoop it all up and scram. I don't like it. The Commissioner won't like it. It stinks. Our Limey friend here is not too happy about this West's death, Mr.

Manager. Maybe she helped him die a little? Would these funds be of a size to tempt a lady?'

The manager swallowed. 'The sum is a large one, certainly. But, so far as my knowledge goes, his death has not benefited her. She already had absolute control of the funds while he was living.'

'What if the money didn't belong to either of them? What if he was authorised to handle this charity's funds privately and wasn't honest, and what if she ain't either? How much dough is there?'

'The sum is large, as I said. Somewhere between twenty and thirty million dollars.'

O'Leary pulled a terrible face. He already had one but this was far worse. 'Freeze it,' he shouted. 'Freeze every goddam cent.'

'But –'

'Don't tell me you've no grounds. I won't buy that spiel. If you haven't any, think of some. The police department will cover you.'

The manager stared unhappily at his Polynesian carpet. 'What I was about to say was not that I had no grounds. I was going to tell you that the funds are no longer here.'

The one occasion when the manager had seen Miss Smith was that very morning. She had come on the dot of opening time and told him how, in view of the tragedy, she had decided not to stay on the island. The securities were portable; so were bundles of bank notes in various denominations. He had asked for a few days' notice to enable him to make proper arrangements. But no. She had insisted on taking immediately whatever was available. Since the bulk of the money had been in bearer bonds what she had taken was virtually the lot. A few hours earlier it had all been there, laid out on his desk.

Hadn't he protested? Yes he had. He told her she would be robbed and offered to send a security guard with her. She had refused, shovelled the lot into a shopping bag, and left. The manager described how he had watched her drive off in a cheap hired self-drive Datsun.

Douglas looked yet another failure in the face. He had

been counting on freezing the ill-gotten gains. The slick planning and execution of the whole operation could only be Ashley's. The clue that he was still alive provided little consolation.

'How did she seem?' he asked.

'Very tired and upset. She struck me as a capable woman on the verge of a nervous breakdown. She told me how she and Mr. West had planned to marry and settle down here and how she couldn't bear the place now. She had arrived from London last night and couldn't wait to leave.'

'Did she say when she was leaving and where she was going?'

'No. I asked her, because I was worried about the money, but she didn't say.'

Douglas thanked the manager for his help and they left. Back at headquarters Sergeant O'Leary said how about pulling her in on a murder rap.

'That's the last thing I want,' Douglas replied hurriedly. 'He's not dead, I tell you. He got out of that boat somehow, or else he was never in it. My only chance of running him to earth is to let her lead me there.'

'It smells like murder to me. With all that dough.'

'Don't you see that if he was going to be pulled in for gold-smuggling it would suit him to be legally dead? The buck-passing between bank accounts was simply to ensure that someone legally alive could collect the money. And she didn't lose much time in doing it. Just as soon as she discovered I wasn't fooled by a put-up death.'

'You ain't suggesting we let her leave the island with thirty million dollars?'

'Why not? We don't know what the bank notes are, but you don't have regulations against exporting securities, do you?'

'We've been known to turn fussy about stolen property, brother.'

'It was given her. Where's the evidence it was stolen?'

'It belongs to that India Fund. Must do.'

'They haven't reported any loss.'

'Where else could it come from?'

61

'The India Fund is registered in England under the Charities Act. It has accountants and auditors. Not even the Director-General could make off with that amount of money.'

'So?'

'So it comes from smuggling gold.'

They had a heated discussion. Then O'Leary telephoned Kaneohe. The detective there reported that the lady in question had made a trip to Honolulu first thing and arrived back shortly before the storm broke.

'Why the hell didn't you report that this morning? Tell us something new, will you? For instance, where is she now?'

Douglas waited while O'Leary uh-huhed into the telephone and rang off with a fraternal obscenity.

'He says his tail has only this minute reported. The storm cut him off. It brought down the wires. It seems they are drying out on the other side and she's packing up to leave.'

'She'll be going to Tokyo,' said Douglas, 'to join George Paget. When is the next flight?'

O'Leary rang the airport. She wasn't booked for Tokyo. She was picking up the same BOAC flight twenty-four hours later. BA 531 that night. It left for Nandi and Sydney at 23.59. Presumably she hadn't learned about George going to Japan.

O'Leary went to the Commissioner's office to report. It took some time. The Commissioner decided to call Paris and speak to *Monsieur le Président*. Douglas was eventually summoned to hear the outcome.

Since there had been no report of a loss of funds by the India Fund, and since the millions of dollars in Miss Smith's bag were therefore likely to be profits from the gold-smuggling which was under investigation by Interpol, the Hawaii police would accede to Interpol's request. Subject to one proviso, Miss Smith and her bag would be allowed to leave the country. If she had to be brought back to face local charges, Interpol would render every assistance.

'There is a personal message to you from your chief,'

said the Commissioner, handing Douglas a typed message.

With the Commissioner speaking no French and *Monsieur le Président* no English, it appeared that the conversation had been a field day for Renée. Her carefully acquired English idioms had caused some puzzlement in mid-Pacific. The message to Douglas read: 'He, the head of this section of Interpol, wished his operative to know that should he, his operative, allow this large quantity of money to disappear subsequent to its export from the United States of America he, the head of this section of Interpol, would personally have his, the operative's, guts for garters. Abyssinia. Renée.'

Abyssinia was Renée's translation of *au revoir*, a rough version of 'I'll be seeing you'. Douglas could imagine several of *Monsieur le Président*'s threats which might be loosely rendered 'guts for garters'.

O'Leary resented the co-operation. He wanted to get his hands on both the woman and the money, and obliging a Limey went against the grain. Grudgingly he agreed to lay on immediate police surveillance at the airport and on Miss Smith's route to it. This would ensure that she didn't do a Paget and vanish in some quite different direction. He also made a reservation for Douglas on BA 531. First class. The tourist class was fully booked.

'Call me if you catch the guy,' he concluded. 'We've death records to keep straight.'

Douglas promised and they even shook hands. Afternoon had become evening. A police car took him to his hotel, where he packed and wondered how to kill the few remaining hours.

From the back window of his room he watched the lights climb the hillside until they disappeared abruptly into low cloud. Hawaii was all contrast. Lights and instant blackness. Sunshine here, squalls there. Polynesia overlaid with America. The boorish O'Leary and the well-spoken bank manager. What was the attraction for Ashley? The comfort? The climate? The remoteness?

Dinner at the Japanese teahouse would be *sukiyaki* on a lacquered tray. Seafood in soy sauce washed down with

Japanese tea, which always tasted of boiled grass cuttings. All very laxative.

He asked the taxi-driver to take him somewhere memorable for dinner. The man chose the Moana, a hotel which stood on Waikiki beach. It provided a setting of coconut palms and the music of cooing doves.

Douglas sat outside under an elderly banyan tree, sipping rum punch and admiring the sea in the grey twilight. The banyan was the reason for the taxi-driver's choice. A notice at the foot of the trunk announced that it was more than a hundred years old and Robert Louis Stevenson had written in its shade. Hawaii was the Sandwich Islands then and Captain Cook had been killed hereabouts. More thoroughly than Ashley.

Towards the bottom of the second punch the lure of beachcombing stole up and settled over him. Why did he busy himself destroying Ashley's life and flushing him out of his hiding place? Wouldn't it be better to give up and stay put? He could earn a living in Honolulu as a language teacher and spend every evening drinking rum and watching the sun take its bath in the Pacific. For a start he could teach the Police Commissioner French.

Every dream fades. If he drank and lotus-ate, he would think. And thinking meant thinking of Ashley, as he was doing now. The exact state of the game between Ashley and Sylvia Smith puzzled him. How could she be an employee of the India Fund if Jack Willingdon had never heard of her? Yet Ashley and women were oil and water.

Take Ashley and Susan. He ordered a third punch and recalled Susan from twenty years ago. That tiresome postwar period of rationing and slowly getting back to normal. He had been teaching then. Instructing small boys in the rules of French and German grammar.

She was dark-eyed, soft mouthed and big-breasted. They were lying side by side on the grass in Kensington Gardens. Somewhere between Peter Pan and the Round Pond. He lay on his back and she on her front, her head propped on her elbows. Their left legs were touching from thigh to

64

ankle. It was the first and last time he had been in love.

'I liked your handsome friend,' she said. 'Tell me about him.'

'I knew him up at Oxford,' he told her. 'And in the army.'

'Was he in Intelligence too?'

'No; before then. It's not important.'

'I didn't know there was a before-then. You never told me.'

'It's not important,' he repeated. 'The war is a bore, and it ended four years ago.'

He tried to change the subject by increasing the pressure on the side of her leg.

'You aren't a hero, are you, and keeping it from me?' As she spoke she dropped a daisy down the vee of his shirt.

'Of course not. It's just that I spent most of the war in India and you've only got to mention the name for people to start yawning.'

'Tell me about it,' she persisted. 'I promise not to yawn.'

Susan believed in Absolute Trust and Telling All. He was always having to bare his breast. But she didn't believe so strongly in Doing All, and he hadn't persuaded her to bare hers. He had been shy with the opposite sex since boyhood and was conscious of gaucheness in handling her. In his late twenties, he should have been more practised. He was floundering like a poor swimmer.

'I'd rather not talk about it, Susan, if you don't mind.'

'You're ashamed of something. That's bad. What did you say his name was? Ashley Something Something?'

'Wyndham West. As a matter of fact we were at school together too. I've known him a long time.'

He raised a hand and stroked her cheek, but she edged away.

'What does he do for a living?'

'He's in the City. I'm not sure exactly what he does there.' This was Ashley's merchant-bank phase, his millionaire-by-the-time-I'm-thirty-or-bust period.

'He seemed very smooth and high level.'

They had been having supper *à deux* the previous evening in Douglas's attic bedsitter in W11. Rabbit pie and Algerian plonk. Ashley had intruded, wanting some business papers in German translated on the spot. They had reached him late and he had to have the gist before dining at the Swiss Embassy to meet a trade delegation from Berne. Immaculate in DJ, he had switched on his instant charm for Susan's benefit and quite bowled her over. When Ashley decided to bowl someone over, he made a good job of it. As a thank-you for Douglas translating he had given her his carnation.

'Ashley's a phoney,' he said. 'He was putting on an act last night.'

The contrast between Ashley's diplomatic high life and his own rabbit pie had been more than he could bear. The evening dress looked new, too, and he wouldn't have minded knowing where Ashley had purloined the clothing coupons for it.

'Nasty.' she said. 'I thought he was by way of being a friend of yours.'

'By way of is right. It's a one-way friendship. He asks the favours and I give them.'

'Oh, Douglas! He was so gay and nice. I do believe you're jealous.' She leaned forward to pick a buttercup and held it to his chin. 'There you are! I thought so. I can see the reflection. You're jealous of him.'

'Don't be silly. That just shows I like butter.' He tried to laugh it off but found he couldn't. 'Seriously, you mustn't trust first impressions. He's not nice at all.'

'He's sweet. And very good-looking.'

'As sweet as a rattlesnake. And don't go getting ideas about Ashley Wyndham West. You may be interested in him, but I can assure you he won't be interested in you.'

That made her angry.

'What exactly do you mean by that?'

'You know very well what I mean.'

'You had better tell me.'

'Very well then.' He became angry too. 'If you insist on having it spelt out, he's about as interested in you as you are in other girls.'

'What a beastly thing to say about a friend! You were at school and in the army and at university together, and you can say that about him!'

'I don't believe you, and even if it were true you shouldn't say it. Have you no feeling of loyalty? He didn't humiliate you by saving your life during the war, did he? Is it something like that you're concealing from me?'

'Something not very like that. If you want to know you had better ask him.'

'It happens to be the truth.'

They didn't part at once. He took her to a Beethoven concert at the Albert Hall that evening and she allowed him to kiss her good night. But the tiff widened into a permanent rift. Their regular meetings became irregular and the relationship steadily less intimate. Before it petered out altogether it became clear that she had taken up with someone else.

A couple of months after their last meeting a letter arrived. He was not to be surprised if he saw the announcement of her engagement to his 'friend' (heavy quotation marks) Ashley. She had taken his advice and asked Ashley what it was he had been too ashamed to tell her. Now that she knew, she wanted Douglas to know that his behaviour had been inexcusable and he should get himself a different job at once. To have pretended that Ashley was the sinner was contemptible of him. She was deeply sorry for him and would always wish him well.

Ashley had struck again.

His headmaster sent for him the next day to inquire whether he felt a change of occupation would do him good and had he thought of something outside the teaching profession.

Ashley yet again.

Susan and Ashley never married, of course, He hadn't wanted her for himself. All he had been after was the satisfaction of depriving Douglas of her. When Douglas last heard of her she had married someone else and gone to live in Hong Kong.

The sun had long disappeared and his glass was empty.

Sounds of dinner being served came through a window behind him.

After the Susan *débâcle* he had never married. Once shy, twice shyer. When the years of mourning passed, he had been taken in hand by Helen. They used each other in an adult way as a physical convenience. He found sex without love sad, but she told him it was better than no sex at all. Before her marriage broke up she had become accustomed to it and didn't care for being without. It was simply an addiction, like smoking or cannabis. He managed to oblige her, by thinking of Susan all the time.

As for the job, the post at that school had also been a first. The war had caught him still at school himself. By the time it was over and he had done a late spell at university he was twenty-seven and without a career. He possessed no aptitude for business or administration, and no qualifications except an arts degree and a teaching diploma. Nothing except his languages.

With Ashley's shadow between him and teaching he had no choice. In the Cold War his wartime intelligence unit was still active and he rejoined it as a civilian. A nine-to-six desk job in a discreet Mayfair office.

Was it irony or justice? He would still have been a teacher if Ashley had left Susan alone. And Ashley? Instead of playing dead and being on the run, he would be safely on course for the inevitable life peerage and a luxurious retirement. Dinner every night at the Caprice or the Moana.

Hunger stirred and he went inside for an Ashley-style meal. Smoked salmon, a rare steak and lush Hawaiian fruits. Let them tear their hair in Montreal when they saw the bill.

Qantas were the local agents for BOAC and a Qantas car picked him up at 23.00. He had phoned before dinner and they decently decided to accord him VIP treatment.

This included generous tots of free Scotch in their Ned Kelly room at the airport. He chose J. & B. Rare. It tasted as smooth as Ashley Wyndham West and that was saying something. The plane was behind schedule coming from

San Francisco but he was mellow and could bear the delay. One of Sergeant O'Leary's men came to tell him that Miss Smith had not skipped out for Tokyo, Tahiti or Taiwan. She was waiting impatiently in the tourist-class lounge. Had she a shopping bag with her? Yes, she had.

How many tourist-class passengers were there, he wondered, with twenty-five million or so US dollars in a shopping bag or stashed about their persons. Ten million pounds it came to, give or take the odd hundred thousand. Her faint familiarity intrigued him, too. If he were an Ashley type he might do a deal with her. She was even the right age to help him end his bachelor days at last.

Through the Scotch mist he remembered that she had tried to kill him once and would no doubt try again.

'Man is born free but everywhere he lives in planes.'

In the balmy Honolulu night Douglas stepped wuzzily aboard for yet another flight. Ashley had said it, of course. It was one of his famous Oxford aphorisms. More of a forecast than a fact at the time, it had come true for both of them. Ashley when he founded IF, Douglas when he began working for Interpol.

A six-hour flight starting at 00.45. Three thousand miles to cover. The equator and the international date line to be crossed. It sounded exciting, but how dreary it proved. The equator and the date line couldn't be seen. Nor could the Pacific.

Even in the comfort of the half-empty first-class cabin he failed to settle himself to sleep. He felt restless with those three thousand miles of ocean in the darkness below. The Pacific was big, as even O'Leary had noticed.

'A little water clears us of this deed.'

Ashley again! On the quiet side of Oahu he had given a practical demonstration. A mock drowning performance was a typical Ashley trick. But how exactly had he worked his disappearing act?

'A little water clears us of this deed.'

He muttered the words to himself. He could hear them spoken in Ashley's voice. Another echo from more than twenty years ago. This time from Oxford. There was comfort in thinking about Ashley. At least it might throw up a clue.

Oxford after the second world war. A university of exservicemen. Elderly undergraduates making the adjustment from killing to learning. They might have run wild, breaking all the rules intended for children *in stat. pup.* Instead they were serious, disciplined, thirsty for knowledge. Where did the balance of good and evil lie in time of war?

70

What was right and what was wrong? Did the end justify the means? Monte Cassino, Nagasaki, Hiroshima. They expected Oxford to supply the answers.

The atrocious food served in the splendour of college halls didn't worry them after army rations. Unblitzed and beautiful still, the run-down colleges provided accommodation of a kind. Doubling up in back-quad attics five minutes from the nearest running water. What did that matter? It was an improvement on a desert bivouac or a barrack room in Indian cantonment lines. In *ersatz* gowns run up from black-out material they read Nietsche beside their gas fires to find out what had made Hitler tick, and Hobbes and Engels to determine the justification or otherwise for their service in Egypt and India.

He met Ashley by chance in the Turl one day. Rumour had reached him that Wyndham West was up, but he was set on never seeing or speaking to him again. They stood for several seconds, face to face in surprise. Then he broke away and took refuge in a second-hand bookshop.

Ashley pursued him. Handsome as ever, brash as ever. Insistent on being loved, or at the very least not hated. They met again at the top of several flights of rickety stairs between shelves overflowing with Victorian sermons. The unsaleable stock from which there was no further line of retreat.

'Dougs! No hard feelings!'

'What four words could have been more in character? 'Dougs' was an infuriating nickname which Ashley had invented for him at school. It referred to some teenage chubbiness round the breasts which had been a cause of embarrassment. No one but Ashley would have had the nerve to use it as the opening gambit in an attempt at reconciliation.

'No hard feelings' was more outrageous still. The tone he used suggested that Ashley was the one sinned against, now in a spirit of Christian charity announcing his forgiveness.

'Some,' Douglas replied without looking at him. He selected a book at random and pretended to rivet his attention

71

on a Lenten address by a long-neglected Dean of Lich-field. 'In fact, quite a lot,' he added when Ashley refused to go away.

'Come off it, Dougsie. Bury the past. India was an un-happy interlude. We were too young. None of us knew what we were doing out there. Kiss and make up, there's a sport. The war's over.'

'No, thank you very much. You knew what you were do-ing all right. The war between us isn't over.' Already Ash-ley had him at a disadvantage again. Frank, open, friend-ship-loving Ashley. Sulky, grudge-bearing Douglas.

'Which college are you at?'

'Exeter.'

He could hardly not answer at all. It wasn't one of the leading colleges, but to him all through the war Exeter had represented the hope of a return to normal civilised life. He had won a minor award in modern languages there at the beginning of the war and had to wait five long years to take it up. Exeter was precious to him.

Ashley wrinkled his Grecian nose.

'Oh,' he said. 'One of these here in the Turl, is it? I can never tell which is which. Isn't one of them called some-thing absurd like Jesus? I would have thought Balliol would have been more in your line. But I remember now. You won a scholarship, didn't you? Of course you did. And you're wearing a scholar's gown. Clever old Dougs!'

'Ashley,' he replied, 'why don't you just b. off? You've done me enough harm for one lifetime. Can't you see I'd rather not continue the acquaintanceship? Go and charm someone else if you don't mind.'

'But I do mind. We've known each other a long time and old friends are the best friends. I'm at Magdalen. Had to indulge in some rather nifty footwork to get in there by special grace and favour. Still, I managed to pull the right strings and invoke the Old Pals and Heroes Act. It's rather a jolly place. Come and see me and I'll show you the deer, dear. Come to tea tomorrow if you're free. You'll enjoy my rooms. They are really rather stylish. Somebody told me they are a bit of what the Duke of Windsor had when he was up.'

It was all too plausibly in character. Ashley, who had passed no entrance exam, had barged the queue of worthy applicants and fiddled his way into the university. Not for him, the interloper, half a back room in a small college of suburban digs a mile or two down the Iffley Road. For a blue-blooded Wyndham West it had to be a royal set of rooms in the most beautiful college of all.

'I'm sorry, but I'm not free.'

'Then I'll come and see you.' Ashley spoke with the gracious condescension of one going slumming.

He kept his promise the very next day. Douglas happened to be in and was helpless against a direct assault. He accepted the inevitable. Ashley always got what he wanted in the end. The smooth talk, the enchanting smile, the ruthless use of both elbows, plus whatever else came to hand— it made an unbeatable combination. Unbeatable by Douglas anyway.

He listened while Ashley talked of his plans for taking Oxford by storm.

Did Douglas not realise that half the people who would be running the country in the next few decades were up at Oxford with them now? They had a unique opportunity to make a generation of valuable contacts.

Ashley would speak at the Union and become President. For that he would have to select a political party. Which should it be? By upbringing he was a Conservative, of course, but Labour might be in power for some time and one didn't want to spend the best years of one's life in the wilderness. The solution was to join the Liberals. They had a large following in the university, and becoming a Liberal had the advantage of not committing one too deeply if one decided later to turn left or right.

'Don't you have any convictions at all?' Douglas inquired.

'Yes, I'm convinced of the importance of doing good. Lots of good to lots of people. And one can't do that unless one gets to the top oneself. I've been reading Kant and his jolly old categorical imperative.'

'Doesn't Kant say, make yourself good so that you can make others happy? Do good yourself, not do yourself good?'

'First do good for yourself, then for others. That's my interpretation. I don't aim to do good works on a piddling scale like a paritsh priest. I must be in a position to command goodness on the grand scale.'

'Knowing you, I can't say I wish you success. You're the most selfish person ever born and not the slightest interested in anyone else's welfare. If you really mean this seriously, then I can only say that your motive is more than suspect.'

'What a meanie you are, and what a low opinion you have of me, Dougsie! But even if you're right, does the motive matter? What makes a good act good, that's the question. I've just written an essay on it and I can tell you. It's not the motive, nor something intrinsic in the act. It's the consequences. Nothing else is relevant. The virtue in an act lies solely in its consequences.'

'So if you kill a man and make other people happy as a consequence you do a good act, provided the sum of their happiness exceeds his loss of happiness. Is that it?'

'That's it. Take political assassinations. If a tyrant is killed and the people set free, the act is a good one.'

'Maybe, but isn't there a difference between political and private acts?'

'There shouldn't be. That's the whole point. Ethics recognises no frontiers. Public and private morality should be identical. A Prime Minister should keep a promise, both as an individual and as a Prime Minister.'

'Well it's nice to have you thinking about right and wrong, Ashley, however late in the day. But it seems to me that all you're saying is that, since you are going to do so much good provided you get to the top, you will be entitled to kill anyone who stands in your way.'

Ashley laughed and continued to outline his programme for success at the university. He had been a good cricketer at school, but cricket took so much time and the competition for a blue might be too hot. Games without blues got one nowhere; so no games.

Except perhaps fencing. He had once won the épée championship in an inter-school competition, and if he could snatch a quick half-blue for this it would look good in *Who's Who* later on. Fencing would fit in nicely, too, with his other great ambition – success on the stage. The OUDS attracted almost as much attention as the Union. If he was to receive the accolade of becoming an Isis Idol it would be wise to have two strong strings to his bow. Naturally he would be going for a brilliant First too.

'I wouldn't talk to anyone else like this,' he concluded. 'It would sound rather boastful. But we've always been special pals, Dougsie, and I need you. Do please forgive me for that business in India. I did my best to get you off. You remember that, don't you?'

'I remember everything about it. All the details are engraved on my memory. You behaved unforgivably and that's that. I don't want to see you any more.'

'To err is human, to forgive divine. Please be divine. Our relationship is too close for enmity.'

He squeezed Douglas's reluctant hand and left.

Over the next three years Douglas saw plenty of him. Who in Oxford didn't? Ashley set out to attract notice and make himself one of the sights. He squandered his clothing coupons on exotic dress and became famous for his leopard-skin trousers, which he wore to lectures and in college hall.

At the Union he made funny speeches, containing carefully prepared mots. In an Eights Week debate he achieved publicity in the national press by successfully proposing the motion that 'In the opinion of this House Christopher Columbus went too far'.

The Liberals didn't mind his trousers as the Conservatives might have, and by working hard for the cause he became President of the Liberal Club. This brought him sufficient support to win the coveted Presidency of the Union, although his election was marred by accusations from the

75

defeated candidate that he had broken the rules by canvassing. A proposal that he should be disqualified was defeated, and the cloud settled eventually on his opponent, as Douglas knew it would. Anyone whom Ashley diddled was liable to be convicted of misbehaviour.

Good-looking, well connected, impeccably poised. Ashley exuded charm from every pore and exploited Oxford's weakness for eccentricity. After the initial shock he had town and gown alike in his pocket. Hearties who scorned him as a pansy for his dress were confounded when he ostentatiously walked out arm-in-arm with the prettiest undergraduettes. The would-be politicians at the Union who wrote him off as a lightweight joker were converted when he routed a visiting member of the government in a debate on the fuel crisis.

He won his fencing half-blue, too, and became an Isis Idol when he achieved a famous hat-trick by capping his Presidency of the Liberals and the Union with the Presidency of the OUDS.

The green-room side of Ashley provided the main outlet for his exhibitionism. Douglas went to see him in Molière and Maeterlinck and various Shakespeare productions in gardens and halls all over Oxford. He played Romeo in New College cloisters. In the balcony scene he made a memorable climb to an upper window, as though taking part in an army assault course. But his most daring role was in the historic OUDS production of *Macbeth* in Christ Church hall.

Ashley played Lady Macbeth in a performance which became a sensation. After the first night the critics hurried down from London and tickets fetched black-market prices. James Agate told the readers of a Sunday newspaper that this was the most exciting Shakespearean performance since Sarah Bernhardt played Hamlet. If he could be persuaded to abandon politics and the certainty of becoming Prime Minister, he wrote, this young man would be assured of a meteoric career on the stage. Gielgud and Olivier would have to look to their laurels.

Douglas bought a ticket and watched mesmerised as Ashley threw caution to the winds and revelled in the ruthlessness of Lady Macbeth. Not to mention the sexual ambiguities. 'Unsex me ... Make thick my blood. Stop up the access and passage to remorse.' Ashley's sparkling eyes flashed and his lipsticked mouth quivered as he demanded of Macbeth: 'Art thou afear'd To be the same in thine one act and valour As thou art in desire.' His uncannily pitched voice – at once husky, sinister and sexy – grew tender when he told the audience: 'I have given suck, and know How tender 'tis to love the babe that milks me.' Douglas almost believed him as he stood there on a dais under the hammerbeam roof caressing his false bosom.

Then came the fury of 'Infirm of purpose! Give me the daggers!' and the heartlessness of 'A little water clears us of this deed'. Finally, the breakdown in the sleepwalking scene: 'Hell is murky ... Who would have thought the old man to have had so much blood in him? ... Here's the smell of blood still: all the perfumes of Arabia will not sweeten this little hand.' Ashley's hand was by no means little but it seemed to shrink as he spoke the words.

'To bed, to bed, to bed.' Applause, applause, applause.

Ashley's Oxford career had its failures as well, but they were less publicised. The brilliant First eluded him. With no academic bent and so much extracurricular activity he needed all his usual luck to scrape a Second. It was touch and go, but his glibness at the viva tipped the scales.

When he went down he capitalised on a Magdalen friendship with a merchant banker's son and took a lucrative job in the City. While deciding whether to become Prime Minister or the twentieth-century David Garrick, he reckoned he might as well fill in time by making his fortune.

Douglas dozed off eventually and woke later with a jolt. 06.50 and Nandi. The other passengers disembarked to stretch their legs in the muggy Fiji dawn.

Preferring not to show himself, he stayed aboard and

watched from the window until they returned. This time there were fewer of them. He scanned the faces anxiously for Miss Smith's. It was missing.

A stewardess protested but he took no notice, scrambling off the plane against the boarding stream and hurrying across the tarmac. From a door in the airport building another straggling crocodile of passengers was leaving to board another aircraft.

Inside, authority was represented by a solitary Indian counter clerk. He was young and clean, like a freshly polished coffee bean.

'Where's that aircraft going?'

'That aircraft, sir? To Auckland, sir.'

'Get me on it.'

'That I cannot do, sir. The flight is fully booked and the passenger list is closed.'

Douglas displayed his credentials. An Interpol identity card with his photograph. A letter from the Director-General of IAA to whatsoever airline it might concern. Incomprehension puckered and glazed the handsome brown features.

'I have to be on that flight. You must do something about it.'

'I can do nothing, sir. All seats are occupied already. Many American ladies and gentlemen are visiting the South Pacific.'

'Then get one of them off.'

'It is not possible. They are a party and their tickets are valid. Their reservations were confirmed in San Francisco and reconfirmed in Honolulu, sir.'

'Then someone else must be taken off. If you haven't the authority, let me speak to the airport manager.'

'But he lives on the far side of the island, sir. He will be asleep.'

'Telephone him and wake him up. Tell him it's an emergency.'

'The only emergency permitted is danger to the safety of passengers, staff or airport property.'

'Let's get this straight, shall we? In the absence of your superiors you are in charge of the airport and you are refusing to accede to a legitimate request by a representative of the police. You realise the seriousness of your position?' Douglas assumed his sahib's voice, recalled from the days when he held the King-Emperor's commission.

'But I am not in charge of the airport, sir. There is a duty officer in the control tower. I will talk to him for you, sir.'

He switched on a walkie-talkie set and explained the situation. The voice which replied sounded English and not to be browbeaten. The Indian contributed deferential 'yes sirs' until Douglas seized the set from his hand.

'Look here. I'm sorry to be insistent, but it's imperative that I board this flight to Auckland.'

'I'm sorry too, but there's no chance of it. The flight is full and it's leaving now.'

'When is the next flight?'

'The same time tomorrow. It's daily, connecting with BA 531.'

'That's no good at all.'

'Then you had better carry on to Sydney. I'll talk to them now and ask them to arrange for you to be put on the next available Sydney – Auckland flight.'

'That's no good either.'

One thing was certain. Once he let Miss Smith out of his sight he would never find her again. She would become Mrs. Jones and grey-haired or Fräulein Wunderbar and a dizzy blonde and would vanish as Ashley had vanished, leaving not even a bank account or a safe deposit behind her.

He could telephone the Auckland police, of course, and ask them to keep her under observation until he arrived, but the police forces of the world didn't exactly spring into instant action on the strength of a telephone call from Douglas in the middle of the night. He had learned that in Hawaii. And with the Smith woman carrying all that money he needed some rather special co-operation. If they discovered it and arrested her, his hopes of unearthing Ashley had gone for ever.

79

In a rage of frustration he continued wrangling by remote control. The invisible white god in the tower would not come down and confront him in person. All he would do to oblige was to order the Indian out immediately to the BOAC plane with a loader to take Douglas's luggage off.

With the Indian gone and the walkie-talkie in his possession Douglas would not give up. He began shouting and the exchanges grew angrier. They also became disjointed, because he lost his temper and forgot the walkie-talkie's system. Did one keep one's finger on the button when talking or listening? He shouted and the white god couldn't hear him. The white god shouted and Douglas missed what he was saying.

'Very well,' he shouted finally, his finger on the button and contact firmly established, 'if you won't let me on that flight I'll have you held personally responsible for aiding and abetting the escape of a criminal wanted by half the police forces in the world. I am formally demanding to be allowed to speak to the head of the Fiji police before the aircraft leaves.'

'Are you threatening me?'

'What does it sound like?'

'Hysteria. How can your criminal escape from an aircraft? I can put a call through to the New Zealand police for you. Meanwhile I'm not breaking passenger regulations and I'm not delaying an aircraft while you go off to Suva and explain yourself to the Police Commissioner. I'd be surprised if he agreed to see you when you got there.'

'Is that your last word?'

'It is.'

'Then sod you.'

'You too. And Interpol, if it employs people like you.'

'You unco-operative bastard.'

The set went dead.

Not a very high-level exchange, he reflected, nor a very fruitful one. He tried to excuse himself on grounds of humidity and lack of sleep, but couldn't stifle the thought how smoothly and effectively Ashley would have handled the situation. Under the spell of his irresistible charm regulations would have been broken as easily as snapping twigs.

Douglas stood on a verandah sweating and trembling. The two waiting aircraft stood on a concrete apron. A wide ribbon of runway ran incongruously through a bare tropical landscape, now lightening with the dawn. A jeep was pulling away from one of the planes with the Indian and his own suitcase on the back seat. In the doorway of the other plane a stewardess was framed, poking out fretfully to see when the steps were to be wheeled away. Douglas felt defeated. His last chance was to do an Ashley.

'Thank you,' he said when the jeep halted beside him and the Indian climbed out. 'Now listen carefully. You are to go over to the Air New Zealand plane and speak to the head steward. He must explain to the pasengers that there has been an unfortunate duplication in the reservations. He must persuade one of the passengers to get off and take the next flight.'

'But there is no other flight today, sir. No person will agree.'

'Then a person must be bribed. Keep the captain out of it, but tell the steward to offer fifty dollars.'

'Fifty dollars, sir?'

'Yes, fifty dollars. US dollars. And if that doesn't do the trick he is to make it a hundred.'

'But who will pay, sir?'

'Your duty officer has personally authorised the expenditure. These are his instructions to you. The payment is not your concern.'

'Then I should speak to him myself, sir. All must be regular.'

He stretched out his hand. In passing it to him Douglas fumbled and dropped the walkie-talkie set. Before the Indian could stoop and retrieve it he picked it up himself, shook it and said: 'Damn.'

The Indian hesitated. The stewardess on the New Zealand plane was waving her arms at him, demanding passenger clearance.

'Sorry,' said Douglas. 'No time for checking back anyway. Jump to it, man. Quick as you can. We mustn't delay the flight any longer.' He mustered the fierce glare of a sahib registering displeasure at a subject person.

The Indian accepted the order in the nick of time. As he hurried across to the aircraft, the walkie-talkie exploded into life again, spluttering fearful oaths and demanding to be told what the hell was going on now. Visibility from the white god's eyrie couldn't penetrate the verandah roof and he had assumed that the set was back in the clerk's possession. That poor meek innocent was being promised the abrupt termination of his employment if the Auckland flight was held up by so much as another second.

Douglas put the set carefully on the ground and scrunched it into silence with his heel. He walked across to the jeep, put his case back on it and ordered the driver to take him over to the aircraft. While they crossed the tarmac, the Sydney-bound plane took off and zoomed low over their heads.

By the grace of God an amenable businessman from Seattle had come forward. He had fluffed the international date line and had an unexpected day in hand. With fifty free dollars for sampling the local talent he was not averse to twenty-four hours in romantic Fiji. He scrambled off with an overnight bag as Douglas scrambled on.

'Well done,' Douglas commended the Indian in passing. 'I will see you get proper recognition for this.'

What would happen to the poor fellow and whether the man from Seattle would ever get his money didn't bear thinking about. The important question now was whether the duty officer had spotted what was going on and been in communication with the captain.

He slid into the vacant seat and prayed. Miss Smith's back was visible six rows ahead. Passengers were buzzing over the extraordinary offer and she could hardly be unaware of the cause of the kerfuffle. A blue-haired Daughter of the American Revolution in the next seat told him that all airlines overbooked by fourteen per cent as a matter of policy. They agreed it was a disgrace and something ought to be done about it.

He quoted another Ashleyism. 'Air passengers of the world unite! You have nothing to lose but your planes!' It fell flat. Lost on the daughter of a different kind of revolution.

His nervousness eased when the aircraft moved forward for take-off. Either the control tower hadn't twigged or it had accepted the situation rather than incur further delay. In either case the pay-off would come in Auckland.

Fiji from above looked sparse and volcanic, dully green and grey. The time was 07.45 and already the temperature had reached seventy-five degrees and the humidity goodness knew what heights. He hoped Mr. Seattle would find lushness and air conditioning somewhere on the island.

Air New Zealand produced forms to keep him busy during the two-and-a-half-hour flight.

While not as particular or threatening as the state of Hawaii, New Zealand wanted him to be aware that it was free from foot-and-mouth disease and other stock and plant diseases currently prevalent in other countries. As New Zealand's economy was dependent on agricultural industry, it intended to prevent the accidental entry of un-welcome diseases. For that reason Department of Agricul-tural officers would be on duty at the port of arrival to advise and assist him.

The assistance he required was from officers of a dif-ferent department. Miss Smith must not be searched for foot-and-mouth in case she started shedding bearer bonds. He had to persuade the police at Auckland not to alarm or molest her until she had led him to wherever she was taking all that money. To Ashley, he fervently hoped.

Prompt attention by the police was ensured in advance. Towards the end of the flight the captain entered the pas-senger cabin and a stewardess pointed to Douglas.

'So you're the trickster,' he said. 'I have instructions to hand you over to the police as soon as we land.'

'I am the police.'

'Then you should get on well together. We are also re-porting your behaviour to IATA.'

'Then our reports should arrive together.'

The words wouldn't have reached her but the exchange could hardly have escaped Miss Smith's notice.

Their descent seemed endless. A cyclone was forecast and the weather grew rough. It was the same storm, start-ing in California, following him to Hawaii, and now hounding him down the Pacific. The plane began jerking up and down like a yo-yo. It flew lower and lower and blinder and blinder through layers of thickening cloud.

They were circling, until Douglas sensed they could go no lower without hitting the ground. He convinced himself that a crash was inevitable. A premonition of death turned his stomach queasy and he closed his eyes to remember something worthwhile from life before it ended.

Instead, while the aircraft lurched and the engine droned, he relived the incident in his life he most wanted to forget. When Ashley had ruined it for him twenty-seven long years ago.

Gulunchi was the name. It sounded like a piece of confectionery. Something between a Crunchie and a Tiffin Bar. Actually it was a small patch of India, remote on the Deccan plateau. A Mahratta village in Shivaji country. somewhere south of Poona.

Nothing had happened in Gulunchi from the beginning of time until AD 1942, when GHQ India Command, looking for a vacant space on the map, decided to rescue democracy by forming a division there.

Douglas travelled from the regimental depot in Delhi with Ashley, George Paget, Jack Willingdon and a red-haired man called Donald Petrie. Five emergency-commissioned second lieutenants. They commanded the advance guard of a force which, when fully mustered and trained, would drive the Germans from North Africa and/or the Japs from Burma.

The journey became a lark. Their compartment was luxurious and cooled by an electric fan playing on an ice-box. While peasants and water buffalo and crops gasped in the heat outside the windows, they played liar dice until Ashley won all their spare rupees. At mealtimes the train stopped for them to eat chicken curries in the cool of a station restaurant, with a small boy pulling a punkah overhead to create a breeze and keep the flies at bay.

They were fit and carefree and making their fortunes out of the travelling allowance. On a permanent posting like this the entitlement was three times the first-class fare. This sum was intended to cover the cost of transporting a household of servants and a stable of polo ponies. But all they possessed was a single bearer each, and these had to be left behind at the depot. To Ashley the system represented a beautiful challenge. He amused the rest of them by concocting a scheme for spending the rest of the war being permanently posted backwards and forwards between Peshawar and Cape Cormorin.

For Douglas the journey offered promise of a new life. Release from the disciplines of OTS and depot. When the Bombay-Madras Express climbed the slope of the Western Ghats he almost believed it was carrying him to Shangri-la.

Even their arrival at the Madras and South Mahratta Railway's smallest main-line station didn't disillusion him. They were going into the field and didn't expect a military band. And just as well. A one-eyed porter and a three-legged cow made up the reception committee. The cow proved to be a permanent inhabitant of the down platform. Too sacred to be put out of its misery, it welcomed each contingent of the new force with melancholy contempt.

Douglas helped to erect his own tent on a bare ridge in the heart of nowhere. The adventure exhilarated him and he felt real happiness for the first time in his life. As second-in-command of a company whose commander was in hospital making a prolonged recovery from DTs, he took charge of successive waves of men as they arrived.

He sited the cookhouse and the latrines, taking due account of the prevailing wind. He supervised the construction of a regimental square for drill and ceremonial parades. He transmitted the CO's daily orders to his men via the subedar and held weekly pay parades, obtaining receipts by means of inky thumbs. Until more elaborate exercises began, he led the company on toughening route marches in the heat of the day. Off parade he exchanged a few words of Urdu with his men. They treated him like a god and he was only twenty.

The evening cool compensated for the day's heat. He

sat in a canvas chair outside his tent in the officers' lines and watched the great red sun sink and the shadows rise. If he survived the war, why should he return to England and grow pasty and paunchy with the rest, living elbow to elbow in a damp climate? A parson's son, he was pacific by temperament. It had never entered his mind that he might enjoy a G. H. Henty life. Clive of India, Havelock of Lucknow, Skinner of Skinner's Horse. In their footsteps – Douglas of Gulunchi.

Yes, there he was. Basking in the interminable emptiness of the Indian plains. Gladly shouldering responsibility for the men who looked to him. Cherishing contentment as a warrior and white sahib. Leading the simple, privileged life.

Some evenings he put on gym shoes and ran across the countryside by himself to the only feature in sight. A hillock with a cave near the top. Inside the cave were bat droppings and an altar for primitive rites. A linggam smeared with red dye. He used to squat between the lips of the cave's mouth and imagine for himself a yogi existence. When the sun was down and the flocks of green parrots had disappeared in the twilight, he ran back to bathe in a tub at the rear of his tent and change for dinner in the officers' mess.

In India everything one did was known, and his solitary evening runs were noted and not approved. The second-in-command, a young regular jumped up to acting major, warned him of the dangers of going native.

'Once you go soft about the country, you'll end up going soft about the people. Then you're finished. India's a cruel place and the only thing the people understand is a boot up the backside. One of the troubles with you ECOs is you know nothing about India.'

'Yes, sir. No, sir.' He knew when not to argue.

But after dinner, while the other subalterns played bridge or poker and made polite conversation to their seniors, Douglas crept away to watch the stars. On parade he drove himself to be a model officer. Wasn't he entitled to some solitude in his own time?

The answer was no. He lived in a community where conformity was the rule and nonconformity a sin. He had joined the regiment and must lead the life it led. For an officer, the life of the mess. Drinking, gambling, horse-play, and fornicating once a month in Poona. Not to conform was to criticise. To criticise was to show disloyalty. To be disloyal was as bad as cowardice; a kind or desertion.

The CO sent for him one day and made his disapproval plain. Douglas had the honour of belonging to the finest regiment in the Indian Army and must uphold its traditions. Otherwise the regiment would have no further use for him.

Among the other officers he was treated on sufferance as Ashley's friend – the bloke who had been at school with Wyndham West and tagged along behind him into the same unit. It was galling to think of Ashley's popularity protecting him.

Ashley himself was a year younger. In the tropical sun, despite the topees they wore, the blondness of his hair had become dazzling. His complexion remained fresh and boyish beneath his tan. He dressed impeccably, even in the field, and carried himself in a smart, brisk, military manner. Although he was far less concerned and conscientious about his men's welfare than Douglas, they worshipped him. If a morale-boosting film had been made by the MOI to publicise the model young Indian Army officer, Douglas had no doubt the part would have gone to Ashley. Wyndham West Sahib was the pride of the regiment.

'You'd do well to follow the example of young Wyndham West,' the Colonel told him. 'There's an officer with a future if he stays in the army. Damn good material. I'd have been glad of him as regular.' What praise could be higher?

Douglas obediently did his best, but day by day India seeped into his bones. A cruel country perhaps, but irresistible. If the bridge-players in the mess were bent on resisting it, what kept them there? Saving the free world from dictatorship? Was India part of the free world? Till self-rule came, could it not be ruled in love, not scorn? He abandoned his solitude and spent more time with his sepoys. The Colonel might suspect him of finding their companionship more agreeable than that of his fellow sahibs, but he couldn't complain. The sepoys were the regiment and part of the raj.

Abdul Rahman was the one who caused his downfall. A Pathan from the Frontier with blue eyes and European skin. A wild staggering lad who cared for nobody and nothing. He claimed to be twenty-five and was probably sixteen – like many of the recruits he had no means of knowing. He had walked into the cantonment in Peshawar one day and announced his arrival from the Afghan hills to fight for the King-Emperor. His village had sent him because the harvest was bad and army pay said to be good. Please would the army teach him how to handle a rifle. He wanted to learn the best way to kill a man because this would be useful when he returned to the hills.

One evening Douglas was inspecting the meal and tasting a chapatti when Abdul Rahman jumped to his feet and put on an extempore dancing and tumbling act. He did it to attract attention and the act proved popular.

The subedar noted that the sahib had been amused and the next morning suggested Abdul Rahman as a replacement for Douglas's batman, who was due for a posting.

Douglas adopted the suggestion, as he adopted all the subedar's suggestions. The man was an Indian and held his commission from the Viceroy, so he ranked below Douglas. On the other hand, since he spoke the language and had been serving with the regiment while Douglas was being born, it was clearly understood by all ranks where the real command of the company lay. Douglas issued orders, but the subedar made sure in advance that they would be the right ones. In event of a disagreement the Colonel would support Douglas in public and the subedar in private.

'If you think he will be suitable, subedar sahib.'

'Most suitable, sahib. Mohammed Khan will train him before he goes. I will see to it myself.'

'He seems rather wild.'

'It is in his nature, sahib, but the regiment exists to tame men. He is not a Punjabi like the others, but he will be a good fighter. The discipline of being an officer's servant will be good for him. You will find him anxious to please you, and if there is trouble he knows that I shall punish him.'

'Very well, subedar sahib. Thank you.'

So Abdul Rahman brought him early morning tea and before he was properly awake seized him by the nose and lathered his face, shaving him perilously with a cut-throat razor while his head was still on the pillow. He bullied the bhistis into punctuality for Douglas's two daily baths – tepid in the morning and hot in the evening. He terrified the dhobi until Douglas's day-time shirt and shorts and evening Khaki-drill jacket and trousers were the cleanest and best starched in the mess. He put the fear of Allah into the sweeper if Douglas's thunderbox wasn't emptied within two minutes.

What the caste system permitted him to do himself, he did with enthusiasm. Polishing boots, sewing on buttons, making the bed. He was a good batman and instantly presumed on it. He ogled Douglas with those wild blue eyes and within a week was running a finger suggestively across his upper arm to indicate that the sahib should reward his services with a stripe.

Douglas resisted. He wanted his chores done, not a personal relationship. But Abdul Rahman, growing as fast in self-assurance as Alice in Wonderland, had other ideas. Broad hints and gestures of blood-brotherhood and secret intimacy were dropped.

'You'd better watch your step with that batman of yours,' said Ashley one day. 'He's making signals clear enough for the Japs to pick up in Assam.'

'There's nothing like that about it. All he wants is promotion.'

'Don't you believe it, dear boy. You know what goes on up on the Frontier. All those Pushtu love songs about boys' bottoms like ripe peaches.'

'Do you mind, Ashley. I've no designs at all on whatever

may be left of Abdul Rahman's virtue and I advise you to keep away. What worries me about him is that he doesn't seem amenable to discipline. The subedar can control him but I don't think I can. Once he discovers that ingratiating himself doesn't pay he's liable to get fed up and desert.'

'You're too easy with him, that's the trouble. Give a Pathan an inch and he'll take a mile. If you can't manage him I'll take him off your hands. It should be rather fun. Like breaking in a horse.'

'In view of your record at school, Ashley, I don't think that would be a good idea at all.'

'For Christ's sake stop being a prefect, will you? We're in the bloody army now. And talking about batmen, not fags.'

Ashley got his way, as Ashley always did. Abdul Rahman was transferred to his company and became his batman and noticeably more docile. After a month he achieved the coveted stripe and flaunted it like a campaign medal or a decoration for valour. There were mutterings among the senior NCO's, who complained of his insolence. Douglas's relief at being rid of him turned to qualms. He still felt responsible for Ashley, and Ashley was riding for a fall.

The affair exploded one night with all the force of a direct hit on an ammunition dump. A noise woke him in the small hours and he switched on his torch to reveal a naked Ashley blundering into the tent.

His first thought was that he must be orderly officer for the night and had overslept. But Ashley's face indicated something different. The debonair hero was in a state of panic.

'It's in my tent.' He spoke urgently, not looking Douglas in the face, his eyes exploring the shadows.

'What's in your tent?'

'You must help me. Please, Dougs!' He was almost in tears.

'Then tell me what it is. Do pull yourself together, Ashley. Of course I'll help you. I always have, haven't I?' While Ashley just stood, he jumped out of bed.

'It may be a scorpion.'

91

'A scorpion? Surely, you're not frightened of that.'
'Or a snake of some sort. A krait.'
'Where is it?'
'On my bed.'
'Has it stung you or bitten you?'
Ashley shook his head.

The story hardly made sense. A scorpion sting could put a man in hospital and a krait could kill, but the resemblance between the two was nil. Neither could climb on to a bed. If he saw them first anyone could bash either of them on the head, and whatever else he might be Ashley wasn't a coward.

Leaving him collapsed on the bed, Douglas put his feet into his boots for protection and picked up his swagger stick.

It was pre-monsoon weather, sultry throughout the night. Like Ashley and most of the other officers he slept without pyjamas, the flaps of his tent open to what breeze was going. In the blackness outside, the sickly-sweet smell of India caught in his throat. Ashley's tent stood next to his in the lines and he had no need of the torch to find his way.

Inside he halted cautiously and played his beam towards the bed. Torch in the left hand, swagger stick at the ready in the right. There was nothing visible underneath and he moved the light methodically over the floor before directing it on to the bed. What lay there was neither a scorpion nor a snake, but Abdul Rahman. Naked and grinning seductively.

A bare glimpse and that was that. Noises sounded behind him and other torches shone. Quick as a krait, Abdul Rahman slithered off the bed and disappeared through the rear exit. A scuffle followed, and a voice in the night. The clipped voice of the second-in-command ordering Douglas not to move from where he stood.

Miraculously, they had landed safely and the voice in his ear telling him not to move was female. Would he please remain in his seat and keep his seatbelt fastened until the aircraft had come to a complete standstill?

Queueing successively for agriculture, vaccination and customs did nothing for his frayed nerves, but the police were soothing. They took him off in a car to headquarters, where an inspector seemed amused by the incident at Nandi. They had already spoken to Paris and would co-operate in every way possible.

He asked for a line to Montreal and confessed to his *contretemps* with Air New Zealand. Montreal tutted and told him not to upset IATA members but expressed more concern about his expenses. He told them how much more secure their members' aircraft would be once they had stopped carrying contraband gold. It was uphill work.

Meantime the police established that Miss Smith had booked in at the South Pacific. They offered to take over her shadowing so that Douglas could get some rest. They even fixed a room for him at a humbler establishment round the corner.

With the promise that he would be told what contacts his party made and when she looked like moving on, he parted from them gratefully and felt less alone. He warned them that round-the-clock observation would be necessary and of her special interest in banks, bullion mechants and India Fund offices.

Having nothing to do but relax, he felt less tired and decided to explore Auckland. His hotel was near the harbour, which ran into the centre of the city where everything appeared reassuringly British. Queen Street intersected with Victoria Street in the main shopping area, with Albert Park close at hand. While he stood at the crossroads the traffic cleared for a pipe band in full tartan regalia making a ceremonial march. He might have been in Liverpool or Dundee.

A guidebook mentioned one difference. Auckland was built among sixty-five volcanos. Like Ashley, they were thought to be extinct. A taxi took him through streets of tightly packed bungalows to one of them called Mount Eden. At first sight it resembled one of the Malvern hills which he and Ashley had been forced to run up and down for a healthy exercise at school. But here the top turned out to be a deep, grassed crater, like an inverted mould for a motte. A bird's-eye view of the town revealed other volcanoes rising among the sports grounds and Coronation Streets.

In the equivalent of Kew Gardens there were blue beds of agapanthus and huge pohoutakawa trees covered with red blossom. In the equivalent of the British Museum were Maori houses and door posts carved with grotesque figures matching those of Europe's medieval masons. A notice informed him that the tongue straight out meant defiance and contempt, the tongue askew meant welcome. The Maoris were Polynesian and he wished he had known the code signs when dealing with Sergeant O'Leary. The Maoris, it seemed, had come from Hawaii some seven centuries before Douglas and rather more slowly. They had conquered the New Zealand aborigines by the simple process of eating them.

Back at the hotel there was no message from the police. He dined at 18.30 and was asleep an hour later. At 03.00 he woke with a bad taste in his mouth. As usual, this proved to be Ashley. By day he could kid himself about his ability to bring the Wyndham West monster to justice. In the small hours he knew that Ashley always won and he always lost. Nature had made them complementary.

He woke again at breakfast-time, surprised not to find himself in a camp-bed at Gulunchi. Sleeping the clock round hadn't refreshed him. He switched on the radio. A cyclone was forecast: his friend from California, Hawaii and yesterday's sky.

'Don't ring us, we'll ring you.' That was what Inspector Macintosh had said. Until the call came he was free.

After breakfast the sun came out, defying the forecast. It had the air of a day for the beach.

A taxi took him across the harbour bridge. Widening work was in progress and the driver complained of the contract going to the Japanese. Theirs had undercut all the tenders from England. The new sections were being made complete in Japan and floated down the Pacific by barge. How could anyone compete, and who had won the war?

Douglas grunted sympathetically. He knew who hadn't won the war. Himself for instance.

He spent the morning in Brown's Bay. Good old Brown. Except for a volcano brooding in the distance, it might have been a cove in Dorset. Typically, in crossing the international date line he had lost a Sunday and not a working day. Today was Tuesday therefore and by way of compensation he had the bay to himself.

At lunch-time he returned to the hotel. A message was waiting. Reception handed him the note. It asked him to ring the inspector's number. Busy and brief, the inspector informed him that another party had joined his party.

While his call was being transferred to a sergeant for the details, Douglas went limp at the prospect of an encounter with Ashley. But the sergeant had better news. The party who had arrived by air from Tokyo and driven straight to the South Pacific was a party by the name of Paget.

So it was George again. And using his own name still.

George the big businessman and philanthropist. George who should have been caught with a consignment of gold and must by now have disposed of it profitably in Japan. George who was surely in charge of Ashley's winding-up operations. Douglas remembered him in his astrakhan hat in Red Square. From earlier days he remembered him in the mess at Gulunchi soaked every Saturday night in Amritsar five-star gin. Aggressively soaked. Piggy eyes and a heavy jowl. A reckoning was overdue.

'Yes,' he said into the telephone, 'that name means something to me. Has he joined Miss Smith openly?'

He had. They were making no secret of their acquaintance. Or their plans. Paget had ordered a hire car and an hour later they both booked out. Before leaving, they inquired about hotels in Rotarua and asked the porter to reserve them two rooms there for the night. Already they were out of Auckland and driving south.

'Rotarua, how can I get there?'

'We won't lose them,' the sergeant promised. 'No need to worry. The car will be checked at regular points on the route. Why don't you stay put and let us report developments?'

'Have they left any luggage at the hotel?'

'No, but they're both travelling light.'

'What is there in Rotarua?'

'Boiling mud.' The sergeant laughed.

Rotarua was the heart of New Zealand's Thermal Wonderland, it seemed. The most natural place to visit. Afterwards one could return to Auckland or travel on to Wellington.

Douglas ran his mind over the probabilities. What were George Paget's intentions towards Sylvia Smith? Friendly or hostile? Marital or murderous? Had he learned about the loot she was carrying? Did she remove it from the bank in Honolulu on his instructions, or Ashley's, or on her own account? Had she told him that he, Douglas, was in Auckland? Was he meant to follow them to Rotarua? If so, did she alone or both of them intend it?

'I'll follow them,' he decided. He had no choice. On past

96

performance it seemed likely that George's designs were as bad as could be. He would surely be a lot safer with Sylvia out of circulation. Not to mention richer.

'As you wish,' said the sergeant. 'It's a long drive. I would advise taking the train. The Wellington night express leaves at four-thirty. We have a special operative at Te Kuiti. If you get off there I'll arrange to have you met.'

A police car called for him at four. The driver handed him a pass valid for first-class rail travel and took him to the station.

His compartment was shabby, and some first-class wag had scribbled on the lavatory wall. A deleted 'not' made it obligatory to use the lavatory while the train was standing in the station. Pillows for the night could be hired for fifteen cents. The natives were friendly, but it was all a far cry from the luxury of a sahib's sleeper on the Bombay–Madras Express.

After the suburban landscape came rising grassland with cows and black and white Holsteins. No mango groves or water buffalo. A Farmers' Supermarket, a Dalgety Loan Wool Store, Wilson's Cement Works. Stations with sedately English names. Then a crop of exotic ones – Papakura, Pukekohe and Te Awamutu.

At Frankton a refreshment stop. The Indian pattern but not the Indian style. No leisurely curry-eating under a punkah. Instead a queue for cups of strong-brewed tea and meat pies in paper packs. With everyone served and aboard again the guard waved the train on. Douglas closed his eyes and returned to Gulunchi.

While the machinery for a court-martial lumbered into action he spent lonely days under arrest, confined to his tent. Meals were brought to him by one of the orderlies in case he should contaminate the officers' mess by his presence. The role of prisoner's friend was refused in turn by Ashley and George Paget. Jack Willingdon begged to be excused. The Colonel had to order the red-haired Petrie to undertake it.

Douglas was allowed to see no one else from the regiment, except the second-in-command when a legal high-up arrived from divisional headquarters to prepare the evidence. The major glared at him for an hour and generally behaved as though in contact with the plague.

Ashley wrote a long emotional letter. There had been a dreadful mistake and he would see that everything came out all right for Douglas. The letter didn't, however, contain a confession or anything remotely incriminating to Ashley himself. Petrie listened to Douglas's version of events with the same expression of contempt as the major had worn on the night of his arrest and at the interview. He could not concieve how Douglas had sunk so low as to accuse a fellow officer for the sake of saving his own skin.

'But Abdul Rahman was in Ashley's bed, not mine. Is it likely he would lend me his tent for the purpose? Use your loaf, Petrie. I was wearing boots, wasn't I? How can you believe I'd just jumped out of bed?'

To Petrie the boots suggested a fetish and made matters worse. He believed that Ashley and Douglas had been sharing Abdul Rahman's favours. Since it was Douglas who had been caught Douglas must stand the racket. Oddly, he seemed to think none the worse of Ashley for committing the same offence but not being found out.

Douglas knew he was paying the penalty for his nonconformity. If he had joined the nightly poker school which the other four made up with the major, if he had buttered up the Colonel, as Ashley did, with earnest questions about the regiment's unutterably boring exploits on the Frontier in the Twenties – if in fact he had tried to be a good regimental type instead of simply a good officer, the affair would have been handled differently. A private dressing-down from the Colonel, a posting to some distant musketry course in Quetta or 'Pindi, a transfer to the second battalion at Chittagong on completion of the course.

Eventually Douglas persuaded Petrie that it was his duty to put forward a defence which Douglas, on his word as an officer and a gentleman, swore to be the truth. Too bad if it had the disagreeable consequence of pointing the finger at another officer, and one who was the most popular member of the mess. He threatened to testify to a lot more about Ashley, both at school and on the troop ship coming out.

'It will do you more harm than good,' Petrie warned him. 'The old man has already announced that he's going to deal with Ashley himself. Even if the court believes you he won't stand for another court-martial. For the regiment's sake.'

As the day approached, Douglas's receding hopes rested on Abdul Rahman, who was under close arrest in the regimental guardroom and reported to be enjoying his notoriety. He owed his stripe to Ashley, and telling the truth would be a new experience for him. On the other hand Ashley had been sleeping with him and denied it. If his pride was hurt Ashley had better watch out.

For hours Douglas rehearsed Abdul Rahman's cross-examination with Petrie. He knew that, when the time came, he would never denounce Ashley in open court or allow Petrie to read his prepared statement. But if the Pathan could be brought to deny any improper association with Douglas and roll his blue eyes at Ashley in full view of the court, Douglas might still be acquitted with honour.

On the eve of the court-martial Abdul Rahman was severely barked at by the second-in-command in the presence of the Deputy Judge Advocate General. The DJAG had been sent by Division to prosecute Douglas and was interrogating witnesses whom his assistant had found unsatisfactory. The major was representing the CO. He spoke Pushtu and had learned the deadliest insults. He used them to slight both Abdul Rahman's honour and his looks.

Abdul Rahman retaliated by telling the DJAG that he had been sleeping with the entire officer's mess. The CO was persistent but impotent. The major indulged in some peculiarly unnatural practices, full details of which he would be revealing to the court in the interest of justice.

The major told the DJAG that, although everyone would know the boy was lying, a scandal would be insupportable. The regiment would become the laughing stock of the Indian Army. The DJAG promised to do his best to suppress any such evidence. He could not guarantee success, however.

The major then ordered Abdul Rahman to withdraw his disgraceful allegations. Abdul Rahman, enjoying the havoc he was creating, refused. The major called him a dog and the son of a dog, and Abdul Rahman called the major the son of a sow and an unmarried sow at that. Reports of the exchanges spread through the camp at lightning speed. The officers' mess, aghast, agreed that it was all Douglas's fault.

That evening, during his sunset airing outside the guardroom under escort, Abdul Rahman, who had been charming the guard commander with tales of Frontier atrocities, suddenly seized the man's rifle, knocked him senseless and ran off into the dusk. He had insults to avenge. Insults which no Pathan could stomach.

Before the alarm could be raised he had reached the officers' lines, entered the major's tent and shot him dead. The shot brought the major's batman and most of the officers' mess at the double. Abdul Rahman had barely time to hack off the major's private parts with a bayonet and disappear with them into the night.

After that the court-martial was an anticlimax. In the absence of the key witness, Ashley made an impassioned speech declaring his unshakable belief in Douglas's innocence and asking to be tried in his place since the responsibility for any misconduct (if misconduct there had been) must be his and his alone. He did not admit to the truth, however, and on Douglas's orders Petrie said nothing to incriminate him. Douglas simply denied the charge and the DJAG, a peacetime barrister, had no difficulty in running legal rings round him and an embarrassed Petrie.

In finding Douglas guilty the President of the Court congratulated Ashley on his gallant and loyal, if misguided attempt to save a friend and fellow officer. Led by young men of such calibre, the regiment, he believed, would quickly rise above the disgrace of this unfortunate incident. As for Douglas, conduct prejudicial to military discipline had undoubtedly taken place. And much more. Infamous and gross misconduct. Here was an officer unfit to hold a commission. He must be cashiered, reduced to the ranks. Innocent sepoys should never have been placed in his charge.

Like all good scapegoats, Douglas stood smartly to attention and listened respectfully to the sentence.

Disgraced, depipped, unsahibed, his stiff upper lip never quavered in public.

The train was running through more enticing country. Rows of eucalyptus. Hills closing in. Hummock's rising out of the ground at close quarters like man-made tumuli. The sky behind the hills changed from orange to lemon and from lemon to Fiji grey. It was after eight when they reached Te Kuiti.

He was met as promised, but not as expected. A blonde in uniform greeted him at the barrier. A well-built girl. Policewoman Irene Hutchins. She gave him a situation report and a late supper and fixed him a bed in a vacant cell.

In the morning they made an early start. It was still a hundred miles or thereabouts to Rotarua. Irene (two syllables) wore a flowery dress. She drove him through English-style countryside under an English-style sky (low clouds).

He noted the differences and asked the names. Among the flora were toi-toi pampas grass and cabbage trees and rimu pines. The black-headed, yellow-billed birds warming their feet on the tarmac were minahs, old friends of his from India and Chessington Zoo, where one had said good morning to Susan in the days of their courtship.

There were fantails and whitethroated parson birds to remind him of his father. Once they slowed down for a family of quail crossing the road. Once they disturbed a hawk feasting on its prey on the dotted line. The other dead creatures on the road were car victims. Not hedgehogs but possums.

Even villages were dying. Bennydale came and went, a community built beside a coalmine which had become uneconomic. The inhabitants were leaving and the main street showed gaps where they had taken their homes with them.

'Are these two armed?' Irene asked.

'I dare say.' More death ahead. He must protect her, but if he could account for George and trace Ashley he didn't mind overmuch about himself. Was there anyone to mourn his passing? Helen? Rene? Susan, wherever she might be? His parents had died long ago. Before the court-martial, praise the Lord.

A pal of smoke and a sickly sulphurous odour signalled the proximity of Rotarua. Irene dropped him at Whakare-warewa and went to make inquiries. He joined a group of tourists inspecting Pohutu, the prize geyser. It played for twenty minutes every hour and a half, but never predictably. It could shoot a jet of boiling water ninety feet into the air, but refused to perform for Douglas.

He wandered among the geysers, surrounded by hot-spring pools and lethal patches of boiling mud. A moon landscape of yellowed rock, white silica terraces and burnt-out sterility.

At the far end of the thermal area the survivors of a local Maori tribe had harnessed nature's spite to domestic use. Meals were being cooked over the mouths of steam holes. Hot baths were there for the taking, but no cold water. Channels had to be diverted on a roundabout course before bath time to allow for the water to cool. A child falling into a pool out of official bathing hours would be scalded to death.

Irene was overdue. He meandered back to a reconstruc-ted Maori village, complete with meeting-house, store-house and sleeping huts, behind a palisade. What could be keeping her? Had they vanished? He stood in the meeting-house wondering why he bothered if no one else cared. Revenge was an unworthy motive. Why shouldn't Ashley have his plaque in St. Paul's and go on enjoying himself somewhere?

By way of an answer Douglas supposed he possessed an inherited moral attitude and more than a touch of obsti-nacy. Since vowing vengeance he had always been defeated, a glutton for punishment. To add to his depression it began to rain.

She appeared at last and all was well. The mere sight of her restored his resolution. Duty called, and he was not alone.

'They've left their hotel,' she said, 'and no one knows when they are likely to get back. I've been to the station as well. A police car is following them and the station's in radio contact.'

'Where are they then? Have they left for Wellington?' The offices of the India Fund in New Zealand were there. He had a suspicion that that was where Ashley might be lurking and where the rendezvous with the others would take place.

'No; they are sightseeing. Up at Lake Tarawera.'

'Sightseeing! Can they go south that way?'

'It's a dead end. Why don't we go to the police station and keep in touch from there?'

A dead end for Sylvia Smith, he didn't doubt.

'If you don't mind, I'd like to see the lake.'

'But they are under observation already. You don't want them to see you, do you?'

'I think they may be expecting me. I wouldn't like to disappoint them.'

She was puzzled but didn't protest. The road wound past two other scenic lakes. One should have been blue and the other green. They were both grey in the slanting rain.

'This is our Lake District,' she told him. 'It's lovely when the sun shines. You're unlucky.'

As if he didn't know.

They passed Te Wairoa and she told him about the buried village which was New Zealand's Pompeii. Tired of being trampled over by tourists and described as extinct, Mount Tarawera had blown its top one day and covered the countryside in ash, lava and mud to a depth of six feet. Today it was being temperamental again, sulking invisibly among the clouds.

While Irene was pointing to where it should have been, a car approached from the lakeside. Douglas scarcely had time to duck. The first car was followed after an interval by another. A second run-of-the-mill Holden.

'Was that them?' he asked. 'Did they see me?'

'It must have been, and I think they did. The other was ours.'

'Are you sure there were two people in the first car?'

The visibility was poor but she described what she had seen and the descriptions fitted. He asked her to turn the car and follow.

'I can't say I'm surprised at your friends not lingering here today,' she said, wiping the mist from the inside of the windscreen.

'It's not the weather,' he assured her. 'It's having company.'

At Lake Rotarua the cars ahead turned right, away from the town. There was an airport beside the lake, Douglas noticed, but to his relief they ignored it. Further on they pulled off the road into the car park of some tourist attraction.

'Tikitere,' Irene told him. 'Otherwise Hell's Gate.'

'We'll wait.'

The rain was heavy now. They watched two figures from the first car run for the entrance. Except for the two cars the place was deserted. They drove in and parked beside the second one. A man got out and spoke to Irene.

'Hi,' he said. 'We heard about you from the station. Do you want to take over? They've spotted us.'

'Does that mean you want to go home for lunch?' Irene was practical.

'Any objection?'

They both looked at Douglas, who shook his head.

'No, of course not. Thank you for your help.'

The car drove away, leaving them alone with the other Holden. They were at opposite ends of the car park, divided by a downpour of Hawaiian fury.

'It's out of doors,' said Irene. 'they can't be going round in this.'

'Can't they?' He reached down, took his automatic from the holster, kissed it for luck and checked it over.

104

'No one told me there was going to be any shooting. I'm not armed. Why did you let the others go?' She wasn't frightened. Just severe.

'I shan't require any assistance. You're to stay in the car.'

'But first you must tell me what's going on. Why have they gone in there?'

'I can think of two reasons. One is that they want me to follow them.'

'To kill you? Then don't be so rash. You don't have to go.'

'That's the other reason. If I don't, the man may take the opportunity to kill the woman.'

'I'm coming too. They can't kill both of us.'

'Yes, they can; and no, you're not.'

He explained how there had to be somebody to follow them if they drove off quickly. If that happened she was not to wait for him. He would make his own way back to Rotarua and wait at the police station to hear from her.

She accepted his orders reluctantly, and wished him good luck. 'You're looking pale. Are you sure you'll be all right?'

He slipped the automatic into his raincoat pocket and patted her hand in farewell. 'I'm a pale person,' he told her. Her solicitude reminded him of the counter clerk at Heathrow.

Hell's Gate was even more weird and sinister than Whakarewarewa. The earth's crust had broken open and the area was a desolate inferno of seething mud pools. There were hot waterfalls, too, fed from boiling lakes. The roots of trees from a primeval forest stood petrified. And no wonder.

He paid his entrance money to a small boy who warned him to keep to the marked track. If he could see the markings. Without hat or umbrella he tucked his chin well into the collar of his raincoat and kept his head down reading the sodden guide sheet. He might or might not be expected, but there was nothing to be gained from advertising his presence. The two ahead were already dim figures in the thermal landscape and he made no attempt to catch them

105

up. So long as they could see someone behind them, his purpose would be served.

The first pool was the Devil's Bath. According to the guide sheet, the water was eighteen feet deep and registered two hundred and ten degrees fahrenheit. The next was named after a Maori chieftain's daughter who had husband trouble and committed suicide by throwing herself in it. The third, Hell's Gate itself, was an enormous boiling whirlpool.

Gushers, steam vents, sulphur baths. Douglas picked a slippery path gingerly between them. One eye on the wonders, the other on his quarry. There were no railings for protection. One false step and a foot would be scalded beyond repair.

The area was large and he became drawn far away from the entrance. Out of sight of the hut and the car park. The two figures in front pressed on. He alternated between hurrying not to lose them and dawdling to avoid getting too close. One of them turned abruptly and he halted in his tracks.

Visibility was so poor that he couldn't distinguish the one from the other. Whichever was looking back was looking straight at him. He curled his fingers instinctively round the handle of his automatic.

All at once they disappeared. Tiring, he limped slowly towards the spot. The path became a bush track. A lush oasis of dense vegetation taking over from the bare rock. Fearing an ambush, he advanced weapon in hand.

It came as he emerged at the head of a waterfall. A bullet ricocheted off a rock behind him. He fired in return and threw himself on the ground. There was no target in view, but at least it served notice on them that he was armed too. He hoped the noise of firing wouldn't reach the car park and inspire Irene to attempt anything heroic.

He wormed behind a rock and waited. If they were both armed and intent on killing him they would split up and attack from opposite flanks. He strained to listen for a tell-tale sound, but the heaviness of the rain made it difficult to hear as well as see.

106

The seconds passed. Were they creeping up on him or was it a warning shot to immobilise him while they escaped? George Paget worried him. In the course of military training they had crawled over quite a lot of India together. No doubt middle age had slowed him up, but he had been an expert crawler in his time. Fieldcraft, unarmed combat and marksmanship. Officer-Cadet, later Lieutenant, Paget had shone at the lot.

Douglas had just decided to cut and run when a cry reached him. A cry to fit the landscape. Desperate and suddenly cut off, as though a door had closed on it. Was it male or female? He couldn't tell.

They must be fighting each other. Perhaps the bullet hadn't been intended for him after all. He picked himself up and ran as fast as his thigh would let him, dodging and stumbling across an open expanse of rock and sulphur.

By a fluke of instinct he stopped a single step short of the hottest pool of all. It was the Devil's Cauldron and the rain was beating into it as though directed by the devil in person. A rock overhung one edge, concealing it from where he came. Balanced on the lip, he looked up and saw a figure running into the distance. He fired, but it ducked and continued to run, zigzagging between the hazards.

Another figure floated on the surface of the pool at his feet. Sylvia Smith face downwards. Another victim for George Paget. The end of his best hope of unearthing Ashley. In a fit of rage he turned his own face upwards, into the rain, and aimed his automatic in the direction of his father's God.

Then he knelt beside the pool and tugged cautiously at the back of the raincoat. If he leaned too far he would be boiled alive himself. Moving down from the lip, he steered the body ashore on to a flat piece of stone. With a shock he saw a pair of men's trousers on it.

Clumsily he turned it over. The flesh on the face was burned beyond recognition.

Which of the two of them was it, this faceless bundle of scorched and sodden flesh and clothes? The build was stocky, the shoulders were broad. Without waiting for it to cool he scrabbled at the clothes, like the hawk on the road worrying at its prey. It was male. It was George. Or had been.

He rolled him back into the pool, singeing the back of his hand with a splash of water. The devil could have his own. Any man's death diminished him, but George Paget's least of all.

WELLINGTON

The boy at the entrance was peacefully asleep among the souvenirs. The car park was empty. Douglas stood, oblivious of the rain, adjusting his mind to the incredible fact that Sylvia Smith had killed George Paget and not vice versa. It was the biggest turn-up for the book since Judith had done for Holofernes.

Waterlogged, he shuffled blindly along Highway 30 towards Rotarua. He hadn't noticed a bullet in the body. Could George have stepped backwards into the pool by accident? It was possible but out of character. She must have taken him by surprise and shoved him in. She was capable of killing, as Douglas knew, and George's death would suit her fine, no doubt. But how was Ashley going to like it?'

He covered two miles before a car picked him up. It deposited him on the steps of the police station. There they put him under a hot shower and lent him some dry clothes. Irene had not reported back, and he decided to keep quiet about the body until he had spoken to her.

When he saw her car pulling up he went out and joined her. She looked him over anxiously.

'Are you all right? What went on in that place?'

'I followed them at a distance,' he told her. 'Then they bolted. They must have seen me and panicked.'

'Were there shots fired? I heard something but couldn't be sure.'

'Shots? Nothing like that.' He couldn't tell whether she believed him.

'They took me by surprise when they came out,' she said 'What with all that rain I didn't see them properly or even hear the car start. When it moved off I followed as you'd instructed. They went down Highway 5 towards Taupo.'

'Is that south? For Wellington?'

'Yes, the main road. I've had the Taupo police alerted.'

'Tell me,' he said. 'Which of them was driving?'

'I couldn't see. The rear window was completely steamed up. Does it matter?'

'It's not important.'

He had come to his decision. If the New Zealand police arrested Sylvia Smith for murder he might never uncover Ashley. Therefore she must not be detained. Nor must he. Therefore he would not report the death. Policewoman Hutchins, bless her, was unaware of it. When discovered, the body would be unidentifiable. It was wrong of him, but not so wrong as letting Ashley go free.

'What now?' she asked.

'A message to the Taupo police to forget it. I don't want our friends to panic any more. Then back to Te Kuiti for us.'

What he really didn't want was for the Taupo police to report only one person in the car. While Irene went inside to pass the message he stayed in the street. What he didn't want either was any questions from the local force.

From Te Kuiti he spoke by telephone to Inspector Macintosh in Auckland. The inspector promised a check on the airports and to let him know if either of his parties booked a flight out of the country.

The next morning he took the day express to Wellington. Irene saw him off and he shook hands with her on the platform. Another woman in his life come and gone. The train was announced as the North Island Main Trunk Railways Scenic Daylight Express Railcar Service. Hs compartment resembled an aeroplane cabin. High-back seats. Trays for snacks. Announcements through loudspeakers. Everything but seat-belts. He might as well have flown.

The journey began smoothly. Gradually his mind eased with the rain and the passing of distance and time. George Paget had suffered the fate of a lobster and Pierre was avenged, but Douglas felt no satisfaction. Only Ashley could give him that.

Before long the train climbed to the central plateau of King Country where, his route map informed him, no white man had been safe a hundred years ago. At the highest point they described three loops and a circle before descending gently past snow mountains to a sandy seascape. Wellington in six hours. Towards the end he dozed.

The effect of the court-martial's verdict had been his dismissal with ignominy from the Indian Army. The humiliation in front of his fellow officers was bad enough, but he minded more about the men he commanded. He had let them down. Lost face for ever. An unforgivable shame in a caste-ridden society.

In a conscripts' war he had to continue fighting for his country. Since a white man couldn't serve as an Other Rank in an Indian unit he had been called up as a private in the British Army. It happened before the president's ink was dry on the verdict.

They hustled him away the same night under cover of darkness. He found himself back at the railway station, where the three-legged cow gave him a withering I-told-you-so look. Both platforms and the area around them were crowded with armed men. All trains were being delayed while they searched every carriage for Abdul Rahman.

Douglas heard later that he had never been caught. Rumour reported that he had escaped disguised in a burqa – the white tent worn by Muslim women which no infidel could peer through without starting a religious war. He was said to have reached home triumphantly with his trophy. In retrospect Douglas thought of him without rancour as the Ashley Wyndham West of the North-West Frontier. Charming, ruthless, and somehow able to get away with murder.

He himself was posted to Multan. A battleground in one of the Sikh wars, it lay blistering on the edge of the Sind desert. Now a punishment station for British troops, a battalion of his new regiment was stationed there for burning down a Bengali village in its cups. Reveille sounded daily at 04.30 and at midday the temperature reached a hundred and twenty degrees in whatever shade could be found.

111

Parades finished at eleven and began again at four. The heat made sleep impossible, either in the midday break or before midnight when the parched earth came off the boil. As the weeks passed he grew wearier and wearier until he caught jaundice and no longer wished to stay alive.

In the cantonment hospital he lay sweating through one insupportable day after another. The living standards of British Other Ranks hadn't improved since Kipling's day and to add to the sufferings of the climate and his illness he had lost his accustomed comforts as a sahib. India was hell and in the world outside – Europe, North Africa, the Far East – the war was being lost. He had no family to mind about his death. Why should he bother to survive?

It was Ashley who pulled him through. The desire not to leave a world where the ungodly still flourished. Who else but Ashley, suddenly aware that he was about to be caught *flagrante delicto,* would have thought to dash out and inveigle an innocent friend into taking his place? Could it be left at that?

With nothing else to do but watch the lizards catching flies on the ceiling, he brooded on paradise lost and plotted revenge. Being neither a Pathan nor a Wyndham West, his would be less savage than Abdul Rahman's on the major. But if India and the Japs spared them both, he vowed he would be even in the end.

During his convalescence an intelligence unit in Simla sent out an SOS for linguists. His company commander took pity on him and, knowing of his scholarship in languages, recommended his transfer.

So Douglas went to Simla and, in the cool above the plains, life became tolerable again. Every morning he woke to a view of the Himalayas rearing up against the distant skyline like a row of vanilla ices. Every evening, as the sun set, they turned to a delicate strawberry. Sunshine on the conifers. Breezes from the Hindu Kush. Paradise regained. He was promoted to corporal, then sergeant, and led a near-civilian life.

News reached him when the Gulunchi division went overseas. It was posted to escort duty, ferrying supplies through Persia and Iraq. So much for action in Burma or Libya. No glamorous fighting for Ashley. No gallant death before they could meet again.

Acting on Irene's advice, he went from the station at Wellington to a hotel near the airport. The White Heron Lodge. It provided him with generous accommodation – a double bed and a sofa capable of sleeping a Muslim's spare wives. From the sofa he rang Auckland and spoke to Inspector Macintosh's office.

A report had been received from the car-hire firm which had rented the car to his parties. The car had been returned to their Wellington garage. No flight out of Wellington had been booked in the name of Paget or Smith. The airport police had descriptions of both.

He thanked them and rang off. What would la Smith do now? Contact Ashley surely. It was half past seven, but Douglas decided on a visit to the IF offices. He took the lock-picking kit from his case and put it in his raincoat pocket.

Crossing the lobby equipped like a burglar, he suffered a shock. A familiar voice greeted him.

'Good Lord, Douglas. What are you doing here?' It was Jack Willingdon and his surprise sounded genuine.

'Business. And you?'

'Ditto. I've just arrived from England.'

They eyed each other appraisingly. Like dogs sniffing.

'Look,' said Jack. 'You're interested in the India Fund in some way, aren't you?'

'Why should you suppose that?'

'You'd better know that I'm here because of a phone call from George Paget.'

'Paget?' Douglas pretended to recall the name from his memory bank. 'A rather tough customer from our Indian days, I seem to remember. Where did he phone from?'

'We discussed him at lunch last week,' said Jack sharply. 'And what does it matter where he phoned from? It was Tokyo actually. He mentioned having seen you on a flight between San Francisco and Honolulu.'

'I wonder why he didn't come and speak to me.'

'I'm wondering one or two things as well.'

'Such as?'

'Such as whether it wouldn't be a good idea for you and George to have a chat. I'm going to meet him now. Why don't you come along? I'd be interested to hear what you've got to say to each other.'

Douglas looked at his watch and appeared to hesitate. 'So George is in Wellington now?'

'He's due. I've just phoned the local IF man.'

'All right. For old times' sake.' George might prove more helpful dead than ever he'd been while alive.

They took a taxi into town. The lights of Wellington ran uphill semicircling the docks and the darkness of the harbour. There was time to kill and they agreed on a quick run round the coast. In a short distance the landscape grew wild and the sea menaced them. Notices on sandy beaches warned of a lethal undertow.

'The landscape's veneer of civilisation is pretty thin, don't you think?' said Jack. 'It's the same with human beings.'

'Speak for yourself,' Douglas replied.

He leaned forward and touched the automatic beneath his trouser leg for reassurance. Jack was dressed every stitch a City solicitor and the taxi-driver seemed no more villainous than most, but Douglas felt a ruffle of fear.

On Jack's order the man turned back through the hills, telling them how the main streets below had been reclaimed from the sea and the old Wellington was up here. Brightly painted wooden bungalows nestled in niches, hanging high above the bay.

The IF man had built his on an almost vertical section. It projected from the hillside and stood on stilts. The sitting room looked across the Cook Straits to the snow peaks of the South Island. Their host's name was Keith Forbes and he received them nervously.

Jack introduced Douglas. 'We ran into each other by accident at the hotel,' he explained. 'I brought him along because he knows Mr. Paget.'

'Mr. Paget has still not arrived. I was expecting him this afternoon. He rang a couple of days ago from Auckland and said he wanted to talk over several matters with me. I am anxious to see him because the Fund's affairs have become rather difficult since Mr. Wyndham West's death. Payment is overdue on a large consignment of wool.'

'There's no need to go into details now,' said Jack with a frown and a glance at Douglas.

'Did George Paget ask you to do something for him?' Douglas inquired.

'Only to book him on an outgoing flight.'

'When and where to?'

'Tomorrow morning. To Sydney.'

'Did you make the reservation in his name?'

'No; in my own.'

'One seat or two?'

'Two.'

Jack protested. 'Will you please stop interrogating Mr. Forbes? The only question that matters is where George Paget has got to. You wouldn't know the answer to that one yourself, would you, Douglas?'

'Why on earth should you imagine that?' Douglas became bland.

'I don't waste my time imagining things. I'm a lawyer. What I deal in are facts. One fact is that George Paget is a punctual and business-like person. I've come all the way from London for a rendezvous with him here today. He assured me he would be with Mr. Forbes this afternoon. If he has been unavoidably delayed, why has he not sent a message? Another fact is your interest in our affairs.'

'I've only one more question to ask Mr. Forbes. When did he last see Ashley Wyndham West?'

'The Director-General was last here six months ago.'

The man was honest and telling the truth. If he knew it. With Jack one couldn't be so sure. He had opened his mouth to say something and then shut it again.

While they waited, Mrs. Forbes served them with prawn cocktails, lamb chops and New Zealand cheddar. A place

115

was laid for George. At ten o'clock Jack gave up and he and Douglas returned to the White Heron.

They continued their session in Douglas's room over a duty-free nightcap.

'Ashley is a villain,' said Douglas. He had decided to put a few cards on the table in the hope of seeing some of Jack's.

Jack, who was sprawling on the sofa, sat up. 'Those four words contain two serious allegations. I was about to tell you to stop defaming the dead, when I noticed the tense. Do you really believe that Ashley faked his death?'

'Yes, and so do you. Otherwise you wouldn't have come fourteen thousand miles on the strength of a phone call.'

'I came because, frankly, Ashley's death has left the Fund in one hell of a mess. It was a very large, personally conducted business and we're still trying to pick up all the threads. George is the senior officer until a new DG is appointed.'

'Who is panicking, you or George?'

'Don't be offensive, Douglas. No one is panicking. It's simply that some rather unpleasant rumours are beginning to circulate and I want to put auditors in straight away to prove to everyone that the books are in good order. As the Fund's legal adviser, I for one can't afford a scandal.'

'I'm not surprised that George should be reluctant about auditors.'

'I've not said that he is. The matter has to be discussed between us in some detail. Also other matters. You, for instance. George seems to think you are a private inquiry agent and we would like to know who is employing you and why. We both hope it's nothing to do with paying off old scores."

'I told you in London. I'm import-export.'

'What is the name of your company?'

'I freelance for a number of companies on an agency basis. I value my independence too much to be employed by any one firm.'

'You wouldn't care to state the names of some of the companies you work for?'

'I'm afraid the work is strictly confidential.'

'You surprise me. Why the secrecy?'

'The work concerns international shipments of certain commodities which it is felt desirable to organise by unconventional means.'

'What is that intended to convey? Could you be more explicit about the kind of commodities?'

'I'm not at liberty to say, but you might think in terms of precious metals.'

Watching Jack's face, Douglas was disappointed. Not an eyelid flickered. Either Jack was innocent of involvement in the gold-smuggling game or else those wartime poker sessions had trained him well.

'Precious metals eh? And how does this concern the India Fund?'

'You had better ask George when he turns up. Or Ashley.'

'Ashley's dead.'

'No, he isn't, and I think you know where he is.'

'Really, Douglas! After that affair in India you've developed an Ashley fixation. I know Ashley behaved badly then. I know he was never the goodie-goodie everyone thought he was. But with IF he did a bloody good job for a whole lot of starving peasants and I'll thank you to leave his memory and the Fund alone.'

'Where is he, Jack? You're in the secret, aren't you? He's somewhere in these parts, I'm sure. Otherwise you wouldn't have flown here to meet George. You would have met in Tokyo or he would have come to London, wouldn't he?'

'Ashley is dead, I tell you. Get that into your obstinate head. The reason I agreed to fly out, if you really want to know, is because a third person is involved. Someone we discussed at lunch last week.'

'The unknown beneficiary? Well, I can tell you you're on beam there. If you take my advice you'll get your auditors in touch with Miss Smith *aussi vite que possible.*'

'When I require advice on professional matters from undercover dealers in precious metals, I'll ask for it. Meantime you wouldn't care to stop lying, would you, Douglas, and tell me exactly what you're up to?'

'Certainly. In exchange for Ashley's whereabouts.'

'This is getting tedious. I'm going to bed.'

When Jack had gone Douglas reassessed the position over a second large Scotch. Jack had put up a plausible performance which it would be dangerous to accept at face value. He was clever and deep and had cheated Douglas once in OTS days. On the other hand, as he had said himself, he had a lot to lose from a scandal. Ashley and George could well have left him out of the smuggling. Yet, knowing their characters, he must have realised that he was liable to be used as a respectable front for fiddling of some kind. Possibly he was only now becoming aware of the nature and scale of the fiddling. With George's disappearance following Ashley's, Jack could be left holding the baby and none of the loot. Douglas tried to feel sorry for him and failed.

He had a bath and went to bed. There seemed little point now in going down to search the IF offices for Ashley. Also he felt below par. The soaking at Rotarua had given him a cold and he dosed himself with quinine.

His alarm went at six in the morning and he rolled out of his super-bed feeling no better. Feverish and nasally congested.

With a grim effort he shaved, showered, dressed, packed and paid his bill before seven. Breakfast could wait, but QF 321, the morning flight to Sydney, wouldn't. He reached the airport in good time, made an inquiry and then sat unobtrusively in the departure hall watching the passengers check in.

No Sylvia Smith, no Ashley. Jack Willingdon instead. He arrived late and spent some minutes at the check-in counter before buying a ticket and hurrying to the flight-gate exit. The final call came a moment later.

New Zealand and Sylvia Smith, or Australia and Jack Willingdon. Douglas felt too fuddle-headed to make the right choice. Ashley must be having a quiet laugh somewhere.

George Paget decided him. With an unreported corpse on his hands he was better out of the country.

'A reservation in the name of Forbes,' he told the girl.

'You've cut it fine,' she said, running her pencil down the list. 'It's two seats, isn't it? Your friend has already boarded. You'll have to hurry.'

He showed his IATA pass and took the boarding card. He went last through the gate and ran across the tarmac, dragging his leg. Inside the aircraft he made a second check. No Sylvia Smith, no Ashley. He took the vacant seat beside Jack Willingdon.

'Mr. Forbes, I presume.' He spoke as soon as his breath came back.

Jack looked up from his newspaper unwelcomingly.

'Oh, it's you, is it? Then kindly tell me what has happened to George Paget.'

'How should I know?'

'How should I know how you know? But unless you tell me before we reach Sydney I shall report him to the police as a missing person. I shall suggest, too, that you may be able to help them in their inquiries.'

They fastened their seat-belts and prepared for take-off.

The Lockheed Electra crossed the Tasman Sea in four hours. The inevitable baby squalled into his ear from the seat behind, and four Australian matrons tippled merrily across the gangway. Jack turned towards the window and refused to speak to him any more.

Douglas's thigh was still aching after his walk from Hell's Gate. The air pressure added to the congestion caused by his cold. He tried to make up for a short night's sleep, but his mind was busy on Jack.

He and Jack were fellow cadets at an Officers' Training School in Central India. They had arrived perilously from England through oceans patrolled by torpedo-happy U-boats. With Ashley and George they formed part of a contingent of eighteen and nineteen-year-olds. Officer material, emergency style. Beardless would-be leaders for the thousands of Indians flocking to the colours whenever the harvest failed.

The frontier grave was still far away, but the going was rough and dysentery took its toll.

In tropical heat they wore boots and puttees and sola topees. Also large black numbers on white cloth tied to their chests and backs, like convicts, so that the perpetrator of any misdemeanour should be instantly indentifiable. They worked thirteen hours a day in a temperature hotter than any they had experienced before. When it came to parading in the midday sun they put mad dogs to shame.

Every day began with a parade on the square. Inspection marching, rifle drill. They were harried by sergeant-majors, who declared their hair to be not short enough, their shave not close enough, their shoulders not far back enough. Douglas's thumbs were criminally prone to stray in front of the seams of his khaki-drill shorts. One morning in front

of the whole parade his chin was denounced by the regimental sergeant-major as reminiscent of a porcupine. The
punishment was a week's extra drill in the afternoons (with
full pack).

Shouldering arms gave him most trouble. He could sel-
dom find the trigger guard with the index finger of his right
hand while looking straight to his front. The assembled
ranks of A, B and C companies would stand rigid in the
dawn while Douglas fumbled for his trigger guard and
the RSM bellowed abuse across the subcontinent. Eyes
steady, No. 84, and feel for it. He was a shirker, a ma-
lingerer. He would have found it soon enough, the RSM
informed Central India, if it'd had hair round it.

An hour's PT followed the hour's drill. Climbing ropes,
leaping bucks, hanging from horizontal bars, rolling on the
floor in a military manner.

Only after this second hour did they qualify for breakfast. By lunchtime, what with weapon training and doubling or cycling across the countryside on fieldcraft exercises,
they had been on parade more than seven hours. The high-
noon high spot was bayonet practice between twelve and
one. Charging and shouting and gouging the innards out
of sacks of straw.

Jack coped conscientiously. George revelled in toughness. Ashley rose above it all with his usual effortless superi-
ority, charming the instructors and mocking them behind
their backs.

After a particularly idiotic lesson in weapon-training
Ashley would invent a new weapon and improvise extracts
from an imaginary training manual in the voice of their
least favourite sergeant-instructor. His most popular in-
vention was the bow and arrow. He would give mock de-
monstrations of this as the secret, war-winning device of
India Command.

'First, we 'ave the parts of the bow, gentlemen. The tip of
the bow, the 'eel of the bow, and the harrow-hactuating
string. Ho yus, gentlemen, get Jerry out of 'is tank and 'e'll
never stand up to cold harrows.'

In the afternoons there were MT lectures, Urdu lessons

and further violent exercise – hockey, squash, athletics. Urdu was the only subject at which Douglas shone. He shared a room with Ashley, and they had Jack and George next door. The four of them shared a munshi who kept a tailor's shop in the town. He cycled up from the collection of shacks known as Main Street to teach them the language over afternoon tea.

'What would you do if the war came here, munshiji?' Ashley asked him on the day they learned of the Japanese invasion from Burma into Assam.

'I would run into the country very fast, Wyndham West Sahib, for of all things life is the most precious.'

Ashley swooped on the phrase and it became a catchword among them. In moments of danger they would call to each other to look out, for of all things life was the most precious.

Unwisely Douglas used it in a company boxing contest when Jack broke a peace pact and in the heat of battle punched his nose with a straight left. They had agreed to satisfy the company commander's blood lust by pounding each other's gloves, but once in the ring Jack became a raging Dempsey.

Douglas's protest did not endear him to the company commander, a man on whom irony was lost. It set the pinnacle on his lack of success. When the time came he passed out with the rest, but not marked for promotion like the other three.

Success for three. Failure for one. An accurate assessment as it turned out.

'You had better come with me.'

They had landed at Kingsford Smith and Jack's voice spoke in his ear. Not a request. An order.

Douglas decided not to argue. Until Sylvia Smith bobbed up again, this was his best plan.

Jack received the prompt acquiescence suspiciously. 'Are you all right? You look like the wreck of the *Hesperus*.'

'I feel like the wreck of the *Hesperus*. But don't mind me.'

Jack hired a car and they drove into the middle of Sydney and out again the other side. It was Saturday. Weekend traffic jams all the way and the temperature in the high eighties. Less than Indian heat, but muggy, humid and enervating enough. Not a day for heavy colds and city centres.

He had visited Sydney often and the harbour bridge failed to raise his spirits. Any progress on the Opera House since his last visit was invisible to the passing eye.

Their destination proved to be the home of the IF man for New South Wales. He lived above a golden bay in a house shaped in a wide V so that every room had a sea view. There were three levels, with a balcony running along the front of each. Above, the roof provided a flat deck for those who preferred their sunworship horizontal. Below, a garden provided a carpet of phlox, petunia and hibiscus. The giving end of IF didn't attract paupers.

Douglas admired, shivered, sneezed and received permission to retire to bed and sleep himself back to health. During the night his old friend the Pacific storm arrived. When he woke it was giving a passable imitation of a monsoon, raining as though set for a month. Sydney was a place where the annual rainfall didn't come in instalments.

Mrs. IF gave him breakfast and he watched her feed a pair of bedraggled kookaburras with cubes of meat. The Sydney newspaper reported that England was paralysed with snow and ice after the coldest night for six years. Jack and Mr. IF were in conference in the next room. Douglas took another dose of quinine and returned to bed.

In the afternoon he got up and the three of them went for a drive. The weather had cleared *pro tem*. Newport, Bilgola, Avalon, Whale Beach, Palm Beach, Pittwater. Resorts with sailing boats and surfies and clusters of dark-brown bodies. At one point they left the car and walked to the head of a steep cliff between coves. The surf spewed over rocks sheer below them. Beyond stretched nothing but Pacific until one came to New Zealand or even, maybe, Chile or Peru. He thought of the wild coast of Oahu where Ashley had taken the plunge. And he kept his distance from the other two.

'If you're feeling better,' said Jack when they returned
123

to the house, 'we'll have another talk after supper.' He sounded far from solicitous.

'Fine,' said Douglas and asked to use the phone.

Things were easier to arrange here. The Interpol office knew him. Sabbath or no Sabbath, he was able to raise Charlie Pyke who had worked with him before. Charlie greeted him with a homely oath, listened to what he wanted, and promised to ring him back.

The call came within a couple of hours.

Point one. The Sydney IF man had no police record. He was a reputable businessman who looked after local India Fund affairs on the side.

Point two. The police in Auckland and Wellington. Neither had anything new on the welfare or whereabouts of George Paget. No one had reported him either dead or missing.

Point three. Miss Sylvia Smith had flown from Wellington to Sydney that morning. She had booked hotel accommodation for the night on arrival. If he desired the pleasure of her company he would find her at the Top of the Cross.

'For one night only?'

'One night of love.' Charlie burst into song. His own rendering of Grace Moore.

'Beautiful,' said Douglas, 'and thanks a lot. When you're next on to Paris, would you tell Renée I'm here? I'll be making a full report in a few days.'

'Where can we reach you?'

'Where do you think? Top of the Cross.'

Charlie made a suggestive noise with his lips and rang off with another rude word. Less homely this time.

Douglas put down the phone excited. The day of confrontation had arrived. First he must avoid getting shot. Then he must extract some information.

By a happy piece of timing Mr. and Mrs. IF had taken Jack down to the beach for a swim. The garage was at the back of the house out of sight. The hired car stood outside it.

He found the ignition key on the dressing table in Jack's bedroom. While there, he picked over Jack's belongings

124

and riffled rapidly through his papers. No firearms, no in-criminating documents. He supposed it would be expecting too much from a lawyer.

He considered a farewell message: 'Go back to England, for of all things life is the most precious.' Good advice probably, but unwise again. Instead he scribbled 'Get Those Auditors In' on a piece of lavatory paper and left it sticking out of a shoe. His bread-and-butter letter to Mrs. IF would have to wait.

The journey into town fractured his nerves. The car drove easily enough, but homecoming Sydney traffic was converging from all over the state. He would have been better off back home on the Brighton road. It was hard to calm himself for the moment of crisis ahead.

King's Cross was Sydney's Soho. The Top of the Cross stood at its highest point. A skyscraper building. Hotel reception was on the seventh floor. The girl there didn't think they had a room to spare. Being superstitious, he wondered whether this was an omen, a sign to keep away.

'It's getting late,' he said, 'and I'm not too well.'

He looked his most haggard and she took pity on him. 'I can let you have 702 for the one night. It's eleven dollars plus one thirty-five for breakfast.'

He accepted it and signed in. The door of the room was in sight and he carried his own bags. TV set, radio, fridge, air conditioning, lavatory, etcetera. He did his usual prowl round, half expecting to find Miss Smith in the shower.

When he returned to ask the number of her room, the girl at reception looked sorry she'd fixed him up. She parted with it reluctantly. Room 1113.

The eleventh floor had a small lobby of its own next to the lifts. He sat on the sofa there, casing the joint's in-mates. There were plenty of comings and goings. The hotel clients seemed to be mostly groups of dumb young men with rugged faces. American troops on leave from Viet-nam.

After a while he took a turn along the corridor and quietly tried the handle of 1113. It was locked.

Was she in or out? If out, could he risk asking at reception for her key? He waited another half-hour and then returned to the seventh floor. A different girl stood behind the counter. Another sign? He went up and asked her for the key.

She looked for it without success.

'It's out.'

'Oh. Then perhaps my friend is in after all. It's not my room.'

The girl gave him a cool stare. 'Have you tried knocking?'

'A little while ago. I'll try again. Thank you.'

'What is the number of your own room?'

He gave it. She was checking on him.

'Would you like me to ring 1113 for you?'

'No, thank you. I'll leave it till later.'

He retired discomforted to his own room and collected his lock-picker. If Sylvia was out with her key she would find a surprise waiting for her when she got back.

This time the eleventh-floor corridor was deserted. He knocked loudly on the door.

'Who's there?' The voice was muffled.

'Room service.' He took out his automatic, preparing to kick the door wide and jump inside as soon as it opened.

The pause was so long he nearly knocked again. Then the door opened abruptly.

A voice said: 'if you're armed, so am I, and I'm shooting first. Walk straight to the window and don't turn round.' A familiar voice.

He walked. It was that or making a desperate dash for it along the corridor. The door banged behind him.

'Keep looking at the view,' the voice warned.

His own room overlooked an uninspiring jumble of neighbouring rooms. This had Sydney spread-eagled below. It was Exeter and Magdalen all over again.

A grid of ribboned lights reflected from the shopping streets in the centre of the city. The pools of darkness hid parks. The Botanic Gardens. The Domain. Hyde Park. He was tensed for the bullet in his back.

A new Manhattan of tower blocks round the stock exchange. Monsters which had outgrown the old business section beside Central Station. An ugly jumble of newspaper offices. The elderly GPO in Martin Place. To keep his mind occupied, he ticked off the buildings one by one. Still no sound from behind.

Money and success. That summed it up. To hell with your family, your school, your accent. To hell with your titles, honours and decorations. How much are you worth? In Sydney money was the measure of merit. An appropriate place for Douglas to die. Someone who had gained no money and made no success.

'Drop that gun on the floor.'

This time the voice was unmistakable. He dropped the gun.

'If I were you I wouldn't shoot,' he said. 'The police know I'm here.' He began to turn.

'Don't turn round.' The voice was urgent.

'Why not?' he asked over his shoulder. 'I'd recognise your voice anywhere. I never believed in your death, Ashley.'

'Clever old Dougs!' That mocking tone.

'Not really. Just specialised knowledge. I'm an expert on you. I've seen the lot. There's no way in which you could ever surprise or deceive me.'

'I surprised you a moment ago.'

'No, you didn't. You were one second faster, that's all. I've been expecting to run you to earth either in New Zealand or here. May I turn round now? I've had enough of the view.'

'Count twenty slowly and then you may.'

At fifteen a door banged. At twenty he turned. Sylvia Smith was standing in the middle of the room with a gun in her hand, wearing a smart two-piece and a Mona Lisa smile.

'Where's Ashley gone?' he demanded.

She raised an eyebrow and kept silent.

'It's important that I speak to him. He mustn't think he can escape by running away.'

She raised the other eyebrow and spoke this time. 'Not so clever old Dougs!'

'Ashley!'

'So there was nothing more I could do to deceive you, wasn't there?'

Douglas caved at the knees. 'If you're not going to shoot me, Ashley,' he said meekly, 'may I sit down?'

'Are you telling the truth about the police knowing you're here?'

'Yes. They know that Sylvia Smith is here too. And I've only just left Jack Willingdon, who is fully primed on my views about your non-death.'

'Thousands wouldn't, but I believe you. You're being frightfully tiresome, Douglas, and I'm really very annoyed with you, but now we've bumped into each other we might as well make the best of things. Take the weight off your feet by all means.'

Douglas sat. Only half believing, he watched Ashley in his Sylvia guise pick up the gun from the floor and throw it on the bed behind him.

'What was that door banging a moment ago?' he asked. 'Have you someone else here?'

'It was simply a little trick to establish whether you'd penetrated my disguise. Search the loo if you don't believe me.'

'Thank you, I will.'

'What a disbeliever you are!'

Douglas crossed the room, pushed open the door and looked in. It was empty. He felt a fool. The same old pattern already. Ashley in the wrong but somehow morally in the ascendant. Himself innocent and floundering. Outclassed. Humiliated. Yet he would need all the old intimacy to save himself.

'Your face is fantastic,' he said. 'I looked at you closely in St. Paul's and at Kennedy, but even now I can't really recognise anything except the eyes.'

'It jolly well should be good. It cost a packet, I can tell you. A surgeon did it for me in Paris. The same one who fixed up one of the train robbers.' Ashley sounded smug about it.

'And the hair is a wig?'

'Of course. There's nothing strange about that these days, is there?'

'No trouble with your clothes or deportment?'

'Not if I keep away from high heels.'

'You walked a bit oddly at Kennedy, but I put that down to a gun in the crotch.'

'My gun was in my handbag. Occasionally I get tired, but the only real problem has been the voice. Raising it a couple of octaves isn't enough. I never dared go and see Jack about the will. Even when I spoke to him on the phone I kept the conversation brief and used a handkerchief to blur it.'

'So Jack's not in the secret? You're working that into the record, are you?'

'Don't be so suspicious. I wasn't talking about Jack, but of course he's not in the secret. I was talking about my voice. You recognised it at once, when you couldn't recognise the rest of me at five yards. I should have gone dumb, I suppose.'

'And illiterate. I ought to have realised from your childish characters that you were writing with the left hand.'

'We can't all be quick on the uptake, can we? Still, I always had you in mind as the one person who wouldn't be fooled. When you started chasing me round the world I felt sure of it.'

After Lady Macbeth and all that, he certainly had been slow. And about the fact that Miss Smith had appeared from nowhere. And about the simplest explanation of those interlocking bank accounts in Honolulu. Ashley and Sylvia Smith had never been seen together. There never was a second person to disappear from that boat. But at least he hadn't been fooled by the death.

'It's flattering to think of myself as the one threat to you, Ashley,' he said, 'but I didn't much care for the attempt you made in St. Paul's to murder me. I quite understand it now, but it puzzled me at the time.'

'Attempted murder!' Ashley raised both eyebrows. 'Come off it, chum. That was nothing more than a friendly

129

warning not to get too close. Can't you imagine how a girl felt at the prospect of having her cover blown, with songs of praise still echoing through the undercroft?'

He laughed and Douglas almost laughed with him out of habit. Ashley had always been witty and good company. That was one of the contradictions which made him such a monster.

'You're a liar,' Douglas told him. 'You'd have been glad to kill me then, as you'd have been glad to at Rotarua, and a few moments ago if you'd thought it safe.'

'If you want to think that of me after all these years, I can't stop you. Please yourself. You came in here with a gun. Who would have been threatening who if I hadn't had one too? It's always been one of your least endearing characteristics, my dear Douglas, to think the worst of people.'

'Not of people. Of you.'

Ashley gave a martyred sigh. 'Anyway I enjoyed the service, didn't you. My only complaint was, the Queen didn't show up.'

'She was abroad, and just as well. She'll be one of the few top people without red faces when this comes out.'

'Nothing is coming out. I may look deliciously feminine sitting here, but get this into your thick head. If you start phoning anyone or making one of your professional dashes, I shall shoot us both rather than face a scandal. Is that clear?' Ashley put on his headmaster face, as though Douglas were a backsliding pupil.

'As clear as you're becoming under that face. I even recognise that expression.'

'Well, you know the form now.' Ashley frowned, then did one of his switches to instant charm. 'Don't let's quarrel. I've been lonely and it's wonderful having someone to talk to. Especially you, Dougsie. I haven't any etchings to show you, but what about my obituaries?'

Before Douglas could protest, he opened a suitcase and took out a fat folder.

'Look at this one, dear boy. *Never in the field of human charity has so much been owed by so many to one man.*
130

Hurrah for Auntie *Times*. And here's the *Statesman* of Calcutta with *The lights are going out all over India*. Dowsing their hurricane lamps, I suppose. A couple of pages in *Time* plus the cover. Not bad going, eh? Even the *Sydney Morning Herald* was reasonably civil.'

'Put them away, Ashley. I'm not interested.'

'But I need your help. I can gather the gist of the French ones, but what about translating the German and Italian for me? These squiggles from *Al Ahram* are hopeless, I suppose, but you can cope with Cyrillic and Russian, can't you? I'm longing to know whether I was a fascist hyena and a capitalist lackey to the end in *Izvestiya*.'

'What does it matter? Where did you get all those things?'

'Where do you suppose? Miss Smith subscribes to a press cutting agency. Now come on. Don't be a meanie.'

Reluctantly Douglas translated some of the clippings, while Ashley commented crisply on the factual errors.

'What a pity I can't write to the editors,' he said. 'Wouldn't it excite them to have the hospitality of their columns trespassed on from beyond the grave? *Sir, I have taken advantage of a passing squid to pen you this missive from the bed of the Pacific ocean.*'

The obituary session led on to other talk. Of the young Americans in the hotel. They reminded Ashley of his army days in India.

'Do you remember that Christmas leave in Bombay? How innocent we were!'

'Don't fool yourself, Ashley. The problem with you is that you were never innocent. Even if you don't remember what happened at school, you can hardly have forgotten that little incident in the Atlantic.'

'You saved me then and I'm grateful still. Really I am. I mean it. I was thinking of it when I decided not to shoot you.'

'Like hell you were. Just as you thought of it at Gulunchi, you treacherous sod.'

Douglas took a step towards the telephone and hesitated. Losing his temper wouldn't do. Nor would getting shot. He must let the talk go on and accumulate some hard evidence. Ashley was ruthless and slippery. He needed playing like a sly salmon.

Ashley tautened, then noticed the hesitation. He relaxed at once and laughed. Abuse hadn't ruffled his poise.

'That's no way to address a lady,' he said, wagging an over-large finger. 'Especially one who's about to pay for a meal for you. I'm hungry and you look undernourished. Let's go out.'

'Do I get my gun back?'

'Certainly not. And what's more, you give a guarantee of good behaviour.'

'Why should I? To you of all people!' Douglas cursed himself for sounding petulant.

'Because if you don't I tie you up and lock you in the loo and run away. Alternatively, you might even fall out of the window accidentally.'

'Who would believe that? You'd have every policeman in the world looking for you.'

'Very well then. A peace pact. Like the one I seem to remember your having with Jack in the boxing ring at OTS.'

'And look what happened then.'

'Your nose bled. Nothing worse. Make yourself at home while I have a bath and change. Then we'll go.'

Ashley scooped up both guns again and went into the bathroom, leaving the door ajar.

Douglas hunched himself in the chair and brooded on his defeat. If only he'd kicked the door in without warning and had the guts to fire as soon as Ashley's voice betrayed him. . . .

They joined up while still at school. In 1941 the army in England was guarding coastlines and railway bridges. India seemed more adventurous, and their training in the school corps qualified them for a special intake of would-be officers for the Indian Army. Preferring not to wait for their call-up, they coughed in front of a medical officer, took the King's shilling and returned to school. The army called it deferred embodiment.

In June they reported to Aldershot for preliminary training. Their contingent was awaiting embarkation, but security forbade any mention of India. If the enemy heard that a convoy was about to sail they would all be sunk. Yet, when the day came, they marched from barracks to the station with topees strapped to their backs. A pipe and drum band led the way fortissimo, presumably to make sure of attracting the attention of every enemy agent in town.

They entrained one morning and detrained the next, crawling and stopping alternately round the country and the clock. Oxford, Nottingham, Newcastle, Glasgow. Destination and route unknown. Douglas passed the time with a *Penguin Book of Times Crossword Puzzles*. Ashley topped up his private's pay with some winnings at pontoon.

Paisley and Greenock in the early dawn. Then Gourock, where they tumbled out and assembled on a platform overlooking the Clyde. They were a shambles. Unwashed, unshaven, unslept. Laden with military paraphernalia like so many beasts of burden. A contingent hardly worth sinking, Douglas thought hopefully.

A steamboat ferried them to one of the waiting liners. A Union Castle giant, formerly SS now HMT. It lay in mid-river in a landscape of grey hills and opened its bowels to receive them with no sign of welcome.

Their accommodation was eight decks down. Lit by arti-

133

ficial light, aired through the blowers in the ceiling, and next to the boiler room. Three full decks below the waterline.

Here, in one mess room, two hundred men were to eat, sleep and somehow exist for up to ten weeks. U-boats permitting. They were to enjoy the use of six basins (restricted to two hours a day) and six lavatories (closed for cleaning immediately after breakfast every morning).

The usual army confusion raged over the allocation of quarters. They began by being moved from side to side and end to end of the room six times. Several hundred men took part in these general posts in a cramped space, all encumbered with kitbag, suitcase, greatcoat, haversack, pack, steel helmet, respirator and anti-gas cape. Not to mention their Boer War solar topees.

At the end of the day Douglas and Ashley, operating in partnership, were among the few who still possessed a full set of the kit they had started with. This took the prize as the worst day of their lives. They couldn't have endured it without each other.

After the last move Ashley had announced that he could stand no more. His gaiety had crumpled and his lips were quivering.

'I'll go mad down here. I must get out. Before we sail.'

'Don't be such an idiot,' Douglas told him. 'You'd be locked up as a deserter. Anyway, how could you possibly go?'

'Through a porthole. I'll swim for it. Under water, if necessary.' Ashley had been *victor ludorum* in the school swimming sports.

'There aren't any portholes. We're under water already. Stick it out. At least we've got each other.'

Ashley, white-faced, accepted the inevitable with a bad grace.

'I suppose this is what that bloody public school was preparing us for. After four and a half years in old Darlybags's house everything else in life is meant to be bearable. *You're both too young to fight but we shall be proud of you, I know.*' He mimicked their housemaster's voice in his fare-

134

well speech. 'All the bastard wants is our names on an honours board among the rest of the glorious dead.'

To cope with the living conditions Douglas found he needed Ashley as much as Ashley needed him. Tables and benches took up most of the space, with a passageway along one side – the side where one blistered oneself touching the boiler room wall. Every night they drew hammocks from a store and slung them above the tables. The slightest motion bumped them into one of four neighbours. With head or feet, or one or other elbow.

Their suitcases were removed to the store, their kitbags stacked behind pipes along the wall. All the rest of their belongings were stuffed into racks above their heads, permanently available for pilfering. When Douglas's knife, spoon and fork were scrounged by an unknown comrade he would have eaten with his fingers for the rest of the voyage if he hadn't had Ashley's to share. These they carried in their pockets and slept with in their hammocks.

After five days at anchor the convoy crept down river without warning one dusk. Past the black pimple of Arran and out into the perils of the Atlantic. 'Trust the navy,' someone shouted at them through the loud-hailer at the mouth of the river. They had no choice. They could only pray, as Ashley did aloud, that it was less of a bloody mess than the army.

The next morning, at boat drill on one of the open decks, they had their first sight of British sea power. The lines of ships in convoy stretched fore and aft to the horizon. An arrowhead of naval vessels led the way. One battleship and six cruisers. A line of destroyers on each flank. Then two more cruisers and, bringing up the rear, an aircraft carrier.

'My God,' said Ashley, 'it must be the biggest armada since 1588! We're going to be all right after all.'

They gripped each other's arms in relief.

Winding their way to the surface through a succession of watertight bulkheads for boat drill, they had already estimated their chances of survival at nil if torpedoed. True, they wore Mae Wests all day and had to keep them within reach at night, but that was the reverse of reassuring. So was the order to sleep in their clothes for the first week at sea. But now survival seemed on the cards again.

The size of the convoy, like its destination, had been secret. Now they counted the ships under escort and calculated. There were between thirty and forty, and they reckoned their own complement at three thousand men.

'A hundred thousand troops. Dougsie. There can't have been an exodus like this since Dunkirk.' Beleaguered for a year off the coast of enemy-occupied Europe, Britain was sending a whole army away to fight on another front. They were a giant symptom of defeat averted.

'Some of us must be reinforcements for North Africa.'

'Round the Cape? One of the stewards swears it's first stop Cape Town.'

'The convoy could split there, and our lot will carry on to Bombay.'

'I wouldn't count on it.' Ashley spat into the sea in disgust. 'Don't imagine you get to India if you join the Indian Army.'

For several days the convoy headed due west until they wondered whether the Indian Army had moved its base to Nova Scotia.

One morning they went on deck to find the battleship gone. The next, the aircraft carrier had disappeared too. They felt deserted and exposed. But safer somehow. The westward course was designed to get them out of range of German shore-based bombers in France. That danger must be over if the carrier had been recalled.

The armada turned south at last. It passed the Azores with its escort reduced to a couple of cruisers and half a dozen destroyers. By then boredom and discomfort weighed more heavily than danger.

Each day was endured lounging at a mess table or lying on a deck. Parades were few for lack of space. Some fitful PT. A sprinkling of lecturettes by officers. Desultory instruction in Urdu. And fatigues. They served as mess orderlies, stripped to the waist in the galleys like slaves.

Housey-housey was the standard recreation. Every deck carried cries of clickety-click, legs eleven and top of the house. Ashley started a poker school, but the stakes were derisory, pay on board being fourteen shillings a week. Douglas found a ship's library stocked with Victorian novels. *Romola* lasted him from the Azores to the Equator.

After a fortnight at sea they were still afloat, and in the tropics. Their remaining escort had been strengthened by corvettes, which suggested that Gibraltar was near. Battle-dress was off, khaki drill was on. At night they were allowed to sling their hammocks on the open decks and breathe air first-hand.

Two incidents broke the monotony. Once the sea grew choppy and the ship rolled and every deck reeked of vomit. The same mess pails were used for emergencies and washing up. Ashley remained prostrate in his hammock for two days while Douglas nursed him. He announced that he was going to die and Douglas had to remind him of his determination to stay alive to spite old Darlybags.

Then one day the escort vessels moved ahead at speed and performed antics like terriers hunting a badger. When the convoy reached the spot it broke formation for the first time. Everyone could hear the dull thud of depth-charges.

They were said to be off the coast of West Africa, approaching Freetown. An area as dangerous as the North Atlantic. A graveyard of U-boat victims.

At Freetown they had their first glimpse of Africa. A low barren shore with parched vegetation. Dry land indeed, and a welcome sight to seasick eyes. But no one from the convoy was allowed ashore.

For five days they sweltered on board inside the harbour boom. Their mail was taken off and they bought bananas and coconuts from natives whose shops were canoes. Bananas cost a penny each, but one could haggle for a baker's dozen by appealing for a free one for the King. Ashley was the only man to get fourteen for a shilling by insisting on one for the captain as well as one for the King and not paying until he received it. It was his first dealing with an underdeveloped country.

On the second day after the convoy sailed he and Douglas stood leaning over the rail. Squeezed behind a lifeboat, they had discovered a private patch of secluded deck. Night had fallen. They watched the sea grow black and searched the sky for the Southern Cross. Ashley's profile reminded Douglas of a medallion of Rupert Brooke. That beauty had died on a troop ship in the First War.

Eeriness came with every dusk. In the daylight the ocean teemed with company, but at night-time they were alone. The convoy moved without a single light.

Permission to sleep on the open decks had been accompanied by the strictest orders about no smoking after nightfall. The tip of a lighted cigarette, it was said, could be seen more than five miles on a dark night. That was all a U-boat required. Patrols on every deck insured against the habitual last fag before turning in.

Low against the swish of the parting water, Ashley's voice laid bare his post-war ambitions. First the premiership. Then, when nationalism had been superseded, the presidency of the world. He would dedicate his life to the service of mankind. There would always be a place for Douglas at his side. His one confidant, now and until death did them part.

Casually he stuck a cigarette between his lips. Douglas, horrified, snatched it out and threw it into the sea. A quarrel blew up like an ocean squall.

'Of course I wasn't going to light it. Do stop nannying me, Dougsie. We're in the army now. You're just a private like me, not a bloody child-minder.'

'I was only trying to prevent you from doing something silly.'

'Well, don't. I'm old enough to decide things for myself, thank you very much, and the regulations about cigarettes are a load of crap. If I were to light up now, I bet you couldn't see a thing from the other side of the deck, let alone out at sea.'

'I wouldn't advise you to try. It's hardly worth the risk of having us all torpedoed.'

'Are you daring me?'

138

'No, I'm not. I'm telling you. Stop being so childish and grow up, can't you? A mentally retarded president won't do the world much good.'

After more wrangling, to prove his manhood and teach Douglas a lesson, Ashley lit up. He resisted all Douglas's pleas and efforts to put the cigarette out and smoked it defiantly behind the shelter of the lifeboat. Nemesis struck minutes later. One torpedo then another shattered the side of the ship.

The explosions were followed by alarm bells. With everyone rushing to boat stations in the darkness, there was plenty of confusion but no panic. The engines stopped and in the sudden stillness the decks were lined with men conscious of being sitting targets. Some, roused from sleep, joined the ranks naked except for their life jackets.

Luckily the water was dead calm. Lifeboats were lowered and orderly queues filed aboard. One of the other ships in the convoy had halted to take on survivors. The ferrying by lifeboat across the open sea went on all night in eerie silence, except for the distant thunder of depth-charges. Douglas and Ashley, shivering, were among the last to be taken off.

In the morning the ship was still afloat with its crew aboard. The ship to which they had been ferried took it in tow. All around them the wide expanse of ocean lay ominously empty. The rest of the convoy had obeyed regulations and abandoned them.

Limping at half-speed, with full anti-submarine precautions, it took them three weeks to reach the Cape. Three fearful weeks of overcrowding and half-rations. Three weeks without possessions, sleeping on wooden decks. Three weeks to realise how protected and comfortable they had been before.

Other ships in the convoy had reported the glow of a cigarette end shortly before the explosions. By the time they reached port every member of the ship's complement had been interrogated in an effort to identify the culprit. Tempers ran high and, if found, he would not have survived to stand trial.

Douglas lied loyally to save his friend. What was the point in telling the truth? The damage had been done. There were savage whispers of keel-hauling. Being an unpractised liar, he attracted suspicion on himself and only his known record as a non-smoker saved him.

Ashley, on the other hand, lied superbly. Once assured that Douglas would not betray him, he became more self-confident than ever. The double escape from drowning and detection he treated as a sure sign of being marked out from the common herd, reserved for higher things. His lack of moral sense filled Douglas with disgust and they drew apart.

The renewal of their friendship was sealed during shore leave at Cape Town. Dry land at long last. Ashley was not to be shaken off. He overcame Douglas's aversion and they made the ascent of the Table Mountain together. By cable car and funicular.

At the top they walked over the craggy surface splashing in their newly issued boots in pools of rain water. After weeks of slip-slopping in plimsolls it was even a relief to be wearing army boots.

Far below them stretched the bay with rows of pygmy houses in the foreground. In the docks the ships of the convoy floated like toys in a child's bath. To the north stood pine forests and mountains higher than they had ever seen. England seemed cramped and flat and far away. Like it or not, they were fellow adventurers. Sentiment and shared experience bound them indissolubly. From childhood and schooldays to army life and near disaster and secret guilt.

'I'm sorry about that cigarette,' said Ashley, squatting on a rock. 'You were right and I was wrong and you saved my life. I don't know what I would do without you, honestly I don't. Please, please let's stick together. Always.'

In those surroundings, with Ashley's hand abjectly offered, how could Douglas reject the appeal? He delivered a short sermon and extracted a promise, though as it turned out he might as well have saved his breath. Ashley solemnly pledged himself to good behaviour for ever.

Blood brothers, they sailed serenely across the Indian

Ocean. No escort, no incidents. Nothing but sunbathing and watching the flying fish. They grew reconciled to troop-ship life. They were young, and the magic and squalor of India lay ahead.

'What are you looking so glum about, Dougsie?'

Ashley had emerged from his beautification in the bathroom. His face was heavily made up. He wore a brocade tunic with matching trousers and stank seductively of Chanel or Dior.

'Am I looking glum? I was thinking about you on the troop ship during the war.'

'Well, try something more cheerful. You're morbid, that's your problem. In fact you look sick.'

'If I do, it's because you shot me in the thigh in London and gave me a heavy cold chasing you in the rain in New Zealand.'

'Always my fault, isn't it? Ashley shrugged and pirouetted. 'How do you like my maharanee gear? I feel dressed to kill. But not you, darling, if you're good.'

'You disgust me, Ashley. Take it off.'

'What a wicked suggestion! Afterwards perhaps. Meantime grub. And do try to behave like a gentleman towards a lady. I've a little Colt in my bag just in case.'

The temperature in the street was Mediterranean. It was past ten on a Sunday evening, but the shops were lit an' open for business. Traffic jammed the road. Hippies and Rest and Recuperation GI's with their girls crowded the pavements. Other girls stood in doorways waiting to be picked up. Among the amateurs and professionals Ashley stepped out like a queen, attracting glances and nudges. To Douglas it was a sickening development from the days when the debonair dandy from Magdalen strolled along the High at Oxford wearing his leopard-skin tights.

They chose an Italian restaurant and Ashley made Douglas order. Canelloni and an escallope in cream. Nothing wrong with Ashley's appetite.

'Nudges but no wolf whistles,' he complained. 'At my age one must get reconciled to being *passé*, I suppose. So what's the use of watching one's waistline?'

'You're not proposing to spend the rest of your life in drag, I hope.' Douglas was embarrassed. The play-acting annoyed him.

'There speaks the school prefect I loved. No; as a matter of fact, if it hadn't been for your untimely intrusion I would have made a man of myself by now.'

'A Wyndham West resurrection?'

'Hardly, dear boy. This would be something altogether new, and it's all planned and ready. In view of your pressing attentions and any possible repercussions from that unfortunate incident at Rotarua, I have been reckoning that Sylvia Smith is due for the quick chop. How was George, by the way?'

'Dead.'

'You're certain?'

'Very dead. No doubt about it.'

'Floating?'

'At first. When I shoved him back his clothes took him under.'

'Recognisable?'

'Not by this time, if that's what is worrying you. Why did you kill him?'

Ashley did his eyebrow-raising act. They were blackened with pencil but not plucked.

'George could be very tiresome,' he said, 'as you no doubt remember. He was the only one in on my little secret and it made him greedy. But you mustn't think I killed him.'

'What must I think then? That he wanted a quick dip and misjudged the temperature?'

'Don't be naughty.' Ashley pinched Douglas's arm playfully, but made sure that it hurt. 'You were the one who really wanted him dead. He was worried about you. I can bear witness to that. In fact you scared both of us, turning up on that flight. At one moment I thought you were going to have me arrested in New York.'

'I might have if I'd realised it was you. Where did George come aboard?'

'At San Francisco. We were to make our final arrangements in Honolulu, but you spoiled all that. Very inconsiderate and rather clever of you. Underneath being such an ass you're really quite bright, Dougsie. I can't imagine why you haven't done better for yourself. Fancy traipsing round the world at your age for a living. And as some tatty underpaid air-express nark.'

'Thank you, and do you mind not calling me Dougsie? Whatever fatty tissue I may have hardly rates beside your falsies or hormone injections or whatever they are.'

'Now I've offended him.' Ashley leaned forward, making soothing noises.

'Take your hand off my knee and stop arsing about, Ashley. Grow up, can't you? It's time you decided which sex you really belong to.'

Ashley laughed, a throaty mid-sex gurgle. 'But it's the dithering that's such fun. Ambiguity is all. Where's the joy if everything is what it seems. Didn't I ever show you my essay on appearance and reality?'

143

'I expect so, but do you mind not changing the subject? We were talking about George if you remember. He made a very professional getaway with that consignment of gold. You must have been mad, carting it round the world yourselves. Or greedy.' Douglas watched Ashley mopping up his pasta as though without a care in the world.

'Gold? What are you talking about?'

'Kindly don't flutter your false eyelashes at me. It won't wash. I know all about you and your charitable works. Not much connection between appearance and reality there either. Don't forget I had a slight brush with George in Moscow, where you were buying illicit gold with all that money donated by widows in Cheltenham to keep the Indian peasantry from starving.'

'Don't be so unjust. How do you imagine IF could have operated if all the money had been misappropriated?'

'Half then. What does the exact amount matter? You've made off with twenty-five million dollars. Plus the price of a substantial amount of gold. Plus plenty more I've no doubt. You used IF to finance your smuggling and now you've milked it dry, haven't you?'

'If so, who's responsible? You! You and your unworthy suspicions. But for you, IF would still be operating. And I can promise you that anything I've managed to salvage for my next life won't be used selfishly. I intend to devote it to doing some more good.'

'What a hypocrite you are, Ashley. Always unselfishly pursuing goodness provided goodness is what is good for you. But not any more. I was despairing of getting enough evidence to convict you of smuggling and misappropriation, but now you've killed George you're definitely not going to be at liberty to enjoy another life.'

'But you hated George, didn't you? You're glad he's dead.'

'He killed a colleague of mine in Moscow. So I might have killed him if you hadn't. But it suits me fine to have my killing done by proxy. And for you to be responsible.'

'But I'm not. I told you that before. He was busy firing at you and in all that rain and poor visibility he stepped

144

back too far. Slithered off the wet rock into a pool of boiling water, poor fellow.'

'Liar! What were you doing while the shooting was going on? Cowering under cover like a wretched frightened female?'

'I resent the cowering and frightened. I was simply bothered about my nylons laddering.' Ashley sniggered.

'You gave him a hefty shove while he was taking a pot shot at me. His attention was distracted and you deliberately pushed him in. That's what really happened, wasn't it? Why not be serious for a moment and admit it?'

'Why should I if it isn't true? You've done surprisingly well so far, Dougsie, but you'll need to work a bit harder if you're determined to have me convicted of something. Why not drop the whole thing? For the past's sake. Come live with me and be my love and we will all the pleasures prove. I've enough money for two.'

'You've enough for two thousand but it won't buy me. I used to like you, Ashley, but I don't any more.'

'Yes, you do. We know each other inside out. Try as hard as you like, it's a bond you can't break. I'm lonely, you're lonely. We need each other again.'

Ashley's new face registered sincerity. His true blue eyes held steady and it was Douglas who looked away.

The words contained a layer of truth. Further talk would lead nowhere more promising. Douglas felt his loneliness. If not to Ashley, where could he turn? Helen meant nothing to him. Susan was lost irretrievably. Sammy had been a close colleague once, but George's killing of Pierre had ended that. No friends, no colleagues, no family. His parents had been killed in the blitz while he defended them from India.

Ashley polished off a cassata, rejected coffee and waited for Douglas to pay the bill. Outside they rejoined the crowds and the night life. Neon lights were flashing and all humanity was on display. Sailors jostled the American R & R men in the hope of picking a quarrel. Beatniks burned joss sticks and sold bangles in shop doorways. Nude photos framed the entrance to night clubs. Barkers announced the glad tidings of unmentionable delights within.

In front of them a middle-aged man staggered and fell on his face against the kerb. Douglas picked him up and dusted him down. Drug-happy, he staggered on.

'*Mesdames, messieurs, voyez-vous les pedérastes extra-ordinaires.*' A leering barker had caught Ashley's attention. The invitation sounded even more wicked in French.

The show was called 'Girls, Girls, Girls!' and he dragged Douglas inside protesting. The enticing photos made it clear that the girls, girls, girls were men, men, men.

Rouged boys danced the can-can. Pantomime dames postured and sang their *risqué* repertoires. a nubile blond-haired beauty performed a strip-tease to a chorus of expectant ooh's and ah's from the audience.

'They always have one genuine girl in these drag shows,' Ashley whispered when the beauty stood revealed in nothing but bra and briefs.

The beauty responded by turning its back, undoing its bra straps and throwing the bra and both breasts over its shoulders. They landed on the stage with a clatter. The beauty stepped delicately out of the briefs and ran off, twinkling its bare behind at the footlights.

Douglas walked out in disgust. Ashley followed, enthusing.

'Sensational,' he declared as they returned to the hotel. 'He had us all fooled. That's what I like.'

'He didn't fool me,' said Douglas. 'Once in one day is enough. Good night.'

They were standing in the seventh-floor lobby. Ashley frowned and put out a warning hand. 'I can trust you to in the past.'

'You don't have much option, do you?'

'Nor do you. You could never turn me in, Dougsie. Think what I mean to you. Think what you've done for me in the past.'

'I wouldn't bank on it if I were you.'

'Is that a threat?' He turned cold and brusque.

'Take it whatever way you choose. You're the one who enjoys ambiguity.'

The lobby was empty. Douglas turned and walked towards his room. Ashley would scarcely be foolish enough to plug him in the back.

Nothing happened. He locked the door behind him. Bluff called. He felt more pleased with himself. There was no need to rush things. He would play Ashley at his own game and win. It was about time.

In the morning Ashley came to his room for breakfast and they greeted each other like a pair of wrestlers wary of coming to grips. Ashley was wearing a sun-frock. He suggested a trip to Bondi and Douglas agreed. Getting there took them less than half an hour.

Sea, sun, sand and bikinis. The red-brick houses stood wall to wall, pretending to be in Bognor or Clacton. Beyond the tarmac of the car park and a ribbon of untended grass the sand was gold, the rollers fierce. Ashley plunged in to show off his prowess at swimming. The undertow was dangerous and Douglas refused to be drawn. One never could tell with Ashley.

Exposure of the body beautiful was the business of the bay. Bronzed flesh spread-eagled. Bikinis were minimal, revealing cleavages in bosoms and buttocks. Ashley wore one with gay abandon. After his bathe he lay on his back drying, as though without a care.

'Are you still thinking of having me arrested, dear boy?'

'Yes,' Douglas told him. 'Arresting you is my job.'

'On any particular charge? George, for instance?'

'Fraud, smuggling, murder and indecent exposure.'

'You wouldn't get a conviction on counts one and two. Insufficient evidence. As you admitted yourself.' Ashley yawned and stretched.

'If you believed that, why did you fake your death?'

'A strictly precautionary measure. You could still dent my halo. But I bet you a million dollars you won't get me convicted in a court of law anywhere in the world.'

'How would you account for all that money?'

'What money?'

'The money made off with by Sylvia Smith. As witnessed by your bank manager in Honolulu.'

'Who is Sylvia Smith?'

'You are. You're registered in the hotel under that name.'

'I shan't be for much longer. Dear Sylvia will vanish. Poof! Like dear George.'

'Which brings us to count three. I wouldn't bank on a jury believing your tale about George slipping accidentally. If it was an accident why didn't you report it?'

Ashley sat up. He looked Garboesque behind dark glasses. His figure was slim and unwrinkled. A towel concealed the bulge in the lower half of his bikini.

'You're right,' he said. 'But I've now remembered what really happened. Before running away I saw you and George shooting at each other. Then you bounding forward. Seizing him, grappling with him and finally hurling him into the pool. Can it be he doesn't want George alive and brought to justice, I asked myself. Then I recollected the Moscow affair and it dawned on me that you were paying off an old score.'

'You wouldn't dare.'

'Have me arrested and see. It would be quite like old times.' Ashley referred to the court-martial as if it were a picnic they had enjoyed together.

Douglas got to his feet. He couldn't trust himself to speak.

'Never mind,' Ashley teased. 'There's always count four. Would you mind doing my back now, dear?' He pointed to a bottle of sun-tan lotion and rolled over on the sand.

If it had been a dagger Douglas would have plunged it into him and damn the consequences. Instead he threw it angrily into the sea.

He put on his clothes and caught the first bus. When he looked round, Ashley was in the seat behind wearing his jazzy floral sun-frock over the bikini. They travelled back together without exchanging another word.

At the hotel a message was waiting. Would Douglas please ring the following number urgently? The receptionist handed it over with the key.

'Come to my room,' said Ashley when he saw the message.

Douglas ignored him and went to his own.

148

Ashley followed, pushing his way in behind. 'Don't do anything rash,' he warned, one hand inside his beach bag.

Still not deigning to notice, Douglas got the number.

'So it's you at last,' said Charlie's voice. 'How's your party?'

'I've got my eye on her.' He watched Ashley move closer in order not to miss what was said at the other end.

'Good on you. Now listen. An Englishman is stirring things up. A toffee-nosed lawyer called Willingdon. Do you know him?'

'Yes, I know him.'

'Well he doesn't care for you much. He claims you're a suspicious character and should be interrogated about the disappearance of a friend of his. Name of Paget. He asked us to get in touch with the New Zealand police. They say they have no information about Paget since you were tailing him at Rotarua. So what's the form?'

'I – I honestly can't say at this stage.' Caught between Charlie and Ashley, Douglas stumbled over the lie.

The line went quiet.

'Hullo,' called Douglas anxiously. 'Are you still there?'

'Just about,' said Charlie. 'That was me thinking and this is what I've thought. Homicide is not my department, but if this Paget is liable to turn up dead it might save a lot of trouble if you weren't in New South Wales when the news came through. That's all. Keep in touch, won't you?'

Douglas promised and rang off.

Ashley laughed. 'Good on Jack Willingdon,' he said. 'I was contemplating doing a bunk and now we can go together. Joint fugitives from justice. Do you know whether there's an extradition treaty between New South Wales and Victoria? Or would you feel safer in the Northern Territories? Come on now. Get packing.'

Douglas hesitated. Orders from Ashley rankled, but had he a better plan? He could feel himself sinking in a quagmire of injustice. The old Gulunchi feeling. To be convicted of George Paget's murder!

Jack must be in league with Ashley after all, he guessed. In Wellington his insistence on Ashley being dead had been

149

overdone. The pair of them were gunning for him together. As legal adviser, how could Jack possibly not have been aware of what was going on inside the India Fund? Also he had been on the boat to India and one of the boys at Gulunchi. How could he pretend not to know Ashley and George Paget for what they really were?

Douglas's past involvement with them would do him no good with the New Zealand police if it came to a show-down. Still less with *Monsieur le Président.* Which of them would disbelieve Jack Willingdon, of Swallow, Braithwaite & Willingdon, City solicitors – bowler hat, black jacket, striped trousers and all? While he regaled the authorities with tales of Douglas's jealousy and malice, Ashley would simply disappear again.

As he packed, Douglas told himself that he must not let go of Ashley. That was the overriding commitment. Fortunately Ashley felt the same. At this stage of the game neither could afford to let the other out of sight.

Arrangements for departure took longer in Ashley's room. Ashley began by stripping to the skin, practising some strip-tease artistry in the process.

'That show last night was terrific,' he said. 'I wish I'd gone to RADA after Oxford.'

'To become the new Gielgud or another Danny la Rue?'

'What does it matter? The play's the thing.'

'For you perhaps. Your things are deception and exhibitionism. But, for some of us, all the world isn't a stage.'

'Poor dull, depressed, downtrodden Douglas! Be gay, not grey. That's my message to the world.'

Ashley was dressing as they talked. First a pair of pants, flowery but masculine. Then a shirt, ditto. A pair of male slacks, pale blue. A transformation scene, except that from the neck up he was still Sylvia Smith.

'Christ Almighty,' said Douglas. 'You look like something from Berlin between the wars.'

'You flatter me, ducky,' Ashley replied and minced into the bathroom.

Until he returned Douglas stared gloomily out of the window. He could make out the bridge in the distance and the Moreton Bay fig trees in the park. The rainy weather had passed and Sydney was sizzling in a February heatwave. What did God think He was doing intertwining his destiny with that of Ashley Wyndham West, the arch-bastard of the twentieth century?

'Another brutal murder. Alas, poor Sylvia Smith. Tell me. How do I look?'

Ashley had returned, make-up and wig removed. His own blond hair was short and flecked with silver.

Douglas appraised him with contempt. 'Not like your old odious self. If it wasn't for the voice I still wouldn't recognise you.'

'How very reassuring of you, Dougsie. That's the first kind word you've spoken since we met. I feel a new man and it's good to know I look it. What fun to be male again! Whatever you may think, I'm not a transvestite at heart.'

'I've never thought of you as anything except queer as a coot and straight as a corkscrew. And I've known for years that you don't have a heart.'

'Nasty!' Ashley wagged a finger.

'And you've cut yourself shaving. Surely you can't be out of practice.'

'I thought one or two nicks on the chin would enhance my manliness. Now stop being a sourpuss and let's go.'

'Where to?'

'You'll find out when we arrive. I'm not having any warning phone calls to your policeman friend.'

He had one large and one medium-sized suitcase, and a small piece of shiny black hand luggage. This was conveniently unisex – either an attaché or a jewel case. He held it firmly himself and waited for Douglas to pick up the others.

'You can bloody well do your own humping, Ashley. You're a man again now. Remember?'

He made for the bathroom door, but Ashley stopped him.

'Can't I even . . .?'

'No, you can't. We'll use a public one later. I shall need

you to guide me through the right door until I get into practice.'

Douglas was puzzled. Could there be something there which Ashley didn't wish him to see? And where was their unknown destination? He tried to put himself in Ashley's new shoes – flashy brothel-creepers. If Ashley hadn't boggled at killing George, why should he boggle over Douglas as soon as the right opportunity occurred? Charlie's phone call might have postponed his plans, but that was all.

Down in the seventh-floor lobby Ashley ordered him to pay both bills.

He objected. 'Won't that look fishy?'

'No fishier than anything else in this district. You inquired about Sylvia when you arrived, didn't you? You and Sylvia were buddies back in the Old Country, weren't you? How can I pay, looking like this?'

'You mean you don't want to be seen by the receptionist?' Douglas realised now that he was being saddled with a second disappearance.

'Of course not. What else do you imagine?'

'Nothing. I'll do it, but what about some money? You have rather more than I do.'

Ashley dug into a pocket and produced a handful of dollar notes 'Here you are. I'll be watching from near the lift, so no surreptitious last-minute messages please.'

The girl at the desk showed no interest when Douglas handed over two keys and paid both bills. They exchanged compliments and he rejoined Ashley.

'You must leave alone,' Ashley told him in the lift. 'Pick me up in the street.' On the ground floor he slid away out of the porter's eye and Douglas began to wonder whether he had made the right decision.

He ordered a taxi. When it came he helped the porter put the luggage aboard. Should he tell the driver to go to the nearest police station? While he hesitated, Ashley climbed in.

'Hullo,' said Ashley for the driver's benefit. 'Are you off to the airport already? I'll come out with you and see you off, if you've no objection.'

153

At Kingsford Smith Ashley scanned the departure board thoughtfully. 'TAA 417 for Canberra. Leaving in half an hour. What about that?'

'Who's buying the tickets?'

'I look after mine and you look after yours. But please don't ask me for more money. I know you've got a free pass. We travel separately and you take the big case. I'm still weak from being a woman and you look more long-distance.'

They queued apart and ignored each other in the departure lounge. Ashley was edgy, as though expecting to be swooped on by police.

Punctually at 15.30 their Electra took off. It climbed steeply over the mud-coloured sea in Botany Bay and swept inland in a wide arc. They sat in the same row on opposite sides of the aisle. Douglas could sense Ashley unwinding. Then the captain announced that owing to an engine fault he was returning to Sydney.

'If this is your doing,' Ashley leaned across and whispered, 'you are going to regret it.'

Douglas shrugged his shoulders. It was nice to have Ashley jittery. 'If things are getting too much for you,' he whispered back, 'what about signing a confession? There's no death penalty in New Zealand. If I can arrange for all your sentences to run concurrently, you should be out and about again in twenty years.'

'Why should I sign a confession when I'm safely dead?'

'If you're so safely dead, why have you got the jitters?' They were snarling at each other now.

On the ground again Ashley dropped the pretence of not knowing Douglas. He wanted him available for killing at close quarters if the police closed in. He demanded that Douglas accompany him to the lavatory. Douglas refused. Already he was regretting his obedience over the bathroom and the bills.

'I accept the fact that you may shoot me out of spite if you're arrested, Ashley. But I can't see your shooting me for not accompanying you to the loo. Why are you so windy anyway? You can see now that it was a genuine fault and nothing to do with me. You're a gent today, so that's the door. I'll wait here.'

He put on his blandest face and it worked. As soon as Ashley's back disappeared from view he ran to a telephone and rang police headquarters. With his usual bad luck there was no one he dared confide in but Charlie, and Charlie took a long time being found.

By the time he reached the phone Ashley was already emerging through the lavatory door.

'Douglas here. We're off to Canberra.'

He dropped the receiver, hurried out of the booth and absorbed himself in a display of Valentine Day cards on the news-stand. That call was something he should have done the previous night and to hell with the schoolboy pact.

For an hour and a half they sat in the lounge side by side without speaking, Ashley pale and savage. At 17.30 a Fokker Friendship took them up for a second trip round Botany Bay. Once more they took separate seats and were not acquainted. After the phone call Douglas decided that he had nothing to lose by continuing to play ball.

This time they flew on down the coast, skirting low cloud before turning inland over Wollongong. Dull green countryside with low hills. Man-made waterholes and a lake or two. Plenty of sheep but few trees or houses.

'Beaut country,' a girl told her boyfriend in the seat behind Douglas's.

Seen from above, Canberra had the same wide boulevards as Washington or New Delhi. Set in the middle of the beaut country in what had recently been nowhere, its artificial lake looked big enough for an inland sea.

They landed casually on a bare plain a few miles out of town. Australian Capital Territory, Douglas noted. Charlie's advice had been taken.

When the passengers gathered to claim their baggage Ashley came forward and greeted him.

'Fancy meeting you here,' he said.

'What a surprise,' Douglas replied drily. 'Do I know
155

your name?' Presumably Ashley had a fresh name for each change of sex and appearance.

'Robinson. Henry Robinson. Surely you remember? Shall we share a taxi into town?'

When the baggage arrived and Douglas moved forward to collect the big case Ashley anticipated him. Under the pretence of reading the label he deftly tore off the identifying tag. They collected the rest of their belongings and hurried to the cab rank.

'Aren't we claiming the big one?'

'Henry Robinson with a load of woman's clothes? What would people think? No; that's good-bye to Sylvia Smith. God rest her sweet soul in peace.'

Behind the play-acting façade Ashley remained a deadly efficient operator. Douglas awarded him full marks for disposing of Sylvia Smith. She had checked in at the Top of the Cross and she had checked out. After that, nothing suspicious and nothing traceable. She might still be in Australia or she could have gone abroad. On a British passport she might have left the country by any one of a number of routes requiring no official record which couldn't be easily evaded. If a search were made who would be likely to remember a woman of uncertain age named Smith?

Instead of taking a taxi into town, Ashley suddenly turned back into the airport building.

'What now?' Douglas demanded. He had his eye cocked for one of Charlie's men.

'Wait and see. Frankly, I don't trust you, Dougsie. You're being suspiciously amenable. You didn't by any chance tip off your Interpol chum while I was in the bog at Kingsford Smith?'

'There wasn't time, was there?' Douglas put on his innocent look.

'Because if you did, there's going to be an anonymous phone call to the New South Wales police telling them that you killed George Paget? That would be a fair riposte.'

'What good would that do you? It would merely start a search for me. And one for Sylvia Smith.'

156

'Then what about another anonymous phone call to the New South Wales police, telling them that you killed her too?'

'Really, Ashley!'

'Really, Dougsie. You left the hotel alone with her luggage after paying her hotel bill. You travelled here alone, abandoning her luggage at the airport. If you didn't kill her, where is she? No one is going to believe that she's now me.'

'If I did kill her, where is her body? You need a corpse to convict someone of murder.'

'Oh no you don't. Remember that steward who shoved a girl through a porthole? He was convicted without her body ever being recovered.'

'There was other evidence.'

'So there is in this case.'

'Such as?'

'I prevented you from going into the bathroom, didn't I? That was because there were what is called signs of a struggle. It wasn't carelessness which made me cut myself shaving.' Ashley smiled at the thought of his own cunning. 'Not enough blood to alarm anyone, but sufficient for the maid to notice. There are a few smears on some of the underclothes in the luggage too.'

If anyone could get a friend convicted of murdering someone who didn't exist, it would be Wyndham West Sahib, pride of the regiment, the hero commemorated in St. Paul's. Douglas knew now that he should have forced his way into that bathroom. His path through life was strewn with the litter of wrong decisions.

'Come on,' said Ashley. 'We're getting out here.'

In a few minutes they had boarding passes for the next flight to Melbourne and were in the departure lounge awaiting the call. Douglas sat considering how much he would mind if Ashley were to kill him then and there. Life was the interval between landing and take-off, as brief in the scale of eternity as their stop in Canberra. Death might not be so bad – if he could take Ashley with him.

157

It took the Friendship an hour and a half to reach Melbourne. Suburban sprawl clothed the ground so densely that they landed among a sea of roofs. They continued to ignore each other until they met by arrangement in the taxi queue. Ashley directed the driver to the Windsor.

'Fugitives or not,' he said, 'we might as well opt for luxury.'

The Windsor stood opposite the Victorian State Parliament House and resembled a palace. They booked in as John and Henry Robinson. Their room was regally furnished and spacious. The private bath and telephone were both eligible for scheduling as historic monuments.

In the restaurant they took luncheon under chandeliers. Outside, the temperature was hotter than an English summer, but Ashley demolished the full *table d'hôte*. Tomato soup, fillet of barramundi, roast sirloin of beef with Yorkshire pudding, strawberry shortcake, coffee. He had ordered the same for Douglas without consultation. Douglas was still moody, not speaking.

'I'm going upstairs for a snooze now,' he announced at the end of the meal.

'To report to your Charlie? Oh no, you don't. We'll take the air together. Exercise will do you good.'

They strolled out into the heat and Ashley ordered Douglas to hire a car. He stood across the road watching while it was done.

'What's this in aid of?' Douglas asked suspiciously when he picked him up.

'Locomotion,' Ashley declared. 'Sightseeing, for the purpose of. I haven't been in Melbourne for years. I'd forgotten it could be as warm as Delhi.'

They visited the museum and inspected stuffed Australian fauna. Families of kangaroos, wombats and koalas grouped in eucalyptus settings. Douglas made no pretence of interest, but Ashley seemed to enjoy it.

The next port of call was the new art gallery, where he admired Tintorettos and Drysdales. Fountains in a court-yard took his fancy too. They threw jets into the air in orgasmic spasms. Douglas sighed and complained that his feet were killing him. He couldn't make up his mind whether Ashley's interest in animals and art was affectation or a blind to cover some sinister purpose. Nothing about Ashley was genuine.

In the park he was allowed to lie on the grass while they listened to the end of a concert in the Music Bowl. After-wards they walked in the Botanic Gardens, viewed the Tree of Separation and found themselves a stretch of Yarra which reminded Ashley of the Thames at Kew.

'I was thinking in the park,' he said, 'about that girl you used to woo in Kensington Gardens. Whatever was her name?'

It was typical of Ashley to have forgotten. He had rob-bed Douglas of her and now couldn't even remember what she was called.

'Are you referring to Susan?'

'Susan! That's it. Are you still in touch?'

'No.' Douglas threw himself on the ground, puzzling whether the question was an innocent one. Susan was his sorest memory.

'I'm not surprised. I never thought she was right for you.'

'Well, you thought wrong. Susan was the one girl in the world for me. My one chance of happiness. At least when you had me court-martialled you did it to save your own precious skin. What you did to me over Susan was sheer sadism. I'd forgiven you often enough before, but I'll never forgive you for that. It's the most despicable of all the crimes you've committed since you made that promise to me on the Table Mountain.'

'What an outburst!' Ashley seemed mildly amused. He was relaxing on his back Bondi-wise but more decently garbed and gendered. 'Don't blame me, dear boy. It's all in

159

the stars. I've only done the best I could and on balance my best happens to be better than anyone else's.'

'You haven't become World President.'

'Not yet, but who says that isn't in the stars too?'

'A man of destiny! Don't you even believe in free will?'

'A figment of the liberal imagination. That's the one important thing I learned at Oxford. There's no free will. Therefore no moral responsibility. We move in predestined grooves like Melbourne trams. *Qué sera sera.* It's all deeply comforting.'

'If that's a classy method of explaining that you're incorrigible, I know it already. I've been wasting my time on you. My whole life, in fact.'

'And you'll carry on regardless. You're incorrigible too. You can't stop. Your character decides, and our characters are all in the genes and a sprinkling of early influences. Wasn't it Freud who said that a character is fully formed by the age of three? After that, however hard we kid ourselves, we can't really do anything about anything. I was born to enjoy Abdul Rahman's favours and you to suffer for it. You were born to find Susan unattainable and I to be the instrument of your frustration. Kismet, Dougsie.'

Ashley finished with a gesture of affection. Douglas rejected it. Ashley looked at his watch and sprang to his feet.

'Time to get back.'

They returned to the car and Douglas drove to the hotel in silence. He could feel Ashley busy plotting.

As soon as they entered the hotel a familiar figure rose from a chair in the lobby. Its eye had been fixed on the doorway.

'Good afternoon, Douglas.' Jack Willingdon greeted him with all the warmth of an iceberg.

'Oh hullo. Fancy meeting you here.' When he recovered from the surprise, Douglas answered casually. His first anxiety was to avoid a public scene.

'Someone kindly phoned and told me where to find you. I wasn't aware of the name you're currently using, but the receptionist recognised my description of you. I've come

160

for a fairly lengthy talk with you, Douglas. It was unwise of you to run out on me like that.'

'Still looking for George Paget?'

'I am. And who is your friend, may I ask?'

Ashley had strolled away unconcernedly but not out of earshot. Jack was sizing him up, but with no sign of recognition.

'Just a friend. A chap called Robinson I met in Canberra.'

'Don't lie to me any more, Douglas. He's no more a Robinson than you are. I've seen the register with both names. Brothers, eh? Are you up to your old Gulunchi tricks? I used to think you innocent.'

'So I was. You've got the whole thing wrong. When I do tell you the truth you won't believe it.'

'Then who is this friend and why are you sharing a room?'

'If you must know, he's a colleague who has flown out to help me in my inquiries.'

'Then I must question him too. You're still trying to involve IF and Ashley Wyndham West's good name in a scandal, aren't you? As the Fund's legal adviser and Ashley's executor I am determined to prevent one. I've not yet been able to establish whether your investigation is genuinely on behalf of some commercial concern, as you alleged, but to me at least, having some knowledge of the background, your motives seem thoroughly suspect. You had better have a satisfactory explanation of your part in the disappearance of someone who happens to be both the Fund's senior official and an old enemy of yours.'

While Douglas was preparing to register righteous indignation, Ashley began slipping unobtrusively away. Jack called to him sharply.

'Perhaps you would join us for a drink, Mr. Robinson.'

Ashley pretended not to hear. Face averted, he continued to move towards the lift. Was this a game for his benefit, Douglas wondered, or was Jack one sex-change behind.

Jack repeated his request more loudly. This time Ashley

was forced to hear. He turned, and at the sight of his face Jack's body tautened, like a hound's picking up a scent.

In the lounge the cream of Melbourne society sat upright in leather armchairs taking afternoon tea. Jack made for a sofa and beckoned to Ashley to sit beside him.

'Who are you?' he demanded in his prosecuting counsel voice. 'Your eyes are familiar. Are you some relation of Ashley's?'

'Ashley? Ashley who?'

It was a bold effort, but face to face and voice to voice even the shining light of the OUDS, James Agate's morning star, couldn't pull it off.

'No!' Expressions of recognition and disbelief scudded across Jack's face.

'Yes, actually.' Ashley smiled mischievously. He might have been playing a parlour game. 'I phoned you last night because I thought it would clear the air if you and Douglas had a little chat.' He snapped his fingers at a passing waiter and ordered three large Scotches.

Jack sat back, flummoxed for words. Douglas leaned forward, elbows on knees, holding his head in his hands to prevent it falling apart. It seemed a situation without a solution, but he now realised that Ashley had been trotting him round Melbourne in the knowledge that Jack was on his way. What was Ashley up to this time?

The drinks arrived. 'Burra pegs for burra sahibs,' Ashley announced. 'Isn't this quite like old times in the mess? The Empire has gone, alas, but the flag, God bless it, flies here still. Shall we drink to the Queen, gentlemen?'

He stood up, raised his glass solemnly and gave the toast. 'Gentlemen, the Queen.'

The others were obliged to rise. One or two loyalists at neighbouring tables struggled reluctantly to their feet and stood to attention while the three of them drank. 'Victoria, of course,' he added.

'I like Melbourne,' he went on in the voice of someone making polite social small-talk. 'They are all money-grubbers in Sydney, but here one feels a lingering sense of values, don't you think? A last breath of the spirit that made the regiment and the raj what they were.'

'Will you stop clowning?' Jack demanded. 'You're a fine one to talk in that way, I must say.'

'Clowning was never further from my thoughts. I'd have you remember you're talking to a posthumous CBE.'

'It hadn't escaped my attention. Perhaps you would begin by explaining how you come to be posthumously alive.'

'That must be confusing to the legal mind. But first perhaps you would care to explain to the Director-General how you come to be here, gallivanting round the world, instead of looking after IF's affairs in London.'

'I've no objection, if you can be serious for a moment. I came at the request of George, who seems to have disappeared in somewhat mysterious circumstances. In Wellington I met Douglas by accident. He palmed me off with some cock and bull story and then disappeared too. I now see you both for what you are. A brace of scoundrels. George Paget, I take it, is – or perhaps was – another of the gang.'

Ashley tutted. 'I realise it must be a shock for you coming across me alive and well and tippling here at the Windsor, but you really mustn't jump to conclusions or be quite so free with your allegations. For one thing it's unprofessional conduct. If I weren't legally dead I'd hire you to sue yourself for defamation of my spotless character.'

'I'm waiting, Ashley.'

'As a starter let me make it abundantly clear that Douglas and I are not in league. Far from it. Douglas is a special investigator employed by Interpol's criminal division in Paris. They have lent him to the security department of the International Air Transport Association. You can't get much more respectable than that.'

Jack rounded on Douglas. 'Is this true?'

Douglas acknowledged it. He sat mesmerised by Ashley's performance. Nimble-witted, brass-faced, steel-cored – that was Ashley. Whatever the emergency, Ashley could cope. Not only cope, but turn the tables. He and Jack appeared not to be in league after all. If so, Jack was wholly

163

in the right, Ashley wholly in the wrong. Yet already Jack was being pushed on the defensive. It had always been the same. In the days of IF's rise to world fame the toughest politicians and brashest television interviewers had never got past Ashley's guard. His public image remained impregnable. Now, with a plaque going up in St. Paul's and statues all over India, a rearguard action against Jack Willingdon was child's play. Watching the master in action, Douglas found excuses for his own weakness.

'Douglas's role in all this,' Ashley was saying, 'has been characteristically devious. I'm sorry to have to say it – and to his face – but he has been hounding me while pretending to be on official duties. And not only me. George too. Anyone wishing to learn what has become of George should apply to Douglas.'

'Well?' Jack demanded.

'I could tell you about George,' said Douglas, 'if Ashley really wants me to.'

'My advice to you,' Ashley interrupted smoothly, 'is not to answer any questions until you've hired a lawyer of your own.'

'My advice is that he doesn't require a lawyer unless he has broken the law.'

'You might also ask him about Sylvia Smith,' Ashley went on. 'Another client of yours who appears to be unaccountably missing. Top sleuth Douglas has all the answers.' He laughed mockingly, doing his imitation of a kookaburra.

'Just you be careful,' Douglas warned him angrily. 'You've spent your life going too far and getting away with it. My advice to you is, don't push your luck any further.'

'Did you hear that?' Ashley appealed to Jack. 'I shall be unaccountably missing myself next.'

Jack inspected his fingernails. 'I find all these innuendoes suffocating. Also I find myself unable to believe a single word either of you say. I regret the misfortune of having served with you during the war. My firm is one of the most reputable in the City of London and I fear, Ashley, that you made use of our acquaintance in the army to provide yourself with a respectable cover for what are beginning to seem extremely dubious activities.'

'If you were deceived, honest Jack – and I don't for one moment admit it – you were deceived in excellent company. I'm glad to have this opportunity of congratulating you on the arrangements for my memorial service. Modesty forbids me to repeat what that dearly beloved Archbishop said, but I shall certainly have it handy as a testimony at the Pearly Gates. Now, what about another snifter?'

'No, thank you. You are not fuddling me with alcohol and I am not leaving without a straightforward truthful answer to quite a number of questions. Since it has become plain that I cannot obtain them without assistance from the authorities you leave me no alternative but to summon the police. You are both to stay here while I make the necessary telephone call. If you attempt to move I shall raise an immediate hue and cry and have you chased down the street like a couple of pickpockets.'

Ashley was far from blenching. 'Middle age and prosperity are making you insufferably pompous,' he said. 'What on earth is biting you?'

'You can't persuade me that there isn't a criminal conspiracy here. And I begin to suspect that you, Ashley, have perpetrated the biggest public fraud since the Piltdown Man.'

'Fraud?' Ashley frowned. 'There you go again, making reckless accusations. Hoax would be the appropriate word and, correct me if I'm wrong, but hoaxes are not criminal.'

'They can be. Particularly where large sums of money are involved.'

'I see. Tell me then, before you make your phone call, how the auditors of IF have been getting on since my untimely demise. If memory serves, everything was shipshape and above board during my lifetime. Should there be any substantial deficiencies now, the responsibility must be that of the executive committee, of which you are a member, and its advisers, of which you are the principal one. I do hope, for your sake, there won't be any unpleasantness.

165

Even criminal negligence would be a bore, wouldn't it?'

'Save your blackmailing breath. No criminal charge against me would stick.'

'Clever old you! You always were a dab hand at keeping your nose clean. However, I imagine if the India Fund becomes the centre of a world-wide scandal your reputation and that of poor old Swallow and Braithwaite will take a nasty knock. Willingdon is a pretty distinctive name. People would always identify you as the solicitor in the IF case. Whatever the law said, I don't suppose they would ever believe you to be as innocent as you claimed. They would argue that you couldn't have been such a complete ass as not to realise something of what was going on.'

'I'll risk all that. It's preferable to a conspiracy charge.'

'Very well. If that's the way you feel, go ahead and call the police. But I think in fairness you ought to listen to my explanation first.'

'What do you imagine I've been sitting here trying to do for the past half hour?'

'Look, I've got a proposition. It's an infernally muggy day and we're all rather heated. We've all of us had a plane journey today, too, and air travel jars the nervous system. Mine anyway. So far as Douglas and I are concerned, we spent the afternoon traipsing round town. We're sweaty and exhausted and were heading for a quiet zizz when you surfaced like an avenging angel. I shall be happy to answer truthfully every single question you feel like asking, but not now and here in a public lounge. We have a car and what I suggest we do is drive down to the beach and take a swim before it gets dark. When we've cooled off and freshened up we'll find a quiet restaurant or come back to our room here if you prefer. Then you can have a question-and-answer session to your heart's content.'

Jack viewed the proposition with suspicion. 'What about Douglas? Does he come too?'

'We're not going to let him escape, if that's what's worrying you. Douglas is an essential member of the party. He is part of my explanation and I'm sure you'll insist on verification.'

'But you've as good as accused him of murder. I don't understand the position. If you are enemies why are you sharing a room?'

'You'll understand, I promise you. All in good time. Come on now. Let's go.'

'You can count me out,' Douglas declared. 'I'm not coming, whatever Ashley says. I don't trust either of you. If you're not going to the police, I shall.' If Jack was doubting him, he was determined not to budge until Jack's own *bona fides* had been established.

'What can you mean by saying you don't trust me? What have I done?' Jack's voice expressed astonishment.

'You've known Ashley and George as long as I have. You shared a room with George at OTS. You were all thick as thieves at Gulunchi. You and Donald Petrie, you both joined IF as soon as Ashley and George started it. Do you expect me to believe that, knowing the two who were in charge, you have been what Ashley rightly calls a complete ass and your part in IF is nothing but wide-eyed do-goodery?'

'Certainly I do. Damn you, Douglas, for an evil-minded snooper into other people's affairs.'

'Some affairs deserve being snooped into. I told you in Wellington, didn't I, that Ashley had faked his death? And you refused to believe me, didn't you? Why should I believe you now?'

'That's enough, Douglas,' said Ashley, calling him sharply to order. 'Or you'll force me to tell Jack that you were blackmailing us and how faking my death was the only means George and I could devise of exposing you. A copper's nark is bad enough, but a bent one is not quite what the old school expects.'

'So that's it!' Jack whistled softly. 'I don't know about the old school, but I suppose it's what one would expect from someone who disgraced his regiment.'

'I'm not saying it's true,' Ashley replied sweetly. He paused for effect. 'Nor am I saying it's not true. I'm merely discouraging Douglas from bringing the police in until we've talked this matter out fully and in private. Tempers

167

are getting frayed and there are two Victorian ladies behind you, Douglas, who are eavesdropping madly. Do let's
have a swim and not involve the local constabulary pre-
maturely. As survivors of that ghastly wartime shipload of
misery, it behoves us to show a modicum of solidarity.'

'Survivors no thanks to you, Ashley,' Douglas was
goaded into pointing out.

It didn't take Jack a moment to pick up the allusion.
'Are you accusing Ashley of being the man who lit that
cigarette? My God! I must say I wondered.'

The look which passed persuaded Douglas that, whatever their past relationship, the pair of them were unlikely
to gang up on him now. Jack had evidently come to the
same conclusion about Ashley and himself. They all rose
together.

'You two go and bring the car round,' said Ashley. 'I'll
fetch some towels from the room. We'll go somewhere
where we shan't need costumes.'

'I'm not leaving the hotel without you. We'll wait in the
lobby,' said Jack. 'If you take more than one minute I shall
call the police.'

Ashley returned quickly enough. He carried Douglas's
small grip with a corner of towel hanging out. His step was
jaunty and his manner schoolboyishly affable.

Twenty miles of city and suburbia.

Douglas drove and Ashley navigated, while Jack brooded in the back, silent as Cortez on his peak. To jolly him along, Ashley prattled pleasantries and reminiscence. By the time they reached open country and coast the atmosphere was still strained but less polluted.

'How much further are we going?' Jack wanted to be told. The change of landscape from fibro houses to tea-trees and banksias was making him nervous.

'It's right ahead. A peninsula called Mount Eliza. Some friends brought me here the last time I was out this way. After the town it's so peaceful and unspoilt it might be somewhere in India. Do you remember Karwar?'

They remembered Karwar. Bivouacking under palm trees on a sandy shore of the Indian Ocean. The division had been on manoeuvres, grappling ineffectually with an imaginary enemy. Douglas recalled that Ashley's manoeuvres had been largely confined to the sea – standing up to his neck in the water, twisting gently on one toe with the tide, planning what life had to offer when the war was over.

'We turn off here.'

Ashley indicated a track running off the coast road towards the shore. After quarter of a mile it ended in a clearing overlooking a secluded cove and the open sea. The sun had gone down in the last few minutes, leaving an orange band running the length of the horizon. Douglas switched off the engine and they sat as though enjoying a Cinemascope spectacular in a drive-in cinema.

'I should have thought this would remind you more of Hawaii,' he said. 'I'm told your house there had a wonderful view.' He glanced round at Jack hoping to discover whether he knew about it, but Jack's face gave nothing away.

Ashley was not to be drawn either. He became expansive about the beauties of Australia. The lure of the outback called, the thousand miles of nothing between Adelaide and Alice Springs where the silence made one's ears sing. He told them how happily he could settle as a yogi on Ayer's Rock, where the view from the top of a thousand-foot-high boulder was the same in every direction. Nothing.

Douglas smiled at the thought.

'Moorgate for me,' said Jack. 'Give me civilisation any day. Some people may remember India as sitting on verandahs drinking burra pegs and watching sunsets like this. I can only think of dysentery, cholera and starvation. That's why I decided to give my services to IF. Since you are so suspicious, Douglas, it may interest you to learn that I have never once charged a fee.'

'I can confirm that,' said Ashley. 'But don't let's start arguing again now or we'll miss our dip.'

'It's too late,' Douglas protested. 'It's almost dark.'

'The water will still be warm. I promise you.'

Ashley stripped off his clothes. The others, chivvied by him, followed suit. The area was deserted and an arc of rock cut off the cove from the adjoining shore. Naked as Adams, they ran across the sand. Ashley was right. The sea had retained the day's heat.

They splashed and floundered in the ink-dark water, rubbing the sweat off their bodies. Douglas paddled on his back, admiring the stars. It was too early for the full galaxy, but he identified the Southern Cross, which he and Ashley had first discovered together on the night of the torpedoes.

According to one of the ancient Greeks, the sea was the mother of all. It existed before land was formed. Plants and creatures were born and died. Sooner or later everything changed except the sea, which went on flowing and ebbing and flowing again. More enduring than rock, it alone in nature enjoyed the secret of permanent survival. That was why drowning was said to be such a good death. Going down for the third time, one felt the embrace of a loving one, the pull of immortality. Or so a philosophical fellow private had comforted him while they waited their turn for a lifeboat.

Did George Paget enjoy the feeling, he wondered. Probably not. George would have been scalded to death before he had a chance to drown. A pitiless death. It ought to be lying heavily on Ashley's conscience, but Ashley had no conscience for it to lie on. Douglas was glad of George's death but would have had him shot cleanly. There was little pain in a quick crunch.

All at once he became conscious of being cold. Floating with his thoughts had kept him in too long. Earlier he had been aware of Ashley doing his semi-professional crawl out to sea and of Jack keeping his distance from both of them. During the drive Ashley's charm had been working overtime – a bad omen. After that it was just as well to have him starkers, with nowhere to hide a gun.

He looked around him. Jack was performing a steady breast stroke, heading for the shore. Ashley had already left the sea and was a shadowy figure disporting itself gymnastically on the sand, apparently engrossed in the exercise of his ageing body beautiful. All the same he was too close to the car for the others' safety. Douglas cursed himself. With Ashley one should never relax.

He decided on rapid action, but as soon as he began moving towards the shore Ashley disappeared in the direction of the car. Jack, finishing his swim with a spurt, reached the water's edge first and doubled across the sand. Douglas, chilled now and with his teeth chattering, wondered whether to shout him a word of warning.

The shot came while he was still wondering. The decisive bark of a single gunshot, followed by deep silence. Then a cry and another shot. The outline of trees and rocks stood out against the sky, but the cove itself lay in darkness. Douglas ran for his life, clambering over an outcrop of rock and throwing himself desperately into a hollow.

171

He could see nothing ahead, but the sound of the shots was familiar. They came from his own gun.

Seconds passed and became minutes. Still he hugged the rock and waited. The nearest houses were a mile away or more. If no one came soon, he would have to make a dash for them, though the faintest noise would betray him. All he could hear, coming from above where the car was parked, was the gentle rustle of clothing.

'Come along, Dougsie. Come and get dressed. You must be perishing of cold, you poor old thing.'

The same teasing, mock-affectionate voice, pretending that nothing had happened. He made no answer.

'Come on now. You're not going to be tiresome, are you?'

The beam of a torch swept abruptly round the cove like a sudden fit of anger. The voice came from behind it.

'If you're thinking of doing anything rash or running away I'd strongly advise you not to. As you may have guessed, there has been an accident. Poor Jack is dead. Unfortunately he was shot with your gun.'

Wet and naked behind his rock, Douglas shivered.

'George Paget, Sylvia Smith, and now Jack Willingdon. Really, Dougsie! Even Interpol can't have licensed you for triple killings. You're overdoing things, dear boy.'

Douglas stopped being frightened and became angry. What had he been doing attempting to bring Ashley to justice? It was beyond his – or anyone's – ability. For the record Ashley would always be in the right. He trusted the stars and his horoscope had cast him in the role of hero. Ashley Wyndham West would never be found guilty of anything.

That left only one way open. What he had planned for George. A private execution. Justice outside the law. Douglas made his resolution as he clung to the rock, determining to make no response. Let Ashley come and find him.

'There's nothing to be afraid of. You surely don't imagine I'd hurt you?' The voice in the darkness gushed with trustworthiness. 'You play ball with me and I'll play ball with you. That's how we were brought up, wasn't it? I need you. You're my mate. We have a special relationship, remember?'

Coaxing, wheedling. Douglas resolved that it would never work on him again. What was it a despairing Darlybags had once said to him in his study? 'I can only believe that boy Wyndham West if I put nots in his sentences.'

'You saved me from being expelled, Dougsie. You saved me from being thrown to the sharks in the Atlantic. You were cashiered in my place. How can you doubt me now?'

Douglas had heard enough. He began slithering slowly over the rock towards the unbearable voice.

'Dougsie, this is too bad of you, playing me up like this. Please trust me. I've all the money in the world. A good slice of it anyway. All I want is to share it with you. I shall be lonely by myself. You've always looked after me. Jack had to go. Don't desert me now.' It was his little-boy voice, the one from the first day at school.

Douglas crept cautiously round it in a flanking movement, aiming to get the trees behind him so that he could attack without showing his silhouette against the sky.

'Very well then. I give you precisely thirty seconds more. After that I'm coming for you with a gun and you can damn well take the consequences. I know you're still there. You can't fool me.' Ashley had run out of soft soap.

Douglas crept on like a turning worm. Then he rose from hands and knees to his feet to charge the last few yards. Immediately he started, his bare foot caught on a sharp edge of stone and he stumbled. A switch clicked and he was flooded in torchlight. Before Ashley could fire he dived for the protection of the car.

Ashley's laughter broke the silence. 'Fieldcraft was never one of your strong subjects, was it? George Paget now, he was the man for dealing with enemy sentries. Tactical Exercises Without Weapons were more your line. Unfortunately in this case I happen to have one.'

Those futile Tewts at OTS! At least Douglas remembered one lesson from them. The element of surprise. He threw a stone from the shadow of the car. It landed behind

Ashley, who spun round instinctively with his torch snapped on. Douglas dashed out of cover as though on an assault course.

Before Ashley could redirect the beam, he was on him, grappling to pinion his arms. The torch fell to the ground and he desperately clutched the wrist of the other hand – the one which held the automatic. He felt Ashley's knee jab into his groin and they crashed together on something unexpectedly soft. Jack's body squelched beneath their weight.

As they rolled over, striking, tugging, kicking and kneeing each other, he could feel that Ashley, fighting like a wild animal, was actually enjoying the physical contact. Douglas forced the revolver out of his hand, but needed both his own to do it. Ashley's other hand was free. He felt it fumbling savagely between his legs. It squeezed and the pain was so agonising that he screamed. The pressure was merciless. It increased and became past bearing. He went groggy, into a tortured daze, and lost consciousness.

When he came to, Ashley, brisk and businesslike, was sluicing him with sea water.

'That's quite enough of that tomfoolery, Dougsie. You'll catch your death of cold lying about like this. Here's a towel. Get your shirt and trousers on. And don't try the wounded warrior act on me. I've a job for you to do.'

The job was to bury Jack. At first his aching manhood made it difficult for him to stand steady on his feet without retching. He dressed from the sitting position until Ashley kicked him upright, to help carry Jack's body to a stretch of sand concealed between two spurs of rock.

'This should be above the high water mark. Get digging and make it deep.'

'There's nothing to dig with.'

'Here you are. This is the best I can do.'

Ashley produced two dustpans. They must have been taken from a housemaid's cupboard when he went to fetch the towels from their hotel room. Proof, Douglas noted, of a premeditated killing. Gritting his teeth, he set to work.

Even with the sand so soft it must have taken him more

174

than a couple of hours. Ashley was busy with the other dustpan a short distance away. His torch was still working but he used it as little as possible. Every few minutes he loomed out of the darkness to inspect progress and order Douglas to go deeper. The bottom of the hole became watery. When Ashley was satisfied they tipped Jack in with a splash.

'What's the other hole for?' Douglas inquired uneasily.

'For his clothes, of course. We don't want him identified too easily. What did you think it was for? There! Does that convince you,' Ashley threw Douglas's gun in beside the body.

'What about your own?' Douglas asked.

'I wouldn't shoot you with that, would I? Not when I have yours to suggest a mass-murderer's conscience-stricken suicide. Don't be so windy.'

'I'm not having my gun in there. I didn't kill him and won't have people thinking I did.'

'Whether it's in there or not it's yours and it's the murder weapon. Nothing can alter that.'

'That's no reason to plant it. I won't stand for it. You're not going to do this to me again, Ashley.' He stooped to recover the gun and was sent sprawling by a kick from behind.

'The gun stays there. I must have something tangible to keep you obedient.'

'If I'm caught you'll be caught.' Douglas had to pick the sand out of his mouth before he could speak and the threat sounded frail.

'Me? I'm not here. It's you who hired the car. Your fingerprints are all over the steering wheel. No one will find any of mine.'

While he spoke Douglas was still lying on the sand, groping surreptitiously for the gun. His fingers closed on the butt at last. This was the moment. In one quick movement he picked it up, turned it on Ashley and squeezed the trigger.

Nothing happened. Another failure.

Ashley enjoyed one of his sardonic laughs. 'That was

very spirited of you, Dougsie. I was beginning to think you'd lost your nerve and wouldn't try it.'

'Then you were wrong for once. If the water hadn't made it damp I'd have had you.'

'Did you reckon on the damp? Is that what gave you the guts to pull the trigger? As a matter of fact I took the elementary precaution of removing the remaining bullets.'

Douglas threw the gun down. It was a sign of defeat. Ashley dropped his handkerchief over it and picked it up carefully.

'Thank you,' he went on. 'You were slow but you played ball in the end. I had expected you to scuffle for it immediately. You had me worried. Don't you realise that I needed your fingerprints on it, dear boy? A gun carelessly left with the body, yet carefully wiped clean of prints. Might that not arouse the suspicions of the State of Victoria? Now we have the murderer's prints on the murder weapon. Incontrovertible evidence.'

Beaten and humiliated, Douglas staggered to his feet and Ashley kicked him affectionately on the shin to emphasize their new relationship.

'Cheer up,' Ashley ordered. 'With a bit of luck it'll be years before they unearth him.'

'Whenever they do, the gun will help to identify him. It'll be traced to me and the police will suspect that he left Sydney to look for me. Is that what you want?'

Ashley considered. 'Perhaps not. It might not suit me either if the gun were found after the body had ceased to be identifiable. On the other hand, we don't want to let you off the hook, do we? Let's compromise.'

They covered Jack up, buried his clothes in the second hole and dug a third for the gun on the other side of the cove.

'Actually,' said Ashley as they returned to the car, 'the murder I'd rather see you punished for is Sylvia Smith's. I wouldn't at all mind seeing the expression on your face when some idiot of a judge sentenced you for killing someone who never existed.

'Most amusing,' Douglas managed to mutter.

'Just my little joke,' Ashley assured him. 'Not to be taken seriously, of course.'

'Of course.'

Douglas drove back to town on the threshold of exhaustion. Before going into the hotel they put on ties and jackets and spruced themselves up. Douglas, under orders, pretended to be Jack and extracted his luggage from the night porter. He established the fact that Jack had not booked a room and managed to get the luggage out into the car. Then he returned and crept upstairs while Ashley distracted the man's attention.

In bed he almost cried. He should have confessed. He should have told the porter to phone the police, and damn Ashley's blackmail. But he just couldn't face the consequences. Ashley's story would be believed. His wouldn't. He had been through it all before.

In the morning it was raining. In Melbourne everything happened in the best English manner. Ashley used it as an excuse for an early departure.

They flew to Adelaide, but when the plane landed he decided they would stay aboard and carry on to Perth. Adelaide was churchy, he said, which must mean choir-boys, but business before pleasure. They would both feel safer after rather more mileage.

Otherwise he was as communicative as a clam. On this flight they were travelling together openly, but Douglas had no idea of their ultimate destination. Ashley seemed deliberately not to have one in order to keep him guessing.

The four hundred miles from Melbourne to Adelaide had taken an hour. The fifteen hundred from Adelaide to Perth, to make them feel safer, took little more than two and a half. They travelled at six hundred miles an hour over the Great Australian Bight with the cloud thinning and the weather improving all the way. Douglas looked down on Mother Sea from thirty thousand feet. He was still in a semi-coma of shock and depression. His spirit was broken and the ache between his legs made him feel perpetually sick.

Below, the colours changed. Red and brown parched earth and red and grey scrubland succeeded the blue and grey of the sea. Carthage must have looked like this after the Romans had sown it with salt so that nothing should grow there ever again. The browns and greys matched his mood of desolation. So, underneath, did the red. It represented, he knew, oxydised iron and the dim but real hope of mineral wealth. Hope deep down. Across the vast desert landscape ran the single ribbon of a dirt-track road. However unpromising the outlook, there was always a way.

In Perth Ashley selected a motel beside the river. Motorway works were in progress in front. Bulldozers and piles of earth heralded riverscaping into parkland and lakeland, to be crisscrossed with feeders for a ring road intersecting with the highway to Fremantle. Ashley sighed at the view from the window of their room and inquired rhetorically what the world was coming to.

With the temperature in the mid-nineties they lunched lightly beside the swimming pool. Alone except for a professional sunbather the colour of seasoned mahogany. He lay as though dead, reminding Douglas of Jack inert, waiting for his grave to be dug.

Ashley appeared to regard both earthworks and sunbather with suspicion. One as some elaborate kind of road block. The other as a police spy.

'You're getting jumpy,' Douglas told him. 'You're imagining things. You'd better get out of the sun.'

'I've got my white patch to tan,' Ashley complained. There was a pale telltale strip across his chest, the shape of his bikini at Bondi. The last evidence of Sylvia Smith.

To avoid sunstroke he swam a few lengths in the pool. When he came out they moved to mattresses further from the mahogany stranger. They lay side by side and Ashley became conciliatory. He inspected Douglas's thigh wound and apologised. Also for the aching groin.

'People don't realise it, but I'm very highly strung. You think of me as calculating, but I often act on impulse. When you turned up at that service I should have taken you into my confidence. Instead I treated you instinctively as a threat to be eliminated.'

'As you're doing now?'

'How could you think it? From now on we must trust each other absolutely, Dougsie. I'm sorry about Jack, but he shouldn't have been so officious. With you and me it's quite different. I'm sorry about roughing you up, but I didn't shoot you, did I? Similarly I've always known that you would never hand me over to the police. How could you after all the past we've shared together?'

How could he after all the traps Ashley had laid for him? That was the right question.

'Promise me you never will.'

Douglas promised.

'Word of honour?' Ashley spoke in a voice which went back nearly forty years.

'Word of honour.'

They searched into each other's sunglasses. Douglas had bound himself without compunction. The promise would be kept. Since Jack's death he had other plans.

'Good,' said Ashley, becoming brisk. 'Then the next thing is to disengage you from your official activities. You must make a report which will satisfy your masters, and then you must resign.'

'How do I live if I give up my job?'

'With me of course. I'm serious, Dougsie. I'm too old to start making new friends. I should be lonely by myself. I need you. I really do.'

'What you need is a scapegoat. You need me to be responsible for your murders. Then, once that's clearly established, you need me dead.'

'I don't. I swear it. I need your companionship and loyalty. You've always been loyal to me, Dougsie.'

'Up to a point.' The point had been Abdul Rahman, reinforced by Susan. 'Where do we live? In India?'

'Too dangerous. With so few Europeans around and my being known there, someone might twig. No; I was thinking of a new Hawaii. Somewhere agreeably remote in the Pacific. Preferably French, where you could speak the lingo and they would leave us alone. Papeete, for instance.'

Douglas felt his skin shrivelling in the sun. For all their past relationship, it was impossible to tell which Ashley really had in mind for him. Papeete or death.

When the heat was over the hump and the evidence singed from Ashley's chest, they put some clothes on and sauntered along the esplanade.

It was Saturday afternoon. Cruise boats were leaving Barrack Square for pleasure trips, ferries heading for South Perth. In the gardens between the town and the river a ladies' cricket match reminded Ashley of his old prowess.

But for the war, he announced, he would have played county cricket for Worcestershire and won the championship for them.

'Not simply for the sake of a ribboned coat,' he added. 'Or the selfish hope of a season's fame.'

'Of course not,' Douglas agreed, his mind elsewhere. Papeete or death. How much did he mind?

'It's the game that counts. You remember my tweakers, don't you?'

'Of course I do. They were jolly good. Seven for seventeen against Marlborough, wasn't it?'

Ashley looked pleased. Douglas felt needed. The odds swung towards Papeete.

When stumps were drawn they walked up the hill to King's Park. Ashley bought pineapple juices from a café and they lay on the grass looking down on the river. Beyond the Narrows Bridge the water formed another lake. Hundreds of sails dotted the surface.

'We'll have a yacht in Papeete,' he promised.

Back at the hotel, while Douglas showered, Ashley switched on the television set and busied himself domestically, making cups of tea from the electric kettle. A foretaste of how they would live together.

The screen came to life with a picture of surfing champions performing acrobatics on giant waves off the coast of Oahu. As Douglas came out of the bathroom to watch, Ashley killed the picture with a snap of the switch, his mood suddenly as angry as the sea.

'Damn you, Dougsie. That's where I should be. I planned it all perfectly and you spoiled it for me. Sometimes you make me sick.'

Douglas at the mirror looked himself in the eye. 'You're not the only one. Actually, I make myself sick.'

'You make everyone sick, but don't go all pitiful about it. It's not your fault.'

'I thought you needed me.' Papeete was receding.

'So I do – depending on how you behave. Now listen to this. What I want you to do is to phone your Interpol pal in Sydney and thank him for his help. Tell him all is well and you don't need him any more.'

'He'll expect more than that.'

'Tell him you're making your full report to Paris.'

'Even so he'll need to be told whether I have any news of George and whether Jack caught up with me. Not to mention what has happened to Sylvia Smith.'

'Well, that's pretty straightforward, isn't it? You have no news of George. You haven't seen Jack. And the Sylvia situation is in hand. You can't say more at this juncture.'

'Very well,' Douglas had resigned himself to a policy of obedience. He picked up the receiver.

'Just a moment.' Ashley took it out of his hand and replaced it. 'First we had better discuss your call to Paris. The report that is going to stop your boss becoming inquisitive. Tell me your precise assignment. Curtains for the alleged Wyndham West Universal Gold Smuggling Ring?'

'To put an end to the smuggling and provide evidence leading to the arrest and conviction of those responsible.'

'Right. On count one you report total success. You are completely satisfied that owing to your persistence and my death the organisation has broken up. There will be no more smuggling. Incidentally, there is no longer any doubt in your mind that I am really and truly dead.'

'None whatever.'

'On count two, gang warfare appears to have broken out among my principal lieutenants. Three men and a woman.'

'Three men? Who is the third?'

'Two then. Or perhaps it's better not to be too specific. The point is that the trail has gone cold and you believe them to have killed each other. You're still checking on the elusive Miss Smith, but it seems that there is no one left to bring to justice.'

'Very neat. Too neat. If I know my boss, he'll smell a very large rat.'

'Then it's up to you to make the story plausible. Wrap

it up how you like. Say that so far as you're concerned the case is virtually over. The lure of the East has got you again and you want to resign without returning to Europe. If he doubts you, that will add weight to your resignation. You're fed up. You've done a good job, no one appreciates you, and you're tired of being mucked about between Interpol having no confidence in you and IATA querying your expenses. Isn't that exactly what you told me?'

'They may ask the local police to check on me. Or they may send another investigator to find out what has been going on.'

'It might be awkward for you if they sent someone, mightn't it?' Ashley veiled the threat with a charming smile. 'On the other hand, a good tale should stand up to investigation. George ought to be unidentifiable by this time, but if the body is suspected to be his it's a fair supposition that Sylvia Smith did for him. Sylvia herself is missing, on the way to being presumed dead. So is Jack Willingdon. His partners in London will probably kick up a terrible fuss, until Interpol drop your hint that he may have been conspiring with the others in the embezzlement of IF Funds. That will soon shut them up.'

They spent the whole evening shaping Douglas's story for plausibility and rehearsing it, with Ashley playing *Monsieur le Président*. He enjoyed the role and grilled Douglas to perfection with awkward questions. The phone calls were left until the next day.

As on the previous Sunday, Charlie wasn't on duty. This time Douglas chose to leave a message. He dictated it carefully and ended by signing off with a grateful farewell to the Commonwealth of Australia and its Interpol bureau, coupled with the name of Charlie.

It was Sunday in Paris too. Also the middle of the night. A double excuse for indirect communication with the chief. Douglas was well aware of the system out of hours. With luck he would avoid *Monsieur le Président's* interrogation. but that was up to Renée. The switchboard operator put him through on an extension to her bachelor-girl apartment at Neuilly. Her sleepy voice demanded indignantly whether he realised the hour in France.

With apologies he gave her his report in the authorised version, translating into French from Ashley's script. Somehow it sounded more convincing in French. He concluded by saying that he had lost Sylvia Smith but was hoping to trace her again. Hence the rush. He would keep in touch.

'You better had,' Renée told him in her special English. 'Monsieur is not pleased with you, *chéri*. He keeps asking why that Douglas does not report. He will demand everything in writing from you. The whole bang shoot. And on one side of the paper only. Two copies, both signed. No details to be omitted. You know the form.'

Douglas groaned. 'Must I, Renée? Can't you be a good girl and tell him I sounded too pressed?'

'Certainly you must. Or do you want me to wake him now? Rules are rules. And we must know where you go. Be sure to telephone on arrival or report to the native fuzz.'

'That's exactly what I've been doing.'

'Canberra? Melbourne? I think not.'

'You sound as though you don't trust me. *Monsieur le Président's* insistence on back-seat driving gets me down. Do you think he would mind if I resigned?'

'Not if it was in writng. On one side of the paper only. Two copies, both signed. *Au revoir*, Douglas. Abyssinia.'

'*Au revoir. Dormez bien.*' He rang off.

'You were splendid,' Ashley applauded. He had been positioned with his ear close enough to hear both ends of the conversation.

'Was I?' Douglas felt like a traitor. He was glad someone was pleased. Renée had unsettled him by not taking his resignation seriously.

They devoted the next two hours to the written report, ending with a formal request for his release from the service. Before signing it Douglas gloomily counted the lies. Any one of them would cook his goose if the truth came out.

'This will crucify me,' he protested.

184

'Nonsense. It puts you in the clear. Any day now you'll be able to disappear without arousing suspicion.'

Douglas silently doubted it. It wouldn't take a trained monster like *Monsieur le Président* long to realise that something was up.

'Why Singapore?'

They had packed up, checked out and posted the letter at the airport.

'Because I have fish to fry there. Also I've a feeling we're time-expired in Australia.'

They had caught the afternoon flight.

Ashley produced a passport in the name of Anthony Beauchamp. Robinson, he explained, had been a temporary, low-class expedient. Beauchamp, a coming-over-with-the-Conqueror name, was the prearranged choice for the reincarnated Wyndham West. Douglas, under instructions, also discarded his Robinson identity. He travelled humbly as himself.

Depressed by the monotony of the sea below, he sat in his window seat feeling his destiny slipping out of his own hands. With Ashley alive he remained without hope of an independent existence. The trauma of the Susan episode had enabled him to make a temporary escape, but now the charm and ruthlessness had recast their boyhood spell.

With his eyes closed he could see the red Victorian buildings of the school where they had grown up together.

Douglas was sent there because the school offered easy terms for the sons of clergymen. Ashley followed him because Mrs. Wyndham West worshipped at the church where Douglas's father was rector.

The school had a system of sheep and shepherds. Douglas had been there a year when Ashley arrived and he became Ashley's shepherd. They were both in Darlington's, whose housemaster had become the pipe-chewing institution known to every boy as Darlybags.

'Wyndham West's mother is particularly keen that you should look after her son,' Darlybags told him. 'He's rather young for boarding school and, having no father, he may not be used to discipline. You know him already and you come from a good Christian household. I rely on you to keep him out of trouble.'

For the first month of a new boy's first term it was his shepherd's responsibility to ensure that he turned up at all the right places at the right times. Classes and chapel. Compulsory games and PT. House prayers and prep. Also that his dress and behaviour conformed to regulations and tradition. During this period any lapse by the sheep made the shepherd liable to punishment.

The month was a nightmare to Douglas. No amount of care could prevent Ashley breaking rules. On the very first day of school he walked back from his classroom to the house with his hands in his pockets – a privilege reserved for school prefects for the past hundred years. Douglas duly received six of the best on his behalf.

'I warned you about keeping your jacket buttoned and your hands out of your pockets,' he told Ashley tearfully. The tears were tears of shame.

'I'm tewwibly sowwy, Douglas. I forgot.' At that time Ashley had a lisp and trouble with his r's. Another cause of shame to Douglas.

'Well, please remember in future. Wyndham West. And don't call me Douglas. We don't use Christian names here.'

'I'm sorry, Douglas.'

They were fourteen and thirteen and life as Ashley's whipping boy was hard.

What made the matter worse was Ashley's beauty. At that age he had gold hair, ruby lips, pink downy cheeks and a pure sexless voice. The celestial image of an angel. Inevitably the music master chose him to sing the treble solo in the Commemoration anthem.

He did it so angelically that he became the rage of the school overnight. In that all-male society he urgently needed protection, and Douglas found his role as shepherd indefinitely prolonged.

Douglas's own attachment to him was idealistic. He saw

himself as the guardian of innocence. Jealous rivals for Ashley's favours saw it differently. Rumours about their relationship spread and multiplied. Douglas doggedly ignored them. He fought the good fight by persuading Ashley to read a passage from the New Testament with him everyday. They remained inseparable. Whatever evil minds might think, he was doing only what Mrs. Wyndham West and Darlybags wished.

The battle was a losing one. Even the armour of Christ and Douglas's best endeavours couldn't protect Ashley from himself. As his confidence and sexual awareness grew he became increasingly responsive to the advances of admirers. His reputation became a school scandal, until only Douglas believed him pure. Every time he doubted, Ashley would wheedle and dazzle him into restored faith.

'You must stand by me, Douglas. You're my only weal fwend. Honestly you are.'

'But is it true what is being said about you and . . .'

'It's a lie. I swear it.'

'On the Bible?'

'On the Bible.' Ashley placed a pale soft hand on the book.

'Then I believe you. Shall we say a prayer together?'

'If you think it will help, Douglas.'

They would kneel on their study floor. The bright blue eyes would be tightly closed, the golden head reverently bowed, but what was going on inside? Douglas dismissed his suspicions as unworthy. He was the chosen substitute for Ashley's father. Ashley looked up to him and he must not fail him.

'Lead us not into temptation,' he would pray. 'Deliver us from evil.'

Ashley's lips would move silently until the end. Then he would join in with a fervent Amen.

One day Darlybags sent for Douglas and lectured him for an hour about Ashley's shortcomings.

'I've spoken to Madam Wyndham West until I'm sick and tired. He simply looks the picture of injured innocence and denies everything. He's a congenital liar and a disgrace to the house. If it weren't for his mother being a widow I would have him expelled.'

'But, sir –'

'Don't argue. Don't make excuses for him. You will learn when you're older that there's no smoke without fire. I've had some experience of boys and this one is the worst of the lot. He's exceptionally talented, but there's a total lack of moral fibre to him. He's the most immoral boy it has been my misfortune ever to have had in this house.'

'I'm sure you're misjudging him, sir. He's still very young and there are some bad influences in the school. The good atmosphere in the house will pull him round.'

'Well, I'm sure of the opposite, and that is why I sent for you. You were his shepherd, I know, and your families are friends, but I am warning you now to have nothing more to do with Wyndham West. Not because I believe everything I'm told about the pair of you, but because your association with him is ruining your school career. So far from your being a good influence on him, he has become a disastrous one on you. Do you realise that you are notorious throughout the school?'

'But, sir! I've done nothing wrong.' It was true, but he couldn't stop himself from blushing.

'At this rate it won't be long before you do, and in the meantime a lot of people believe you have. You must stop associating with this boy. If you don't you will become contaminated. Corrupted.'

The interview made Douglas all the more determined not to abandon his charge. He reported it to Ashley, who pulled a face and did his imitation of the housemaster uttering fatuous platitudes while failing to light his pipe.

Somehow Darlybags washing his hands of Ashley sealed the bond between them. It reinforced the need for someone else to stand *in loco parentis*, and Ashley in gratitude promised to make life easier for Douglas by behaving more discreetly. They still bickered. Their attitudes and interests were poles apart. But the cement had set on their friend-

189

ship. Darlybags shook his head over them and regarded them openly as lost souls.

Douglas's career at the school survived. It became respectable but undistinguished. He was never good at games, but he won the closed scholarship to Oxford in a thin year by sheer hard work. On the heels of this success he scraped home as a school prefect.

Ashley, by contrast, blazed like a meteor. In addition to his Hollywood looks he was blessed with a quick brain, an eye for a ball, and plenty of guts and no scruples in the scrum. A core of masculine toughness underlay the girlishness, and he rapidly developed from a cherubic chorister into a heroic athlete. Awesome tales of his disreputable escapades faded into whispers, thanks mainly to Douglas's efforts.

There was the day, for instance, when Ashley was awarded his First XI cricket colours at the unbelievable age of fifteen. He had taken the opposition's last five wickets for no runs. Then, batting at number eleven, he kept his end up for forty minutes in an undefeated partnership with the captain, to win the most important match of the season by one wicket.

At midnight he was still in partnership with the captain. They were discovered in the pavilion by the groundsman 'in their birthday suits and up to no good'. Only a swift bribe could avert a report to the headmaster and inevitable expulsion. The captain vanished in a panic, and it was left to Douglas, woken in the small hours by a trembling Ashley, to arm himself with his few precious pound notes, climb out and conclude some delicate negotiations. Ashley swore undying gratitude, the Captain of Cricket never met Douglas's eye again, and the money was never repaid.

The coming of the war blighted Ashley's promise. By 1941, when he should have been both Captain of Cricket and Captain of Football, he and Douglas were bound for India. Darlybags had breathed a sigh of relief to see them go. The house, he said, had had its narrowest escape from scandal in a generation.

Douglas got no thanks for saving it.

He opened his eyes to find Ashley viewing him as though he were a risky speculation.

'What are you plotting, Dougsie?'

'I'm not plotting anything. I was thinking about school.'

'That godforsaken place! Cold baths and going for runs up those blasted hills! Sadism and sublimated sex! I shall always be haunted by Darlybags – not to mention Marly-bags, his moustachioed mate.'

'He came to your memorial service.'

'To gloat, I expect. Just think of it. I'm a credit to the house after all. Having a boy memorialised in St. Paul's must have made his entire career worth while. Imagine the pain you would have caused him if you'd unmasked me. Think of the cancellation of all those places reserved for Little Willies whose dads want them to go to an establishment which turns out Wyndham Wests.'

They reminisced in a 'do you remember' vein until a storm distracted them. Lightning flashing across the Javanese jungle like Ashley in one of his tantrums. Over Sumatra the sky darkened like the Apocalypse. They flew blindly through cloud with seat belts fastened.

'It's your weather again, Dougsie,' Ashley complained. 'You're a bloody albatross.'

Douglas discovered to his surprise that the prospect of crashing didn't worry him. He couldn't conceive why a premonition of death had made him uneasy over Auckland. Could it be that he had been looking for Ashley then, and now he had found him?

Eventually the lights of Singapore appeared. The plane made a jerky two-point landing on a runway set in a grove of coconut palms. Customs and immigration were undemanding. They drove into town past ramshackle Chinese and Indian stores.

They passed the night at the Cathay. Ashley was secretive. In the morning he arranged a meeting time for the evening and disappeared. With Douglas's resignation in the post they appeared to have reached a stalemate. Now was not the time for either of them to make a move.

All the same, when Ashley was safely out of the hotel, Douglas picked the lock of the case which accompanied him on every aircraft flight. As he suspected, it was crammed with bonds and currency notes, presumably from the bank in Honolulu. Probably some had already been banked in New Zealand and Australia in the name of Beauchamp. If so, there were still plenty left. He decided not to disturb them and relocked the case without straining his mathematics by counting.

What had to be done without delay was the setting down of the truth. On Cathay Hotel writing paper he wrote it all out. A bald account in officialese and no attempt at self-justification. The facts damned Ashley and they damned himself. As he sealed the envelope and put it in his pocket he recalled Darlybags's warning about contamination.

Getting it all off his chest left him feeling as though he had undergone major surgery. He went out in a post-operative condition and lunched Chinese. Shark's fin soup for a starter.

Afterwards, by way of delaying tactics, he inspected the town and its citizens from a bicycle rickshaw. The world's fourth largest port, the rickshaw pedaller boasted in pidgin English. On the streets were Chinese, Malays, Tamils, Sikhs and English, but mainly Chinese. The shops bore owners' names like Ah Chum. The world's ocean shipping was anchored in the harbour, but Chinese junks monopolised the Singapore river.

Summoning his courage, he asked for the main police station and inquired there for his Interpol contact. If the man was in, he would hand over the envelope. For safe custody. If the man was out, Douglas wouldn't trust anyone not on his official list.

To his relief the contact was out. Instead of the envelope Douglas left a routine check-in message to be transmitted to Paris: nothing further to report.

That was Ashley's position too. In the evening they dined Indian, on curried shrimps and chicken with all the

192

trimmings. Ashley concentrated on eating. He was tense and terse and preoccupied. Over the coffee he made the announcement that they would be leaving in the morning.

This time their destination was Kuala Lumpur. A Malaysia Singapore Airways Comet took them there in forty-five minutes. They rose over the Straits of Johore in a rainstorm and landed in sticky jungle heat.

Again Ashley disappeared and again Douglas mooched. The humidity sapped his resolution, and when he called at the police station to report he didn't even take his envelope with him. Again Ashley was fretful in the evening and gave orders for a dawn departure. Douglas asked no questions. He was waiting.

They drove out in the first light. Past the Strawberry Hill Mogul railway station, the goldfish farms and orchid nurseries, and the tin mine's rickety complex of wooden ramps. Their return journeys to airports were like a repeated film run backwards.

Their aircraft for this hop was the Silver Kris Service to Bangkok. It took off over rubber trees and the last of the tigers in the hills of Selangor and landed in a plain of rice fields and waterways.

'The bastard had better be here,' Ashley muttered while they waited in the customs building exasperated by the formalities, the language, the currency and the confusion over collecting their baggage.

'I take it you're looking for your third man,' said Douglas, probing at last.

'You can take it how you like it. Things were a darned sight easier when people knew me around here. I've got you to thank for this flaming face-lift.'

'Never mind,' Douglas soothed him. 'Money talks, and we're not short of that, are we?'

Their hotel in town backed on to the river, and Ashley's money bought them a room the size of two squash courts. He sent Douglas into lunch while he made a phone call.

The grillroom on the top floor overlooked the river and the klongs and the Temple of Dawn with its guardian monsters. When Ashley came he was in one of his moods.

'So he's not here?' Douglas asked at the sight of his face.

'Who's not here?' The snarl would have done credit to a temple dragon.

Douglas thought he knew the answer but decided not to risk mentioning the name. If his guess was right the victim had red hair and it would be best not to intervene. Why should he care if he wasn't yet top of Ashley's list?

Over coffee Ashley left to make another call and returned in a better temper.

'Not here,' he said briefly. 'But I've traced him to Hong Kong.'

They checked out, Ashley paying for the unused room with lordly unconcern. His surplus ticals and satongs he scattered among the hotel staff without bothering to work out their value.

'Don't we even stop for me to report to the police?' Douglas asked in the taxi. He still had the envelope in his pocket.

Ashley shook his head. 'At the pace they go here, you'd be detained a week. How I hate Bangkok!' He glared out of the window at a street of brothels and night clubs. One of them was called Doctor Stephen Ward's Massage Parlour.

'It's Rest and Recuperation again,' Douglas pointed out. 'Your sort of town I'd have thought.'

Ashley curled his lip. Bangkok's staple industries were opium and prostitution and he found them degrading. Less classy than gold-smuggling and male strip shows, Douglas supposed.

They had booked their flight from the hotel. Thai Airways International this time. A Royal Orchid Caravelle to Hong Kong. Take-off was scheduled for 17.30 and they passed through customs without a hitch. Ashley, as always, carried his case of loot with professional nonchalance.

After some more than usual engine-revving and taxiing up and down runways, they were airborne by 18.00. Ashley called for Scotch to drink himself back into a good temper. Douglas, remembering Loud-mouth's advice over Windsor Castle, ordered his champagne with cognac.

'Where are we going after this?' he inquired, when Ashley seemed sufficiently mellow.

'Taipei and then the south Pacific. But first we've got to get your resignation accepted. Hong Kong is where you disappear.'

'My Honolulu.'

'Not exactly. There's no need for you to die like I did. Dramatics are not your line. You simply change your identity and become untraceable.'

'Suppose I'm recalled to Europe to be interrogated?'

'You refuse to go. You've done your job. You've reported fully. You've resigned. Who do they think they are? You're fed up with the lot of them.'

'They'll be suspicious. I must have a likely pretext.'

'Of course they'll be suspicious. Interpol is suspicious by nature, isn't it? I think a woman is the best bet.'

'Not Sylvia Smith? A spot of resurrection?'

'Don't try to be clever, dear boy. That's not your line either.'

'Very well, but shouldn't I know what has become of her?'

'You lost her in Bangkok.'

'In Doctor Ward's Massage Parlour?'

The champagne and brandy were sending Douglas light-headed and Ashley's withering glare failed to wither.

'You had better be serious. You're going to have to phone Paris tomorrow.'

'But they probably won't have my letter yet. And when they check the immigration records they'll find out that Sylvia Smith never entered Thailand.'

'Then she must have used an assumed name, mustn't she? You're meant to be the expert on this sort of thing. If the story doesn't wash, the truth will all come out; and actually you murdered her in Melbourne, if you remember. It's more than somewhat in your own interest to be convincing.'

'What about my woman then? I fancy something Chinese. If she were Red Chinese she could carry me off behind the bamboo curtain. That's the most effective method of disappearing. By train to Canton.'

'But you sent your resignation in from Perth, Dougsie. Where there aren't any Chinese. Red, white or yellow.'

'So I did.'

He fell asleep and dreamed of nickel heiresses and sheep-shearers' daughters. When he woke up it was night. Patterns of lights welcomed them from below. The lights of the island and the harbour, circling the darkness of the peak. The lights of Kowloon on the mainland, sparkling between the sea and the black, brooding hinterland.

The airport was crowded and taxis were scarce. Ashley secured one with effortless ruthlessness, outplaying a pregnant Chinese with three small children and ignoring a patient queue of two dozen behind her.

As they left Kowloon on the car ferry he pressed a fistful of US dollars into Douglas's hand.

'What I have to do here may take a few days, Dougsie, so I'm going to have to trust you. On reflection you had better not ring your boss till I tell you. Meantime don't do anything foolish, will you? It would be a pity to spoil everything now, when we're nearly home and dry.'

'Roll on Papeete.'

'Exactly. Now, while we're here we shan't know each other. We'll both stay at the Hilton so that keeping in touch is easy. But separate rooms.'

He paid off the taxi short of the hotel and sent Douglas on ahead to book first.

In his room Douglas fell asleep again without bothering about food. It wasn't only the drink. The strain of playing dangerous games with Ashley was wearing him down. He felt near the end of his tether. 'Hong Kong is where you disappear.' 'There's no need for you to die.' He recalled the precise intonations of Ashley's voice. They were meant to reassure, but with Ashley you never could tell. Even if you were Douglas.

In the morning things seemed brighter and killing, or being killed by, Ashley unthinkable. Outside his window a bustle of ferry boats threaded between cruise ships and ocean-going tankers. Beyond stretched the Kowloon waterfront and, over to the right, tower blocks on the island itself. Ashley would be enjoying the view immediately below. The close-cropped turf of the Hong Kong Club cricket ground.

Douglas turned to examine the room itself. All it lacked was a woman. He considered the possibility of something more bedworthy than the dream of a sheep-shearer's daughter.

More than twenty years had passed, but he still remembered the name of the man who had taken the girl he should have married to Hong Kong. Ashley had considerately sent him a cutting of the wedding announcement and had fun over the absurdity of anyone being called Mrs. Bullock.

Fumbling with the pages of the Hong Kong telephone directory, he could smell the scent of her body in the park.

The directory listed Mrs. Susan Bullock. He asked for the number and lay back on the bed overcome by an attack of nervous expectation.

When the ring came, the voice was hers. He announced himself hesitantly, stumbling over his own name.

'Douglas! It can't be! Well, I never! What are you doing here?' She sounded pleased.

'Just passing through. I remembered your married name and thought it might be nice to meet again. You're not free for lunch by any chance?'

She was. Lunch would be lovely.

'And your—'

She cut him short. 'I'm on my own.'

'Oh! Well, one o'clock at the Hilton? Would that suit you? Or is there anywhere else you'd prefer?' He felt as gauche as a schoolboy making his first date. How smoothly Ashley would have chatted her up.

Still, he managed it somehow. One o'clock at the Hilton.

She rang off and he took Ashley's money and went out more excited than he could remember since they parted. Someone had been pleased to hear his voice again.

Des Voeux Street was gay with banners and fairy lights celebrating the Chinese New Year. The characters were incomprehensible, but picture symbols proclaimed the Year of the Cock and he could read the English rendering of the New Year greeting. *Kung Hay Fat Choy*. At first he had thought Fat Choy was the affluent owner of a chain of stores.

The sky was bright too. All the omens were auspicious. 'I'm on my own,' she had said.

He found the underpass beneath Chater Street and boarded the ferry. On the Kowloon side he windowshopped up and down Nathan Road, hovering between opals, ivories and silks. The Ocean Terminal Building had other wonders of the East on display. Swiss watches and German cameras at knockdown prices.

In the end he bought her a jade brooch. It was far more expensive than any present he had ever bought before, but Ashley could afford it. He also bought a present for himself. A new automatic.

She turned up on time, looking smart in a green cheong sam. He pumped her hand and she kissed him on the cheek. She was soft-eyed still and larger-breasted. The upturn of her lips reminded him of his mother's. She had worn well and he hadn't. They reminisced over cocktails, feeling their way.

'What a terrible thing about Ashley Wyndham West,' she said.

'What about him?'

'His death. Surely you must have heard about it. It was in all the papers.'

'His death? Oh yes. Hero of the nation. Of course I read about it.'

'So it still rankles. Poor Douglas! I realise he misled me about you. He let me down badly, but the greatest men have human frailties, don't they?'

'If you don't mind, Susan, I would rather not talk about him.' They hadn't been together five minutes and already Ashley was intruding.

Over the meal he established that her husband had been a lecturer at the university and died the previous year. Instead of going home, she had stayed on, doing a job as clerical assistant in the registrar's office.

'What about you?' she asked. 'You went back into Intelligence, didn't you? Are you still in that game?' Her eyes looked anxious. On his behalf.

'Something of the sort. Nothing very grand or dangerous. I've not made much of a career, I'm afraid.'

'Nor have I. After nineteen years here what have I got? No husband, no children, and a job suitable for a teenager. Not that I mind. I like it here. Why worry if you're happy?'

199

'I worry because I'm not. I shouldn't mind about things, but I do.'

'Poor Douglas again! I'm sorry. I do hope you're not implying that it's my fault. That letter was virtually dictated by Ashley, but I should never have sent it. It was unforgivable of me.'

'Not of you. Please don't think that.'

She listened sympathetically while he told her of his peripatetic life and how he had never married. She was astonished to learn that he still lived in the same slummy attic flat at the foot of Notting Hill. Her sympathy deepened his sense of failure.

Before she left they arranged to meet again in the evening. He pressed his gift into her hand.

'Don't open it now,' he begged. 'It's only a little how-do-you-do-again present to match your dress.'

He did it clumsily, not at all in the Wyndham West style.

They met for lunch and dinner for the next three days. Carefree, Ashley-free days. The brooch went over big and he continued to spare Ashley no expense. Or rather, he supposed with a qualm, those widows and children who had contributed their pennies to the India Fund.

When Saturday came she asked him to take her out on a trip through the New Territories. At the Kowloon railway station they bought tickets to Sheung Shui. It would take an hour each way and a first-class return cost nine shillings. He felt like a cockney taking his girl to Hampton Court or Southend and thought he would propose when they reached the maze or the beach or whatever Sheung Shui had to offer.

They travelled on the line he had mentioned to Ashley. The exit for defectors to Canton. It ran first through lightly wooded hills and between strips of cultivated allotments. This was the lung and market garden of the Crown Colony. Timidly he held her hand.

After the harbour at Tolo and the new university the train climbed into more open country. Each station lay in an oasis of British culture – football and basketball pitches where Chinese played Western games in English school uniforms. He asked Susan whether she liked children, and she did. He had worked out her age at forty-one. Not quite past child-bearing.

At Sheung Shui they were evicted and the train went on to the frontier with only locals aboard. At Susan's suggestion he hired a car. The road lay through duck farms and fish farms and petered out at a police station. The driver swung off it up a track and came to a stop on the crest of a ridge.

'That's China,' she said, nodding at the view. 'I come here from time to time and I wanted to bring you.'

A barbed-wire fence stretched along the bank of a winding river. The plain beyond ended in a jagged line of hills. Three white watch-tower blocks dominated a small town in the foreground. Not a human being in sight. A forbidden area presumably. China seemed as placid as the Welsh marches seen from the hills of his schooldays.

'What is the town?' he asked.

'Shum Chun,' she said. 'There are guards in the towers to prevent people escaping. Alex, my husband, helped in escapes. He used to drive out here at night when the message came through that one was due.'

'Did he work for the government?'

'Officially the Hong Kong authorities weren't involved, but they connived at what Alex and his organisation did. What they would never do was help in an emergency. For fear of reprisals. When someone got stuck on the wire, he stayed stuck.'

Her voice faltered, revealing the purpose of the trip. It was a pilgrimage.

'Is that how he died?' They wouldn't play Western games on the far side of the wire.

She nodded. 'He went down one night to help some poor wretch. The Chinese sent up Very lights and machine-gunned him. They even came across afterwards and took his body. I've never had it back.'

He tightened his grip on her arm, not trusting himself to say the right words. They were no longer alone. The dead and vanished Alex lay between them. Doing an Ashley.

201

'I just wanted you to know,' she said.

'That he was a hero?'

'No, no. What happened to him. That's all.'

'In case I was thinking of asking you a second time to marry me? Well, I was. You represent the happy life I should have had and lost. But I see now I'd be too much of a comedown after Alex.'

'Don't be silly. You've always been too modest. You're as much a hero as he was. I know the work you do must be dangerous, whatever you pretend.'

'If I married you I would give it up.'

'What would you do instead?'

'Teach again. That was my vocation.' He took out a newspaper cutting. 'There!' It was from yesterday's paper. A vacancy in the university for an assistant lecturer in French and German. 'The money's not much but I could top up with some private tuition.'

'I know about it,' she said, 'and I thought of you. But would an academic life suit you?'

'Would I suit it? I've an Oxford degree but little teaching experience. How could I start now giving lectures on Racine and Heine?'

She reassured him, but it wasn't until the train ran into the outskirts of Kowloon that he summoned his courage to make the proposal.

'I don't want to be a bore, Susan, but is there any chance of your marrying me? Whether I put in for this job or not?'

'I'm very fond of you, Douglas,' she replied. 'You've a forgiving nature.'

'Please forget the past. I couldn't stand your saying yes out of a sense of guilt. Anyway it was Ashley's fault, not yours.'

'I can't forget the past. Any of it. It's sweet of you to ask me, but that's why I'd like to think it over. May I let you know when I get back from my leave?'

'How long will that be?'

'A couple of weeks. I'm not going home. Only to my brother in India. Is that too long?'

'What's a fortnight after twenty years?' He tried but

202

couldn't conceal his disappointment that she hadn't said yes at once.

Outside the station a newsboy thrust a paper at them. BRUTAL MURDER: BUSINESSMAN SLAIN. The big bold headline ran right across the page. Chilled, he stopped in midstride.

'Petrie,' he said, digging in his pocket for a coin. Like Paget, Petrie had stayed East after the war. Becoming IF's representative in South-East Asia.

She took the paper from him and read the name. Donald Petrie.

'How did you know? What's going on? You told me your job isn't dangerous. Did you . . .?'

'No, I didn't. But I know who did.'

His tone shut her up. They walked through the streets under *Fat Choy* banners and parted with yet another shadow between them. Ashley, Alex, and now the redhaired Petrie.

As he deduced, Ashley was waiting for him in his room. His key had been missing from the porter's pigeon holes and the deduction was elementary, my dear Wyndham West.

By that time he had read the newspaper account in full. A British businessman by the name of Donald Petrie, resident in Singapore, had been fished out of the harbour. Drowned after suffering head injuries. Wallet and watch missing. Thought to be the victim of robbers who had perpetrated similar attacks on other well-to-do visitors.

Half fearing a trap, Douglas tested the door handle of his room. Finding no resistance, he took out his automatic, threw open the door and jumped back sideways into the corridor.

'Windy?'

Ashley was sitting in the armchair wearing a gold silk dressing-gown covered in scarlet dragons.

'Who wouldn't be with you at large?' Douglas concealed the gun and came in. He closed the door and sat on the edge of the bed. 'Poor old Donald.'

'Petrie? Yes, I noticed it in the paper too. Sad, isn't it? I

203

seem to remember he was prisoner's friend to you in that spot of unpleasantness during the war.'

'For want of other takers. And a fine hash he made of it. In collusion with you no doubt.'

'How very unfair of you, Dougsie. It's that mean vengeful streak in your character coming out again. Donald did his best for you. He was thoroughly conscientious in the true North British tradition.'

'Which is why he died?'

'Which is why, like you, I can't pretend too much sorrow that he's kaput. I've known him almost as long as I've known you. He was the only person besides George and Jack who could have put two and two together.'

'That's the fourth member of your Gulunchi poker school to come to a violent end. Abdul Rahman got the major and you've done for the others. Now you're the only survivor.'

'Don't be so crude, dear boy. Petrie was killed by a gang of thugs. Tongs they call them here. If you doubt my word that I didn't kill him, I can only assure you that I've a cast-iron alibi.'

'That I can believe. Also that you didn't kill him yourself. In the true Chinese tradition you paid to have him killed.'

Ashley sighed and assumed his martyred smile. 'Are you intending to be tiresome about this, Dougsie? Because if so, don't bank on your indispensability. I love you deeply, but I love myself more.'

'If Petrie's death had been a worry to me I would have prevented it. I guessed who you were after. So far as I'm concerned, he's another smuggler who won't be smuggling any more.'

'You heartless brute.' Ashley switched to his shocked face. 'That makes you an accessory before the fact. And you're wrong about him being a smuggler. George and I were very careful to keep Donald ignorant of the gold business, though I fear he was beginning to suspect.'

'Then I'm sorry about him after all. What happens now? Who are you planning to kill next?'

204

'No one. I said three men, didn't I? This one rounds it all off. Your colleagues at Interpol won't miss Donald's connection with IF, so you must make up another instalment of your story for them. Suppose you spoke to Donald yesterday and he told you how Sylvia Smith was after him. Suppose he killed her and dumped the body out at sea, without of course realising that she had already paid a tong to have him killed.'

Douglas registered doubt. 'Suppose you undergo the cross-examination, not me. Much better know nothing about it and let them draw their own conclusions about Sylvia Smith. We wouldn't want to be delayed by an investigation.'

'Certainly it's time to move on again. Will they be nosey about your reasons for staying in the Far East?'

'I don't think so. I don't intend to be too specific about anything.'

He had decided not to tell Ashley about Susan. Not until his escape was fully prepared. The reaction might be severe, and he had to be fully prepared for that too. Meanwhile Ashley seemed genial and relaxed. Too relaxed.

They agreed that he should tackle Paris through the local Interpol bureau. He left Ashley lolling in his dressing-gown and went straight there. The officer in charge was an English inspector with an Eton accent and a Clark Gable moustache. He and Douglas didn't take to each other.

'There's a long delay on calls to Paris,' he said when he had listened to Douglas's story. 'You could be kept hanging about here for hours. I have to speak to the Criminal division about another matter. When they come through I'll mention yours too. You want confirmation of the acceptance of your resignation? Where can I reach you?'

'At the Hilton.'

'That's a bit pricey, isn't it?'

'I couldn't find anywhere else in a hurry. I'll be moving in with my girl friend in a day or two. She's at the university and I'm applying for a job there. I'm a linguist, you know.'

'What is her address?' The question sounded like an accusation.

'I'll give it to the hotel if I move before I hear from you.'

'You won't leave Hong Kong before we've been in touch again, will you? Paris might have some questions for you.'

'No, no; of course not.'

He sensed that Clark Gable found the assurance over-eager. With a man like that he dare not risk getting involved by claiming any knowledge of Petrie's murder. It was unwise to leave a loose end, but safer to write later, simply mentioning Petrie's association with IF in case it might be relevant. He could hardly claim not to have noticed the newspaper reports.

On the way back to the hotel he took out his envelope. There had been no question of handing it over to Inspector Gable. A confession now would ruin his new life with Susan. He nearly tore it up and put the pieces down the drain, but second thoughts warned him that it might still be a weapon against Ashley.

The next day he spent in the hotel waiting for the Inspector's call. Susan was unavailable. She had announced that she would be busy all day clearing up and packing for India. Ashley, immaculate in yachting gear, went sailing. As they still didn't know each other in public, they exchanged news of their plans casually in the breakfast room.

In the evening he rang the Bureau. The inspector was not on duty but a message had arrived from Paris. Douglas's resignation was accepted. With immediate effect. He must keep in touch with the Hong Kong office in order to complete the necessary formalities. *Monsieur le Président* was being suspiciously obliging.

He shook hands with himself nevertheless. Except for Ashley he might be free, and if Susan would say yes he had no further interest in Ashley. Not even in Ashley's death, he realised with surprise. Disengagement was all he asked. Would Ashley consent?

During the night he came to another decision. A showdown with Ashley would be explosive. If the worst came to the worst, it could be fatal. He must avoid one.

Susan was leaving for Delhi by an Air France flight in the afternoon. He had arranged to meet her at her flat in the morning, have lunch there and take her out to the airport. His decision was to go with her.

As soon as he appeared at breakfast Ashley broke the rules by hailing him. Openly, as one far-flung Englishman to another.

'This gentleman is joining me,' Ashley told the waiter between grumbling about the size of his eggs. 'Can't Hong Kong chickens do better than this?' he demanded and sent the man away for more.

'Well?' he asked.

'Nothing yet,' Douglas lied.

Ashley had had the gist of his interview on Saturday with the inspector and now listened intently to all the details. Douglas said the expected call must come in the course of the day and he would wait in again. Ashley announced that he would be enjoying another day's sailing. They were to rally in his room in the evening. If the call was satisfactory they would be off to Tahiti in the morning.

When Ashley was safely off the premises Douglas bought a ticket for Delhi from the Air France office, paid his hotel bill and checked out.

'Why the luggage?' asked Susan in surprise when he arrived at her flat.

'I'm coming with you. Do you mind?'

'But what has happened? Why didn't you mention it before? Has something gone wrong? Something serious?'

She was flustered, anxious for him, searching behind his eyes for the truth. It had been foolish of him to make her suspect him of responsibility for Petrie's death.

'It's nothing like that at all,' he assured her. 'My resignation has come through and I'm a free man.'

'So soon? That's marvellous. I'm so pleased. It will be lovely sharing a holiday. I'm sure my brother will put you up.'

She was genuinely pleased. He could hardly believe his luck. They toasted each other over lunch and he kissed her.

At Kaitak the airport seethed with assorted humanity. Half the population of Hong Kong seemed to be booked for an afternoon flight. Lufthansa were leaving for Van-

couver, BOAC for London, and China Airlines for Taipei.
Air France was nowhere, until they discovered their flight
being serviced by Royal Cambodian Airways. Douglas felt
glad to be out of the IATA jungle. He still had his free
pass but honesty of a sort had made him pay the fare out
of Ashley's loot.

Armed with boarding passes, they moved towards the
departure lounge and the crowd became even thicker. They
joined a long queue, scarcely moving. The delay worried
him. He had to stop himself looking over his shoulder for
a pursuing Ashley.

Life was absurd. He had started from Heathrow as the
pursuer. Now, on the other side of the world, although he
had done nothing wrong and Ashley nothing right, the roles
had become reversed. Why should he be the one feeling
guilty? It was typical of their whole association. He was
glad to be done with it. As soon as Susan finally agreed to
marry him he would send Ashley a farewell telegram. He
passed the time concocting it. Marrying Susan Stop Assure
You Lips Sealed Stop Goodbye Goodbye.

It took them twenty minutes to reach the immigration
officer's window. At the very moment when their exit forms
were being stamped he became aware of someone elbow-
ing through the queue behind. Sickeningly aware. The familiar voice hailed him gruffly.

'Hullo there! I've just made it, as you see.'

Ashley proffered his form for stamping and passed
through the barrier with them. Susan was staring at him,
but he was wearing dark glasses and appeared not to notice
her.

Douglas's first instinct was to throw his arms around
Susan to protect her. His second was to run away, but how
could he escape? There was no re-entry behind, and boarding aircraft was reserved for those holding the right passes.
To cut and run across the tarmac would be to invite arrest
– with a full confession in his pocket.

'Aren't you going to introduce us?' It was Susan speaking.

He apologised and fumbled for words. 'This is, er,

Anthony Beauchamp, a friend of mine. And this is Susan, my fiancée.' At the word fiancée he set his jaw defiantly and watched Ashley's face for danger signals.

'Well, hardly fiancée.' Susan corrected him with a smile. 'Douglas and I are old friends who've been getting re-acquainted. I've been living here for some years. What about you, Mr. Beauchamp? Haven't we met before some-where?'

'It's very ungallant of me,' said Ashley in the same gruff voice, 'but I can't recollect having had the pleasure.'

'There's something about you.' After so many years Susan was slower than Jack but she looked puzzled.

Douglas plunged in. 'I can guess what it is,' he volun-teered. 'Do you remember Ashley Wyndham West?'

Ashley slid a hand unobtrusively beneath his jacket. Un-der the left armpit.

'Anthony's a cousin of his,' Douglas went on hastily. 'There's said to be a family resemblance. Perhaps that's what you noticed.'

'A second cousin,' said Ashley. 'I never knew him.' He spoke hoarsely, clipping his speech. Anything to disguise his voice.

Before Susan could reply, the flight was called. In the bus to the plane she found a seat. The two men stood, al-lowing themselves to be elbowed along out of her earshot.

'Go away, can't you. You leave me alone and I'll leave you alone. It's all over, and about time too.'

'Stupid Dougsie! Didn't it cross your sleuthy little mind that I might be having you watched to see what you got up to? How obliging of you to buy a ticket from the airline office at the hotel, so that I could be sure to get your desti-nation right. You miserable specimen. You can't even do the dirt on a pal without ballsing it up.'

'I'm not doing the dirt on you. I swear to you I'll keep your rotten secret till I die, if only you'll get out of my life and stay out.'

'And what about the fair Susan? Rather part-worn now. Fancy your returning to that piece of vomit! She deserted you once for me, remember? We were pretty close then. She must have recognised me.'

'Of course she didn't.'

'So you say. How can you be sure?'

'I'll soon find out. It won't be hard. She'll tell me.'

'Meanwhile, since you're so forgiving, you must forgive me too if I stick around.'

Inside the Boeing they sat in a row with Douglas in the middle and Susan by the window. Ashley, anxious not to let her hear more of his voice, devoted himself to *Portnoy's Complaint.*

Douglas spent the time desperately reassembling his thoughts and scattered plans. He loved Susan, and all he had succeeded in doing for her was endangering her life.

She interrupted him from time to time. To point out Hainan and the Gulf of Tonking. Then Vietnam and Cambodia. Vietnam from above appeared green and peaceful. Across Cambodia wound a great brown snake. The Mekong river.

During stops at Phnom Penh and Bangkok Ashley kept with them but not near enough for conversation.

After Bangkok came the four-hour hop to Delhi. Douglas identified the lights of Rangoon. Then, craning across Susan's chest, he tried to pick out the jungle from the Bay of Bengal. At last, beside the dark curl of the Hoogly, an enormous flickering camp-fire welcomed them back. Calcutta!

He and Ashley had returned to India. What, he wondered, had become of Abdul Rahman.

Calcutta behind them, Douglas settled down to doze. Fears of what lay ahead and sniggers from the next seat kept him awake. Ashley was enjoying Portnoy. Confident and carefree as ever while Douglas fretted. Those sniggers came straight from boyhood.

Douglas had heard them first in the middle of a wedding service. His father was marrying a pair of young parishioners in his Saxon church in the byways of Worcestershire.

The bride had come up the aisle on the arm of her father, who was the local brewery owner. Behind her came an angel-faced boy clutching her train. He was five, golden-curled, and dressed in white satin. While the voice was breathing o'er Eden a dog which had nosed its way into the church lifted a leg against the side of the pulpit. An obscene yellow stream ran across the stone flags before the verger could usher the animal out. While the adult congregation sang on regardless, the page's sniggers acted as a descant. Douglas, genteelly bred, was left wide-eyed with shock.

Ashley's mother had recently moved into the large house beside the church. It was the rectory in Victorian times, but in the Twenties Douglas's father could not afford the upkeep. The Wyndham West establishment included a cook, a parlour maid, a nurse for Ashley, a daily woman from the village for the heavy housework, and a gardener called Harris whose duties included boots and knives.

Even so, Ashley's mother complained of poverty. She was a widow in reduced circumstances. She had no butler, footman, chauffeur or tweeny. Not even the customary boy for the boots and knives.

By the end of the reception Douglas and Ashley were sliding down a mossy slope together in the brewery owner's

211

garden. The white satin suit became green in the seat, and though the toboggan race without toboggans had been Ashley's idea, Douglas, being six and a half, duly received the blame. His first dose of taking the rap for Ashley.

It made no difference. He had been swept off his feet. He dreamed of going adventuring with his new friend and woke up afraid lest Ashley had died during the night. But later the same morning Ashley's nurse arrived to invite Master Douglas round to play.

With the house went a large garden and a strip of woodland beyond. Here they hunted wild beasts with bows and arrows and refreshed themselves afterwards by lighting fires to bake potatoes in the ashes.

On the big lawn they played croquet. A game for cheats, as Douglas discovered. Ashley always won, until one day Douglas looked up from playing a shot and caught him nudging his ball nearer the hoop with his foot. At first Ashley was all denial and put on an act of injured innocence. Then he worked himself into one of his tantrums, calling Douglas rude names. Finally he became brazen, admitted to cheating and appeased Douglas with a piece of stolen cake. Another pattern had been set.

Sex first reared its head in the woods. In the middle stood a shed which could not be approached without the warning crunch of twigs. This Ashley declared to be a hospital. Here, taking it in turns to be surgeon, they performed operations on each other. Each in turn prodded and probed the forbidden parts of the other's anatomy with skewers and threatened gruesome amputations with rusty shears.

Ashley's mother grew suspicious of the goings-on in the woodshed. Invitations to Douglas pointedly ceased. It was made plain to his parents that he had come under a cloud for corrupting the innocence of dear little Ashley. His father kept a charitable silence, but family prayers suddenly concentrated on the importance of standing firm against the Devil and all his works.

The expulsion led to a period of secret assignations. Of Douglas scrambling over the garden fence instead of knocking at the front door. He exhausted his precious stock of humbugs bribing Harris into joining the conspiracy.

'It's all very well for you young villains,' the gardener grumbled, 'but what's going to happen to me, Master Ashley, when your Ma finds out?'

'You can twust me, Hawwis,' Ashley lisped.

Harris smiled and ruffled Ashley's hair. He was a handsome hero to the boys and had a way of his own with Mrs. Wyndham West. He was familiar and knowing and one day answered Douglas's whispered inquiry about Ashley's father with the breathtaking story of the piano teacher. Douglas couldn't imagine anyone like a piano teacher daring to probe the forbidden parts of Ashley's mother.

When she duly caught him in the garden and Harris was accused of 'conniving at deceit', the gardener rode out the storm unashamed. The row lasted for ten terrifying minutes and when, a month later, Douglas was allowed to resume his visits officially, he was surprised to find Harris still lord of the potting shed. It was a relief to his conscience. Jobs were hard to come by in the Depression.

'Hawwis is lazy,' Ashley pronounced when they discussed the great scene. 'It would serve him wight to be unemployed.' Also, Hawwis took liberties. The hair-ruffling rankled.

In point of fact, if the garden was neglected, Ashley was to blame. Harris provided him with more companionship than Douglas did. He could bowl straight. He could teach a boy to ride a bicycle and shoot with an airgun. He looked after Ashley's succession of pets. Mice, guinea pigs, rabbits, even a snake.

When Douglas was introduced to the snake Ashley made him put out his hand to stroke it.

'Don't be a coward,' Ashley goaded him. 'It's only a gwass snake. It won't bite you. Cut my thwoat if I tell a lie.'

It took the snake less than a second to prove that Ashley should have his throat cut. A scar on his finger remained to remind Douglas of the most painful moment of his childhood.

The minute he stepped out of the aircraft at Palam, the old fragrance of Mother India caught him by the throat again. A heavy scent of dung and death in the night air. It had been the same thirty years before when they disembarked from the troop ship in Bombay harbour. The odour of ordure, Ashley had called it then.

Susan's brother met her in the customs hall and at once invited Douglas to stay with him in the British High Commission compound. He was a bachelor and rated a house with more than one spare room. Ashley hovered hopefully but succeeded only in cadging a lift to the Ashoka and an invitation to lunch the next day. Not until they had dropped him did Douglas drop his guard.

In Susan's brother's house he caught the last whisper of the raj. His bath was run for him and announced like a meal. Drinks before dinner were served on a tray and glasses refilled unasked. Dinner appeared and disappeared without the need for any effort apart from walking from one room to the next. Roast peacock and crème leechee. Sher Khan the bearer presided over their comfort. Even Mrs. Wyndham West in the balmy Twenties and Thirties hadn't done as well as this.

In the morning Sher Khan brought Douglas tea in bed and collected his dirty clothes. The dhobi would wash them and have them ready to wear by the evening. This was life before the deluge of Douglas's court-martial.

He thought of his attic in W11 and wondered how he would be able to manage on an assistant lecturer's pay. Even in Hong Kong the old-style raj had gone the way of the dodo. The days of living in Hiltons were over. So was the mirage of lotus-eating in Tahiti on Ashley's absconding funds.

From his bed he could see the Union Jack flying over the High Commission and the royal coat of arms high on the main building. Inside the compound, Susan's brother had told them over dinner, lay a complex of offices, houses and blocks of flats. Gardens and tennis courts. A hospital and a swimming pool. One could spend one's whole existence in the enclave, being born in the hospital and married in the consul's office. There were no facilities for burial or cremation.

Was one of their bodies to be carried out for disposal? With Susan involved there could be no more peace pacts or pretences about Papeete. In the past, from the croquet lawn onwards, Ashley had always won. But not this time. Not when Susan's life was at stake too.

The silent bearer reappeared to take away the tea and announce his bath. A coloured Jeeves impeccably ministering to the needs of master and guests. He was what Douglas had never succeeded in being – a true professional.

And probably a better detective too. Always aware where you were, what you were doing, what you would want to do next. Nothing could be hidden from Indian servants. From Douglas's accent Sher Khan and the others would recognise him as a pukka sahib. One glance at his luggage and clothes would reveal his poverty. They would all be busy drawing conclusions about his relationship with Susan from the fact that he hadn't slipped into her bedroom during the night.

At the risk of the bath water getting cold he stayed in bed until the impeccable Jeeves had finished laying out his clothes. One thing he was keeping to himself was his automatic. It had slept in its holster under the pillow and now it went into the bathroom with him. After his bath he checked it over and strapped it round his ankle, concealed beneath the leg of his slacks.

Ashley came early for pre-tiffin drinks and focused all his charm on Susan, not seeming to care now whether she recognised his voice. Ashley gay, Ashley reckless, there were danger signals. Douglas sat wary and glum watching her respond to the sparkling chatter.

'You quite remind me of your cousin,' she told him.

Ashley Wyndham West?' Ashley inquired coolly. 'I'm not in that class, I'm afraid.' His eyes were still hidden behind dark glasses.

They eulogised Ashley together while Douglas listened tight-lipped.

'I don't think Douglas agrees,' said Ashley.

'Dead heroes are best,' Douglas replied.

'Really, Douglas! Don't be so sour,' Susan told him.

Ashley took her into the garden, his arm round her waist. Douglas followed.

They amused themselves identifying trees and birds, Ashley showing off his knowledge. He pointed out neems, flamboyants and ripe green papayas. Ring doves and hoopoes. A black-headed, red-bummed bulbul. Then he moved to flowers.

Douglas, who could scarcely tell a daisy from a delphinium, was outclassed as usual.

'Anthony must have gardening blood in him!' Susan exclaimed admiringly.

Instead of replying, Ashley bent down to examine a flower. To Douglas, alert for any unusual movement, the gesture was false. Susan might be right, he realised. How, all these years, could he have believed in the piano teacher while Harris himself was filling the role of father everyday?

'I do believe he has,' he answered.

The flick of a glance from Ashley was proof. Douglas could see the golden curls being ruffled and Harris's affectionate smile. He remembered his surprise at the gardener surviving the scene of wrath. When had Ashley been told or put two and two together, he wondered. And how deep a dent had it made in his ego?

Overnight, it seemed at lunch, Ashley had invented a whole past for Anthony Beauchamp. When Douglas tried to embarrass him with questions he put up a performance worthy of his Lady Macbeth.

Inquiries about family were brought to a full stop by the information that he had recently and tragically lost his wife. Having come into money, he was consoling himself with a trip round the world. There were hints of a family business which he was too ashamed of to discuss. His local knowledge came from having served in India during the war, but his service had been with a hush-hush intelligence unit which couldn't be talked about.

After lunch he made no move to leave and Douglas was

determined not to allow him a second alone with Susan. The three of them were still sitting in the shade of the verandah when Susan's brother returned from his office for tea.

'Now it's cooler,' he offered, 'why don't you take the car and make an excursion?'

The offer was to Susan and Douglas, but Ashley accepted. 'I vote for the Ktub,' he announced.

The Ktub Minar. Douglas remembered it. The most beautiful fragment of the past Delhis which littered the plain. The historic plain where the conquerors' route from the north-west narrowed between the Himalayan foothills and the Rajputana desert. The tower had attracted suicides. Because of the tapering it was said to be impossible for a body to fall from the top and land clear on the ground.

'I expect Susan would prefer the Red Fort,' he said, 'or Humayun's tomb.' But Susan allowed herself to be persuaded by Ashley's show of enthusiasm.

Passing through the hall to the car, Ashley picked up his unisex bag.

'You won't want that,' Douglas told him. 'Why not collect it when we get back?'

'It contains my camera,' Ashley reported. 'We might get a good picture or two.'

Douglas knew what else it contained and that Ashley had no intention of returning. His flight would already be booked, his escape route prepared.

At the car they wrangled over who should drive. Ashley wanted Douglas to, while Douglas said that since he had no international licence Ashley must. For once Douglas won. He opened the door of the driver's seat for Ashley and contrived to put a hand under Ashley's armpit as he stepped in. The gun was there.

'What are you feeling me for?' Ashley muttered angrily and pulled himself away.

He spoke for Susan's benefit and she treated Douglas to a sharp look, recalling the old accusation. She took the front passenger seat and Douglas shared the back with Ashley's bag. He tried surreptitiously to open it, but the lock held.

217

Ashley. drove carefully. Susan's brother had warned them that the festival of holi was being celebrated. Small boys would be throwing coloured water over each other and passers-by. Like April foolers they were meant to stop at midday but didn't.

A gang with blotchy faces and stained shirts ambushed them in a village and bombarded them with bladders. It needed quick work with the window-winders for the inmates to save themselves. They emerged with the bonnet of the car sporting an abstract pattern of streaks and blobs in bright yellows, blues and greens. Douglas took advantage of the incident to transfer his automatic into a pocket unobserved.

At the Ktub he and Ashley wrangled again.

'Who's for going up?' Ashley demanded. 'It looks nice and safe.'

'Please yourself,' Douglas told him, 'but Susan and I won't.' Whatever the safety precautions, he wasn't leaving *terra firma* in Ashley's company. Nor allowing Susan to.

'Nonsense. You look peaky after your cold. A good clmb is what you need. It'll help you with your weight problem too.'

'I've an injured thigh.'

'Poor you! Come on then, Susan. Race you to the top.' As Ashley issued the invitation he took off his dark glasses.

'Didn't you hear me? Susan is not going up!'

Susan, embarrassed, hesitated between them. She was looking reproachful at Douglas and puzzled at Ashley.

'Anthony,' she said, 'I want to ask you something.'

'Don't,' Douglas begged her. He gripped her arm and turned her back towards the car.

The grip and the tone of his voice frightened her. She allowed herself to be led. Ashley shrugged and followed them back.

'Well, it's a nice day for a drive,' he said. 'I'll find you somewhere else, where your thigh won't bother you.'

They drove a few miles and he stopped at another ruin. Stone walls and bastions stretched out of sight along an escarpment of rock. He leapt out, seized Susan before Doug-

218

las could, and helped her up the slope to the entrance. Douglas behind could hear him feeding her with snatches of history.

'Citadel of the Tughlaks,' he announced. For a few years this had been the capital of a dynasty of shahs. A disgruntled saint had cursed it and made the water undrinkable. Uninhabited but indestructible, it had stood alone in the landscape for centuries.

Susan was entranced, the tiff at the Ktub forgotten.

'But it's marvellous! It could be Norman or Crusader. I never expected anything like this in India.'

Ashley led her on, dazzling her with expertise. He made comparisons with Berkeley and Krak-les-Chevaliers, with the Cyclopean walls at Tiryns and Akbar's deserted capital at Fatehpur Sikri.

Once inside, they were high. A tumble from the walls would mean broken bones. To his dismay Douglas saw Ashley run ahead, stand on the highest part of the ramparts and beckon Susan to join him.

Evening was darkening the sky along the ridge. Frowning on the moment of truth. Apart from a solitary hawk overhead they had the place to themselves. Douglas shouted to Susan to stay where she was.

Despite his urgency she took no notice. He could only watch while Ashley distracted her by pointing to a tomb in the valley with his left hand while his right crept under his shirt. Grimly Douglas took out his own automatic. His hand was trembling. He tried to steady it, but what was the use? He could never risk a shot with Susan in the line of fire.

'I'm sorry about this, dear boy.'

Ashley's voice rang clear. Its message was unmistakable. To Susan he might have been referring to the tiff, but Douglas knew better. Ashley had outwitted him for the last time.

'Please let Susan go.' Douglas felt his flesh goose-pimpling, but his voice was under control.

'She's yours. Come and get her.' Ashley hugged her tight, pretending to flirt. Using her as a shield.

Douglas calculated. Ashley would let him come to within six yards. Then he would fire. One shot for Douglas, one for Susan. He would wipe the gun and put it in Douglas's hand. Then drive to the airport with his bag, and be away. He would have paid his bill at the Ashoka before coming to lunch. The master mind left no loose ends.

'Come on. What are you waiting for?' This time the Ashley teasing voice, last heard on the beach at Melbourne.

Douglas waited. A movement on the ground close to the others had attracted his eye. He called to Susan to stand still and began to run.

He ran, not towards them, but to his left, keeping the same distance from Ashley. While running he brandished his automatic and this made Ashley step a couple of paces to the side to keep Susan between them. It was a small movement but enough, bringing him within striking distance of what lurked on the ground.

The abruptness of the movement frightened it into an attack. It slithered over the rock and its head flashed. Ashley screamed and fell to the ground, clutching his ankle. Before he could recover, Douglas was on him and had seized his gun.

'What was it?' Susan asked in a panic.

'A krait,' Ashley moaned. 'Didn't you see it? Douglas did.'

'A krait's deadly, isn't it? If you saw it Douglas, why didn't you warn him? What are you doing standing there with those guns? It won't come back, will it? Why don't you help me get his shoe and sock off?'

Her voice was hysterical, but Ashley's sounded worse.

'Suck it,' he shrieked. 'Suck the poison out before it gets into the blood stream. Suck, damn you, suck.'

'That won't be any use,' said Douglas coolly. 'It's in the blood stream already. I'm afraid a krait bite is fatal.'

'Don't listen to him. He's trying to kill me. He wants me dead.'

Susan had the shoe and sock off and was kneeling, about to suck the wound. Douglas prevented her by force. He pushed her away and they struggled while Ashley moaned and floundered, frothing with pain.

220

'You're not to,' Douglas told her.

'Leave me alone, will you?'

'You'll poison yourself.'

'That's for me to decide.'

'I won't let you. It won't do any good.'

'I do believe he's right. You're trying to murder him.'

'Look, I know about kraits. He's a dead man already.'

'There must be a serum. Are you going to prevent me getting him to hospital? Because if so, I shall scream till someone comes.' She jerked violently and pulled herself free.

'Hospital,' Ashley moaned. 'There's an antidote if you're quick enough.'

Douglas knew what Ashley's decision would have been if their roles had been reversed. Success brooked no scruples. But Douglas had been made differently. He was a failure.

'Very well,' he conceded weakly. 'Let's take him to hospital.'

They lugged the wounded Ashley to his feet and he hobbled desperately towards the gateway, one of them supporting him on either side. The citadel loomed grey in the twilight and the sky shone bright pink above. As they half carried him down the slope the last of the sun set behind the grove where the Ktub stood.

Douglas thought of the twilight parakeets at Gulunchi. They reminded him of another krait, the one Ashley had invented to lure him into the tent with Abdul Rahman. The childhood scar from a different snake was hidden under Ashley's clutching hand. Douglas's triumph was due, an accident foreshadowed. Why let mercy spoil it?

Infirm of purpose, or to oblige the woman he loved? What did it matter why he was saving Ashley's worse than worthless life? To show he was trying, he drove towards New Delhi at the speed of a demented Sikh. Ashley lay sprawled on the back seat with his head on Susan's lap. Spasmodic groans announced that he was still alive.

When they were near the hospital Susan said quietly: 'He's Ashley Wyndham West, isn't he?'

'Yes,' said Douglas, 'but don't let him realise you know.'

'I thought he must be. I was going to ask him at the Ktub. When I saw just now how much you hated him, I knew I must be right.'

The bitterness was understandable, Douglas supposed. He decided not to defend himself. Later he would explain everything to her. It needed time and, coma or not, Ashley couldn't be trusted not to be listening.

The duty orderly at the hospital asked how long it had been since the bite. When Susan told him he said there was still time and she burst into tears of relief. She wouldn't move from his side or let go of his hand. Douglas was the odd man out.

A doctor came to examine the wound. He shook his head when he heard what the snake looked like.

'Certainly it was a krait, but we have no antidote. Our serum is for other snakes. This one is the deadliest. You must go to another hospital. It is beyond the old city. The orderly will go with you and show you the road. You must hurry.'

Ashley had become delirious. He heard what was said but refused to accept it. 'Serum,' he cried. 'You must have serum. I must have it.'

'Sir, we have no serum for kraits here.'

'Bloody India!' Ashley moaned. 'Bloody inefficient wogs!'

'The fault is not India's. It is your country's, not mine. A British organisation supplies this serum. We are promised consignments and they do not come. If they were not promised we would buy for ourselves and the serum would be here. Do not blame India, please. Blame your own India Fund.'

Ashley closed his eyes. Two sad-faced sweepers carried him to the car on a stretcher.

Susan comforted him with her tears in the back while the orderly sat beside Douglas. He gave directions and shouted out of the window at buses and bicycles and bullock carts to clear the road. The bright holi patterns on the

222

bonnet belied the emergency and people waved back at them good-humouredly instead of moving over.

The journey seemed endless. After long obstructions caused by festival crowds they reached the second hospital with Ashley unconscious. Nearly all the staff appeared to have taken the holi holiday. The single duty doctor was occupied with another emergency. When he came at last it was too late. He made a brief examination. Ashley was dead.

The hero of the sisterhood of nations made a handsome corpse. He lay on the bare string charpoy with his sightless eyes still proud and a curl on his lip. Challenging and defiant. Serving notice on Douglas that he had not done with him yet.

'Who is next of kin please?'

The doctor had invited them into his office. Susan was in a state of collapse but refused assistance from anyone, Douglas most of all.

'I am,' he said. 'Mr. Beauchamp was my half-brother.' He lied easily and sensed her contempt.

They endured a long session of form-filling. 'You must please arrange disposal of body,' the doctor told him.

'My brother was a friend of India,' said Douglas. 'He wished to leave her his body as a parting gift. You may keep it.'

'But this is not teaching hospital.' The doctor was a Hindu and shocked.

'Then please pass it on to the medical faculty at the university.' Ashley's precious body dismembered by Indian students would be some atonement for his sins. That would knock the sneer off his face. Behind him Douglas heard Susan sob.

The formalities over, they walked out into the night.

'That was a beastly thing to do,' she told him. 'First you aim to shoot him. Then you kill him by not warning him about the snake. And finally you refuse him a Christian burial. I don't believe being cut up for medical research was his wish at all. I think you just made it up out of spite.'

'Let's discuss it later, shall we? We're both a bit shocked.'

'If he really was Ashley that makes it even worse. There seemed something familiar about him all along, but you put me off by saying he was Ashley's cousin. I suppose you caused some terrible accident which made him have face surgery. Not that I would believe what you told me. You were always jealous of him. Now you've murdered him and you're gloating.'

'It was Ashley and I'm not gloating. I'm only glad because he would have killed both of us. He knew you'd recognised him. What do you imagine he was doing on that ridge?'

'Warning me for a second time not to marry you. He took that gun out in self-defence. After he was bitten you wouldn't even let me suck the poison out. If I had, he might still be alive. You killed him just as you killed that man in Hong Kong. I thought you were kind and gentle and rather pathetic and all the time you're nothing more than a filthy murderer. A hired assassin. Killing your friends for money.'

'Believe me, Susan, it was Ashley who was the murderer not me.' Defensive, pleading, his tone rang untrue. She was slipping away from him. He prayed in vain for a small ration of Ashley's glibness.

'You're a practised liar,' she said. 'I've heard you at it more than once today, so why should I believe you now? You've assassinated him and arranged to have his corpse mutilated. Now you're going to spin me a tale to murder his reputation. Well, I shan't listen. I despise you. I hate you. More than anyone else in the world. How could I ever have thought of marrying you? I hope he haunts you. It's you who should be dead.' She was hysterical, bewitched still by Ashley's fame and charm.

They were standing on the pavement and she spoke without caring who heard. The row was a free show. A scruffy assortment of loin-clothed men and boys gathered round them. Walking wounded from the out-patients department in need of a tonic.

He made a last effort. 'Listen to me please. Why do you think Ashley had to take a false name? He was using the India Fund to make his own fortune. He was a con-man, a crook.'

'I'm not going to listen to you. Ashley may have done something wrong, but nothing can excuse what you've done to him.'

She broke away, climbed into the car and slammed the door behind her. Douglas struggled to follow but the right words wouldn't come and she refused to let him in. Apart

225

from his mother she was the only woman he had ever loved and Ashley was still depriving him of her. Defeated, he handed over the ignition key, but remembered to retrieve Ashley's bag. He hoped the students would chop Wyndham West Sahib into little pieces and feed him to the hospital cat.

As she drove away with a furious grinding of gears one of Ashley's favourite sayings came into his mind: 'Never run after a woman or a bus, dear boy. There'll be another along soon.' But not for Douglas there wouldn't.

He turned back into the hospital and asked for the doctor. A nurse showed him to the medical superintendent's office. Several surgeons were in conference. He apologised for intruding and explained who he was.

'Dr. Mehta has been telling me about your brother,' said the superintendent. 'A sad case, sir. If only he had been brought here directly! Half an hour earlier and we could have saved his life.'

'You did all you could and I would like to show appreciation by making a donation to the hospital on his behalf.'

'That is a kind thought, sir. Our patients and our buildings, they are all of them poor.' The other doctors tittered at the little joke.

Douglas forced the lock on Ashley's bag, took out the camera and spilled the rest of the contents on the desk. As he had suspected, it still represented the bulk of Ashley's loot. Round the desk a dozen dark eyes widened at the sight of bundles of bearer bonds and bank notes in assorted dollars. Dollars US and dollars Australian. Dollars Straits and dollars Hong Kong.

'It's all yours,' he said.

There were gasps.

'But that is many lacs of rupees,' said one of them gravely.

'Many crores,' said another.

'It will build us a new wing.'

'A new hospital.'

'Many new hospitals.'

226

'It is too much,' said the superintendent, mopping the sweat of temptation from his forehead. 'We cannot accept such a sum without investigation and formalities.'

'My brother held it in trust for a charity,' Douglas told him. 'It was intended for a purpose like this and he had the right to dispose of it as he wished. I can assure you the gift is a genuine one. Please accept it.'

'Your brother is a benefactor indeed,' said the superintendent. 'I will speak to the governors. If it is accepted and hospitals are built with the money we shall name them after him.'

Douglas shook his head. 'That would not have been his wish. He was an admirer of the founder of the India Fund and that is the name he would have wanted to be commemorated. You will find a way to accept the money?'

The superintendent swallowed. 'That will be our hope, sir.'

Douglas shook hands with each of them. Brown grateful grasps. When he left they were tittering again and fingering the notes unbelievingly.

From the street he looked back at the makeshift buildings huddling round a central block built to commemorate one of the Queen-Empress's jubilees. India could do with something better for her teeming sick. A chain of Wyndham West Sahib Memorial Hospitals would close the India Fund account.

Holi made taxis unobtainable and he was lucky to find a tonga. Jolting through Chandni Chowk and past the IF offices in Connaught Circus, it took him more than an hour to reach the High Commission. The pony backfired pungently every few hundred yards.

Sher Khan greeted him with the news that the memsahib was in her room lying down and had given orders not to be disturbed. The sahib, working late, had returned to the office.

Douglas rang the airport, packed his battered bag and wrote a note of thanks to his host. For Susan he could not bring himself to leave a message. Two desertions were more than one too many. Her accusations and refusal to
227

hear his defence had numbed him like a local anaesthetic. Now he was feeling the pain. Less lucky than Ashley, whose anaesthetic was general and permanent. Ashley would have burst into her room and talked her round. Douglas had already resigned himself to her being lost beyond retrieval.

Sher Khan sent the sweeper for a taxi and accepted the traditional *baksheesh* with dignity. Douglas diverted the taxi past Humayun's tomb. He would never return to India. Never meet Abdul Rahman and the others who once respected him.

Outside the town the air was soft after the day's heat. His visit had lasted twenty-four hours, no more; yet he was glad to leave.

'Ashley is dead,' he kept repeating to himself. Goodness knows how long the inquest would have delayed him. He had had to promise Dr. Mehta that he would stay. 'A practised liar.' Susan had been right about that.

Air France had brought him. Air France took him away. Blessed be the name of Air France! The smoothness of the night flight cushioned his despair. In three and a half hours he reached another world. Teheran. A further three and a half and still another. Lod. At Teheran it had been 02.00. At Lod it was the same. They were flying against the clock. Space was real but time had stopped. Was death real when life stopped? He wondered how Ashley was getting on.

At Lod he disembarked on impulse. At Delhi he had been purposely vague about his destination. Not having enough of Ashley's money, he was using his IATA pass again.

Sammy, who had been Pierre's friend, was on the list of official contacts. A sergeant in the Special Branch, he still did work for Interpol. Douglas rang his night number and an hour later he appeared in a police car.

'Welcome to Israel,' he said without enthusiasm. 'What's the emergency?'

'Me. I'm in trouble.'

'Oh?'

'I'm sorry to have got you out of bed just for my sake, but can you fix me up for the night? I would like to talk to you in the morning.'

'I'm off to Jerusalem in the morning.'

Sammy was stiff but took pity on him. He and his wife had a tiny flat in Tel Aviv and Douglas spent the night on a mattress on the floor. Over breakfast he said that Douglas could come to Jerusalem with him if he wanted. A bomb had exploded in the university the previous day. He had some interrogation to do, but they could talk on the way.

Douglas accepted humbly. With Ashley gone, any human contact was welcome. 'I'm afraid I'm being a nuisance,' he said. 'I hope you don't mind.'

Sammy looked him over like a suspect and said politely how glad he would be of the company. Douglas wouldn't have a sympathetic audience, but at least Sammy was a professional and would understand.

While they drove through orange groves and vineyards and fields of rotting Russian lorries captured in the June War, Douglas began the story of his troubles. It was a gloomy confession and Sammy listened without comment or question. In the Latrun valley, which had been no-man's-land and a desert, he interrupted to point out the result of two years' work. Cotton bushes, sprinklers watering young crops, acres of early vegetables ripening out of season under polythene for the European market. It was March and the sprinklers had to keep going until the khamsin brought the last of the rain before summer.

'Men died here in the war,' said Sammy proudly, 'but look what has happened as a result. If death is inevitable, who would not prefer to die so that good should come of it? We must look on the bright side, Douglas.'

'Yes, of course. I'm tired, I suppose,' Douglas replied, and Sammy clapped him on the back to dispel the gloom.

Externally the bright side seemed to be uppermost. After the New Year in Hong Kong and holi in India it was purim in Israel. This time a festival of children's fancy dress. Instead of throwing coloured water, they paraded.

229

The streets of Jerusalem were full of pocket admirals and midget gypsy dancers. Sammy dropped him at the Damascus Gate after they had arranged to meet for lunch.

The winding alleys and narrow bazaars of the Old City failed to charm. Some of the smells could compete with a tonga pony. He found no consolation in the Church of the Holy Sepulchre, supposed site of the Crucifixion. Nor in the Dome of the Rock, where Abraham was said to have prepared the gruesome sacrifice of Isaac.

The Wailing Wall depressed him further. At each of these holy places people were praying. Christians, Mohammedans and Jews. To Douglas all their faiths were savage myths. Man had created God in his own cruel image.

He wandered out of the Old City and toiled up the Mount of Olives. Sammy's jeep was outside the Intercontinental. Inside, Douglas treated him to smoked goose's breast and shish kebab with the last of Ashley's loot. He finished his story.

'You're right about being in trouble,' said Sammy. 'I can't even count the number of regulations you've broken, and *Monsieur le Président* doesn't forgive those who lie to him. Are you sure he has accepted your resignation?'

'Subject to the red tape.'

'It won't stop him having you disciplined. Or arrested. You can be sure he will find all this out for himself in the end. If I were you I would just fade away and hope for the best.'

'But where would I fade to?'

'Why not go back to India and do good works? Organise an India Fund which isn't a racket.'

'But I can't organise things as Ashley could, and I don't believe India's my country.'

From across the valley of the brook Kidron the golden dome of the mosque glinted at him and he raised a smile in return. This was all he was good at. Sitting and admiring. The Welsh marches from the downs above his school. Atlantic nights from the deck of a troop ship. Sunset at Gulunchi. St. Basil's cathedral from his hotel window in

230

Moscow. Humayun in Delhi. Views and buildings made better friends than people.

'I'm sorry about Pierre,' he said. 'I really am. I should never have let that girl hold me up. If you had gone to Moscow instead of me he would still be alive. Have you forgiven me?'

'No,' said Sammy, 'but I'm trying. What do you want me to do for you? Make your peace with the boss?'

Douglas nodded. It was cowardly but that was his reason for stopping off. Ashley would have managed it for him, but who else was there to help him now? No one but the undesirable Helen, waiting in London to gobble him up. He sighed and put a crumpled envelope on the table.

'My confession,' he announced. 'All but the last bit, which I'll add. It explains four violent deaths and one disappearance. Ashley Wyndham West, George Paget, Jack Willingdon, Donald Petrie and Sylvia Smith.'

'If you take my advice you'll destroy it. It's better not to have things in writing. I remember what you've told me. I'll ring him up.' Sammy threw the envelope back.

'You speak as though I'm a criminal. Except for not reporting things, I've done nothing wrong.'

'Do you believe that yourself?'

To avoid replying Douglas paid the bill. The stop-off had been a mistake. He had come hoping for sympathy and been met with disbelief. Sammy would do what he asked, but without friendship, without the understanding he had expected. Ashley had at least understood.

On the journey back to Tel Aviv they stuck to safe topics like Arab terrorism. Sammy was efficient. He had discovered the identity of the university bomb-planter.

After a second night enjoying the hospitality of his floor Douglas rose at five and a hired car took him away. As it neared Lod, a gigantic orange sun hurried up from behind the hills which hid Jerusalem. He was grateful for this spectacular farewell from the city of unbelievable faiths.

BOAC's flight 719 from Sydney left it behind in a matter of seconds. Soon the plane was out at sea, bumping and boring through cloud. According to the captain they were flying at a height of 31,000 feet and a speed of 545 m.p.h. No need to hurry for me, Douglas replied to himself.

Cloud deprived him of Rhodes, but the mountains of Greece were visible. He spied on what had been the ancient city states in their private valleys and remembered having to help Ashley with his Greek compositions.

Across the Adriatic clouds closed in again over Italy until great slabs of sugar icing began to appear and a whole panorama of Alps glistened in sunshine. Pygmies compared to the peaks above Simla.

The view of France became patchy, with Paris hidden. His conscience stirred as they flew over it. Orly was where he should be landing. Perhaps at that very moment *Monsier le Président* was sitting like a long-nosed lump of granite with the receiver jammed against his ear. Long distance from Tel Aviv. Renée would be enjoying herself.

Beachy Head was the harbinger of home. His heart sank with the aircraft as they glided down among the red roofs of Hounslow and taxied to rest in the inevitable rain.

No one was waiting to meet him. At Lod he had thought of having the flight number telephoned to Helen but decided against. What was it she had said when he left? He must get himself another job. They must talk about things. His heart had sunk then, but now he wasn't so sure. He had no job, no Ashley, no Susan. Life offered nothing but Helen. By a happy chance he had arrived on a Saturday, their night together.

The usual quota of airport staff were on strike, but not the customs. In view of his now ambiguous status he didn't want any bother from them. The automatic he had taken from Ashley at Tughlakabad resembled his own. Douglas carried it in one raincoat pocket and his Hong Kong purchase in the other.

Was it his imagination or did immigration examine his passport and face more closely than usual? The customs man seemed knowing but made his chalk mark with no

more apparent interest than the standard questions about
tobacco, alcohol and gifts. With passengers humping their
own baggage and no buses running the general chaos may
have helped. Safely through, Douglas stood in the taxi
queue for an hour and a half thinking of nothing but
Helen.

At Norland Square he rapped on her door on the way
upstairs. No reply. His own flat smelt fusty. She usually
aired it for him once a week when he was away. He threw
his bag on the floor and himself on the bed. Sleep was the
brother of death.

As soon as he woke he noticed the letter on the desk. The
writing was hers. He tore it open and read through four
effusive pages. She had married the major!

Her excuses were kindly meant but offered no comfort.
The major lived in the flat below hers. Helen's and Douglas's love-making sometimes shook his ceiling. He had
once written a pompous note of protest which she laughed
at and pinned above her bed as a testimonial. He must
have become her Saturday night stand-in during Douglas's
trip. Now she actually preferred the brainless, scarlet-
cheeked military buffoon.

Douglas saw his new life in shreds. He lay on the bed
despising himself for minding about being rejected by a
woman he had never wanted. Ashley would have made a
caustic comment or two.

St. James's struck five across the roof-tops. On an impulse he rang Paris and demanded to be put through to
Monsieur le Président himself. *Priorité.* The sacred weekend could go to hell. Renée protested shrilly and it took
some time. When he came through at last, the great man
spoke like God affronted.

He had received an *incroyable* report from Tel Aviv. A
report *plus incroyable* than any received in all his police
service and the entire history of the criminal division of
Interpol. It confirmed the decision he had already reached:
to order a full-scale investigation into Douglas's activities.
He required instantly a new report in writing. Douglas
must be prepared to return to the other side of the world to

aid inquiries and inquests and suffer the consequences of his actions. He need not deceive himself that Interpol would protect him in any manner whatsoever.

Douglas ate humble pie. The circumstances had been peculiar, certainly, but he could explain everything. Might he please withdraw his resignation and come to Paris?

Emphatically not. It had been no part of his duties to leave corpses behind him in every country he visited – and fail to report them. Never had a man proved himself less fit to be an agent of Interpol. Mendacious reports. Personal feuds. Complaints from IATA about his extravagance. His resignation at a time of financial stringency was the only point in his favour.

'But I put an end to the gold-smuggling.'

'That occurred before you left London. It ended with your friend Mr. Wyndham West's disappearance. Why did you hide from me the closeness of your relationship with this man?'

'I told you I knew him, and it made no difference to my work, except to make it successful. I brought him and his associates to justice for you.'

'Not for me. For yourself. And justice belongs in a court of law. Since Mr. Wyndham West is dead he remains innocent, whatever you may allege. It was not for you to find him guilty. If he committed a crime he should have been tried and convicted. You mistook your role, my friend.'

The voice of God droned on. It might have been a judge's summing-up at the end of Douglas's trial.

'But I have no money and no other job to go to,' he pleaded. 'I only resigned to humour Wyndham West while collecting the evidence against him.'

'That is your misfortune.'

Douglas continued pleading and in the end God half relented. At IATA's expense.

'They have requested a special investigation into an outbreak of ticket forgery. Since you have already been seconded to them for some months, you would be the most suitable person to undertake it. The appointment is temporary only, however, and would be subject to your being made available for any inquiry arising out of the Wyndham West affair.'

'And afterwards? Would Interpol take me back?'

'Never.'

Douglas groaned to himself. Interpol felt the same about him as Susan and Helen. 'Would IATA take me on those terms?'

'On my recommendation, perhaps. We shall see.' There was a pause. 'Stay in your apartment please. You will be telephoned.'

Renée made the call an hour later.

'You wicked Douglas,' she said. 'Nobody loves you. What is it you have been up to?'

'Have I got the IATA job?'

'Yes. For six months. So that he will know where to find you, he says. You must report in Montreal on Monday morning.'

'This Monday!'

'And write your new report before you go. *Monsieur le Président* demands the truth. The whole truth and nothing but the truth, if you can manage such a thing. Two copies, *chéri*. On one side of the paper only.'

Douglas put down the receiver. They were treating him like a criminal, graciously granting him his livelihood for another six months. He tore open his crumpled envelope in a rage and added two more sheets to what he had written in Singapore, not caring how far any of it incriminated him.

What did it matter? He was a self-confessed accessory before and after plenty of blood-stained facts, and it seemed unlikely that the ticket-forgers would oblige by providing him with an itinerary which would fit in with his heavy programme of inquests. He counted the tally on his fingers.

Hawaii for a revised version of Ashley's first disappearance. Rotarua for George. Sydney or Canberra for nonexistent Sylvia. Melbourne for Jack. Hong Kong for Petrie. Delhi for Ashley second time round. The time-table would have to be staggered for his benefit, each police force dissuaded from detaining him until they'd all had a fair share.

In Holland Park Avenue, when he posted the report, it was raining with pacific fury. The urge for a last gastronomic fling took him to *Chez Moi*. He should have known it would be full on a Saturday night. Instead he had to make do with a nosh-up at Mick's Cafe in Shepherds Bush.

The night passed without much sleep. In the morning he repacked and, with no Helen to transport him, caught a taxi to the airport. The rain hadn't stopped and the Sunday paper provided its weekly fare of wars abroad and strikes at home.

Air Canada flight AC 845 was due to leave for Montreal at twelve noon. He checked in shortly after eleven. The girl at the counter handed him his boarding card and wished him a good flight. Once again he watched his luggage disappear like a coffin from a crematorium chapel. Was it on its way to Montevideo or Monaco?

'You're getting too old for this sort of thing,' Helen had told him. 'A tatty underpaid air-express nark' was Ashley's description. He was always in flight. Or in transit. Always going west these days. He thought wistfully of the Moana's banyan tree and the dream of beachcombing in Waikiki. Then the lure of drowning in the sea off Mount Eliza. And how he had wanted to end it all in the war, jaundiced in Multan.

The labour dispute had delayed flights and the departure lounge was overstocked with fellow travellers, none of them departing. The seats were all occupied and he stood uncertainly, alone in the crowd. Life had become empty without Ashley. The whole world was one big departure lounge and, thanks to him, Wyndham West's last flight had been called. The voices he heard were not those around him.

'You got a grudge against the guy or something?' O'Leary in Hawaii.

'But he's so gay and nice. I do believe you're jealous.' Susan in Kensington Gardens.

'I am warning you to have nothing more to do with Wyndham West.' Darlybags in his study.

'Try as hard as you like, it's a bond you can't break. I'm lonely. You're lonely. We need each other.' Ashley in Sydney.

'Sometimes you make me sick.' 'Actually I make myself sick.' 'You make everyone sick.' Ashley and himself in Perth.

'Nobody loves you.' Renée from Paris.

He struggled into the gent's and was conscious of a Pakistani cleaner staring at him. Then smiling and speak to him. Soliciting in a public lavatory. Not listening to the words, he shied away in revulsion. It was the final straw.

Sentimentally he chose the lavatory where he had read *Paris-Match* before taking off for Honolulu. The voices kept coming.

'We move in predestined grooves like Melbourne trams.'

'Of all things life is the most precious.'

'If I were you I would just fade away.'

'I hope he haunts you. It's you who should be dead.'

He had taken Ashley's life. Susan and Helen had both deserted. There was no one on earth to weep for him and God was a figment of faith.

He took his automatic out of the holster and pointed the muzzle at his heart. What was good enough for Jack Willingdon should be good enough for him. He squeezed the trigger slowly as he'd been taught.

A clean job would have been out of character, but at least he didn't miss. The floor came up and hit him on the chin. Painlessly. The chill of the pan soothed his cheek and he felt more comfortable than he could remember. Why hadn't he tried lying on lavatory floors before?

The banging on the door sounded like the distant drums of the regiment he'd disgraced. Goodbye to all that! He watched with interest a river of blood curl into a pool of some poor marksman's urine. His last vision before unconsciousness was of the five-year-old Ashley wearing his white suit.

The Pakistani cleaner forced the door. He had entered

England illegally the previous year and never expected to see an Englishman he had known in the days of the old raj. So far from soliciting, he had been expressing joy. Lonely in a foreign country, he took Douglas in his arms and hugged him. Then, dripping with Douglas's blood, he ran out into the departure lounge calling at the top of his voice for a doctor.

His name was Abdul Rahman and he was weeping. Weeping for Douglas.

*A Selection of General Fiction
from Sphere Books:*